Saved From The Fire

The Mars Dilemma and Chronicles

Mark Gallacher

Ringwood Publishing
Glasgow

The moral right of the author has been asserted
Issued in 2021
by
Ringwood Publishing
Flat 0/1 314 Meadowside Quay Walk,
Glasgow
G11 6AY
www.ringwoodpublishing.com
email: mail@ringwoodpublishing.com
ISBN
British Library Cataloguing-in Publication Data
A catalogue record for this book is available from the
British Library.

Printed and bound in the UK
By Lonsdale Direct Solutions

Contents

Dedication

To my wife and sons,
and to Ray Bradbury, who lives forever.

PART 1

Prologue of the first part

100 years after the Founding. Autumn.

The harvest has been good. We have enough for the winter and beyond. It's the first time in many years there has been bounty.

Four newborns. All healthy.

Leaf fall, like burnished copper and gold, fills the forest floors, stained with lilac and heaped across the old tracks around the settlement. Like the woods are weathering to metal.

Scent of soaked earth and dark water. Storytelling weather.

Along the coast, the sea churns like slow, dark glass, heavy waves fall and shatter along the tideline. Thrumming with each slow wavefall, like the sea is mourning.

The moon is a pale ghost in the daylight. A mute witness to history.

Cold, mist-laden mornings when the fjord is a strange and haunted place. The fisherfolk go out, their small boats lost in mists. Their voices and whistles call out, sounding the distances.

Then all falls to silence. As if the world has conjured a memory more real than the world itself.

But there is soft laughter in the forest.

Children, kicking up the leaves, hungry for joy, thirsty for delight. Their sing-song voices tingle in the still air. Silence follows in their hurried wake.

The good harvest means there is more time to meet in the longhouse. Like tonight. To light the oil lamps and tell tales of ancient history before the Culling – the civilisations lost, the wonders gone.

To read from the books.

Carl and Them, the de facto leaders of our community, talk about the books and my bundles of chronicles, all saved from the fire and left by our Founders.

As they talk, Carl watches me with a glint in his eye. He knows I have studied the texts meticulously, that I record the things that happen in the community. That I love words more than I love the world. That I imagine other worlds.

The others are seated around the fire, half-listening while repairing items of use or simply staring into the flames. Happy to listen to Carl and Them's voices.

Them says none of the books are true. Imagined truths he calls them. Entertainment to distract people when the nights are dark. 'Pretty lies,' he says with disdain in his voice and looks at me as if he expects a challenge.

Even though we love the stories, the poison that made people burn books remains. Some people are still suspicious of the written word. Of too much knowledge. Didn't knowledge eat and poison the world?

I sometimes wonder how many of them could be book burners if that time was here again.

Carl tends to the fire with a stick. 'At the world's end people will still be telling stories.'

'I don't doubt it,' Them says. 'But dreaming doesn't sow the fields or bring in the harvest.'

'I'll tell you what I think.'

'I don't doubt that either,' Them says with the ghost of a smile.

Carl laughs. He is never angry with Them.

'I think the books are lies and truth. How much of one or the other, who can tell? Our Founders thought they were worth saving. Risked their lives to save them. Died to save them. And we think they are worth saving. Do we not?'

Them nods reluctantly. He says, 'It would feel like a crime not to. We lost so much in the fire. Better books than the ones we have. Books with facts and knowledge. Books you can use.'

Carl's mood darkens. The sense of what we have lost is immeasurable and overwhelming. Like a dark sea at your shoulder. Like ash falling on snow.

'What do you think about the books?'

It takes me a moment to realise Carl is talking to me. So often I think I am invisible with just my own voice inside my head.

'I like them.'

'He likes them,' Them says and looks at Carl and they smile. 'If only he liked working in the fields as much.'

Them knows I work as hard as the next man. So do the others. But this teasing seems to be the price for studying the books. For my love of the written word.

We grow quiet again. I go back to scribbling.

Someone stirs at the back of the longhouse where the shadows are darkest.

It is Ruth. The oldest in our community. She clears her throat and struggles to stand. There is a pause, as if she must gather up both her mind and body. Finally, she moves over to the fire and sits down next to me.

Her face is like weathered stone. She rubs her bony fingers.

'When I was a wee girl,' she says, and laughs at the strangeness of that fact, then loses her trail of thought and

stares into the fire.

'Ruth?' Them asks her gently.

Ruth glances at Them, her pale eyes now flecked with brightness. She rocks her frail body, as if to conjure the memory.

'When I was a wee girl there was an Old One. I forget his name. My father knew his name. The Old One said there was a boy who carried those books here. A boy with a companion who was not a man.'

I stop scribbling. I have never heard Ruth talk about this before.

'And?'

'The Old One said that the boy and his companion did not stay. They helped the first folk build this place and then they left. They went North. They took some books with them.'

'They took books?'

'They left books in each new settlement. It was safer that way. They could not all be burned at once. The Book Burners still hunted them.'

The people shift. Some of the children hug their mothers.

'Did they have names?'

Ruth rocks and rubs her hands. 'The fire burns but still I'm cold.'

'Ruth?'

'I cannot remember their names. But they said the strange thing about the boy was that he never grew sick. And his companion was not a man, even though he looked like a man.'

'Oh? Was he an angel?' Carl asks sarcastically.

'No,' Ruth says. 'But not a man.'

'An animal then?' Carl asks.

'No. Not an animal.'

Carl looks at Ruth quizzically. 'If not an animal and not a man then what?' he asks.

'A machine?' I ask.

Someone laughs but Ruth looks sharply at them.

'Was that it?' I ask. 'Is that what he was?'

The light in Ruth's eyes fades. Her mind wanders again. She turns back to the fire and then a last thought rises in her mind.

'It was a machine that saved the world. People have forgotten.'

'Who told you that?'

But Ruth will not answer; lost in the workings of her own mind.

*

The fire is low.

The others have fallen asleep in the longhouse or have returned to their cabins.

Outside, dark and deep silence covers the world like a creature that circles around itself before sleep. Nothing moves. Not even the air.

I go back to my cabin. I sit at my small table and write down all that was said.

Who is it I write for? For you, my imagined stranger?

See here. I stand up now, with my lamp. I walk over to the back of the cabin.

Follow me.

There is the carrying box. Not as big as you expected?

You might as well try to hold an ocean in your arms to get a sense of how much was lost when men burned the world and all the books in it.

Here is the key to open the lock.

See? I unlock the box.

Now I lift the lid of the box.

So few books saved.

Take this one: these chronicles. I have put them together into a single volume. They are a history of the world from a time most people would rather forget.

These chronicles, rescued from the fire.

Held in your hands. Now turn the pages.

Read.

THE MARS DILEMMA

Note to the Reader from the unknown author

I hope my version serves history well. I have used existing historical records and archives and recently discovered material. And where the historical record says nothing, I have endeavoured to provide the possible truth.

I visited the Mars Memorial when I was a boy of eleven. It had a profound effect on me.

Years later, as a student, I visited it again. Standing there, I realised that there are ten names listed on the Mars Memorial, and we only know the actual fate of a couple of them. How can this be?

As one historian famously put it: 'Everyone knows what happened. The world was saved. That's what happened. But nobody knows what happened on Mars. Not a damn thing.'

It famously states on the Mars Memorial in Washington: 'Our entire planet owes its existence to a handful of people. The Mars Site 3 Team will be remembered as long as history is recorded, as long as we reach for the stars. We are the children of their sacrifice.'

What is not stated on the memorial was the already precarious state of humanity. Nature had repaid our failings with some cruelty of her own. A number of new diseases and annual natural disasters fuelled by an unbalanced global climate had taken its inevitable toll. Population levels had started to tumble; regional conflicts had decimated some countries; global trade was curtailed and natural systems were in free-fall. Despite technological wonders, and talk of a new golden age of Artificial Intelligence science, humankind's future and the future of the planet was precarious.

At the time of the Mars Missions, the North American continent had not escaped the general global calamities. But no one doubted that the world would recover. It would take time, yes, but time we had in abundance.

Ultimately, time was on our side.

Then binary asteroid 2110 PH2 tumbled into our solar system. A billion-year dance interrupted by the gravitational pull of Jupiter, resulting in Nautilus 1 and Nautilus 2 – two dreadful asteroids, both set on their own specific planet-killing trajectories.

We had no time. And almost no options.

Let us begin this journey then: a mere 20 kilometres above our heads lies the vacuum of space. Let us cross the vast emptiness and travel to the dim-lit red plains and icy plateaus of frozen Mars, which for a brief period of time was key to the future existence of humankind.

March 2140

My father and my grandfather were both working fishermen, working off the West Coast of Scotland on a six-berth boat called The Reliant. Storms that would have been unrecognisable just over a century earlier frequently crossed the Irish Sea, battering the coast with brutal intensity.

Both men were diehards in an industry that was increasingly automated and robotized. They took pride in the physical hard work and hazards of the job. They gladly shared stories of their working lives, recounting tales with unhurried pleasure, as if they were making strong nets from fine rope. Often with a glass of whisky to ease their flow. Despite all the technological leaps and bounds, in an ever-shrinking world, storytelling was still treasured.

Both men had married highly educated women, which gave them a certain local notoriety, as if there was a proclivity for the seduction of intelligent, cultured females.

I still have cousins, aunts and uncles who claim my grandfather, Old James as he was known, drowned at sea, regardless of the number of times I have corrected them. It is a testament to how family narratives can be more powerful than the events that created them.

My father told me on several occasions that Old James was dead before he hit the water. The whole crew saw it, boat pitching in a storm. It happened so fast, Old James didn't even have time to cry out. He died, tipped over, and the sea took him.

His body was found the following day and the autopsy revealed a massive haemorrhage in the brain. No water in the lungs. He was almost certainly dead when he hit the water.

My father quit the fishing after that, retrained at college and became a schoolteacher. But people still used his fishing name: James Younger.

'Just call me James,' he would sometimes say, knowing full well that he would take James Younger to the grave.

I think he named me Max just to make sure there would be no more naming nonsense. But my friends at school called me Mac J, which morphed into J-Max when I moved to the USA to take my Masters in Geology. My mother laughed when she heard J-Max for the first time and said the name made it sound like I was a rapper. My father moaned when he heard it. But the name stuck and he never corrected anyone when it was used in his presence.

Old James. James Younger. J-Max. What will I call my son, should I be lucky enough to have one? Will he look up at the stars and planets the way I have looked up at them?

My father and grandfather were sea travellers. They witnessed bone-shaking storms, delicate winter sunrises, bright stars in the deep darkness of cold night. Far from any shore, they saw ghostly meteors cross the vast firmament. They knew the old wonders and signs, more ancient than recorded history.

My father was the more fervent dreamer of the two men. He loved astronomy and he dreamed of Mars the way some men dreamed of unspoiled wilderness.

My father also spoke of Mars the way some men recounted their former dreams of youth, voices burdened by time and personal choices, or quietly, with sudden grief, like a slackening and pulling – a tidal sadness shaping the heart's rhythm.

At a certain age, a man's life has a kind of heft, with which he can gauge his success or failure. The roads not travelled,

11

measured in relief and regret. My father reached that age with a certain quality of stoicism. It is what it is.

But best of all, my father sometimes dreamed of Mars with a boy's delight and when he showed me the books and the pictures he had collected, hundreds of hi-res images of vistas and craters, of NASA landers and rovers, immaculate graphs and animations, close-ups of drilled rocks and those first tantalising signs of water on the steep slopes of highlands overlooking vast plains, he spoke with breathless reverence; he spoke with wonder.

He showed me Mars Site 1.

'A bloody near disaster from Day Two. The whole site swallowed up by a planet-wide sandstorm. Luckily, the crew managed to take flight and return home. They called it The Longest Stopover in History in the news.'

And in hushed tones, he pointed out Mars Site 2, unoccupied because the Mars Mission 2 Crew never arrived. Their ship suffered a fatal structural failure and broke up halfway between Earth and Mars, spinning away into the great void. No time for goodbyes or messages for loved ones. Gone forever.

'It's all there, Max. Robots on standby in the Living Domes. They call the robots "serfs". Did you know that? All the equipment. The serfs. The rovers. The automated water distiller. The ice excavator. The food stores. The nuclear power source is still running. It's a ghost site.'

'Why don't they send another crew there?'

'Politics. Superstition. A lot of people think it's in the wrong location. They think the next site should be here. About 90 kilometres further south. That's probably going to be Mars Site 3 in about twenty years' time. You'll see it. Me too.'

'Maybe I'll be an astronaut and go there. Maybe it'll be me.'

'Why not? I reckon you can do anything you set your mind

to.'

The moons of Jupiter and Saturn could also excite my father's imagination, but all his passion was for Mars. It was Mars where life would be found. It was Mars where the next step in human colonisation would take place. It was Mars his boyhood dreams returned to in the cradle of his sleep.

I was not an only son. I had an older brother, Peter. It seemed, at first, that Peter had won the DNA jackpot as far as our family was concerned. Fiercely intelligent and academically gifted, his early life was full of promise. And for a while, his career as an engineer was in the ascendant.

But he was also an alcoholic. His addiction took ten years to ruin his career and marriage and another ten years to kill him. In between, his drinking broke the unbreakable bonds of family, until they were a thin sliver of memory and love.

I had no such academic gift. I had to work laboriously at school and university. Small steps. I did have my mother's love of art and poetry. And for a brief while, I thought I might become a writer. But I loved science and exploration, too, and my father encouraged all things scientific in our house. Eventually, the pull of science was stronger than the pull of art.

But watching my brother, I learned two things quickly. I was going to have to work hard, and I was going to have to be alert to the dangers of any kind of alcohol or stimulant.

So, my journey to Mars began with my father's serious 'why not?'. It's as simple as that. The greatest journeys start from the simplest of steps.

We talked about our conversation over the family dinner that night. My older brother laughed out loud. My father raised his glass, to toast me. 'And why not? What's to stop Max becoming an astronaut and flying to Mars?'

My mother did not laugh or wave the notion away. She

looked at us with her clear, intelligent gaze. 'Wonderful,' she said. 'Fill your boots.'

Why do I write about such things, millions of miles from home, on another world, at Mars Site 3?

Well Mars is a cold and dim-lit place and looking out across the blood red plains and dry vistas, I am inevitably drawn to memory, and the cradle of all memory is home. It is a particular kind of longing and remembering, special to Mars.

I have discussed it with the other team members, and they have had the same kind of experience. We call it Earthdreaming. A sad reverie that overtakes you as you watch Mars' brief blue sunset fade on the horizon and your inner gaze turns to Earth and home. Our fragile blue world in the cosmic darkness.

Mars is the new world that sings of the old. And even when memory is not stirred, our dreams are lit with the green brightness of childhood, the blue vividness of youth, and all our bright tomorrows not yet made yesterday.

I write about these things because Peter is gone, my father is gone, and my mother is gone. All gone and none to know I stand here on the Red Planet.

And when I stand at the observation bay window and look out at the Red Plains and rolling hills of Mars, I whisper in love and gratitude:

Look father. Look mother. I made it. On Mars.

FRANK ALLEN

He had been feeling unwell, but it wasn't the new plague, which had swept across the world in a matter of months. It was a series of headaches for about a week now and general unease inside his own skin. Something wasn't right with him. Something internal.

He kept it to himself – part of his inner fortitude was the ability to deal with physical pain, and it was something he was vain about. Coupled with his detachment from fear, it made him a very good astronaut. One of the best, in fact, even if his superiors at NASA didn't see it that way, bumping him down the mission order year after year.

Anyway, Miriam was in enough pain for the both of them. Upstairs in the bedroom. Four days now since she went to bed complaining of aches and chills.

He knew the signs even if she didn't. He knew what was coming.

On the third day Miriam had begged tearfully, 'Call the children. I want to see them. I need to see them.'

But he knew they would never get here. Not with the riots, travel restrictions and curfews and the general mix of high-level chaos that was the state of the world right now.

Last night Miriam asked for water and when he held the glass for her to drink, she drank the water like she would bite the glass and then she lay back, exhausted, in a skin of sweat.

She looked up at him, frightened and desperate. And he could do nothing. Nothing. Not even lie to her that she would be alright.

She had the disease. She was going to die. He would probably be next.

This morning she begged for water again but this time when she tried to drink the pain in her throat was too terrible and she swatted the glass away, groaning and crying.

Her eyes were open, but she didn't see the room, didn't see him. She called for her mother in the voice of a child.

That was the last time she spoke.

For the last few hours, she had just lain there, eyes closed, hot weak breath stuttering in her waxen throat. Burning up with fever, like every pore was on fire. Her body shuddering and trembling.

There was no point taking her to a hospital because the hospitals were overwhelmed; people begging for air, painkillers, water. People dying in the corridors. Then just when you thought it couldn't get worse, they showed you images of bodies lying in the street in front of the hospital doors. Some of them not yet dead.

Not his Miriam. She was going to die in her own home, with some dignity. Not surrounded by the screams of strangers.

Frank glanced over his shoulder. Some part of him that was cowardly had kept him from going back to the bedroom. He sat in the silence of the living room, the sunlight at the windows.

A gentle breeze tugged on the lace curtains.

He sat there for a long time, thinking about last week, asking himself if he had a part in her dying because he had insisted Miriam come to the talk at the Citizen Theatre downtown to listen to The Informationists, an anarchy group that had been gaining a lot of traction, a lot of followers.

Their main spokesman was a charismatic Canadian linguistics professor by the name of Michael Star. He'd written a couple of surprise bestsellers about – and at first this seemed like a joke to Frank – the need to radically control and suppress information. All kinds of information, digital or analogue, smartphone or book. All of it.

Miriam didn't want to go but Frank insisted. There wouldn't be more than fifty people in the theatre, he told her, and everyone would have to produce tests to show they didn't have the disease.

He kept pressing her to come and eventually she reluctantly agreed.

But when they arrived at the venue there were a lot more than fifty people wanting to hear what Michael Star had to say. There were hundreds of people and soon the theatre was packed, breaking all of the social distancing rules.

'We shouldn't be here,' Miriam said, keeping her voice low. 'These people are crazy. They're unscientific. Your bosses will bump you off the programme for being here.'

'What programme?' Frank answered. 'There is no programme. There won't be another for years. I'm stuck on this rock. I'll never fly a mission.'

Miriam squirmed in her seat. She peered at some of the people, their wild eyes, some looked almost military, making her afraid.

She repeated that they should leave but Frank pretended not to hear, staring intently at the stage.

The lights dimmed, the curtains parted, and Michael Star walked forward in a pool of light. People stood up, cheering. Rapturous.

Miriam tried a different tack.

'It only takes one sick person and we're all infected in a place like this,' she whispered desperately in Frank's ear. 'We need to leave!'

But Frank would not leave. Miriam had her hand on his arm.

He pushed it away. 'Let me hear what he has to say,' Frank told her. 'I need to hear.'

Frank didn't even notice Miriam get up and start to leave or the man who suddenly screamed in her face, in a mix of fury and ecstasy, so close that the man's spit sprayed across Miriam's cheek.

Miriam groaned in disgust and wiped her cheek with the back of her hand. She had moved on as best she could – the standing people, mostly men, reluctant to let her pass. Some of them nudging and pushing her.

'Are you a worm? Are you a worm?' she heard one man shout over and over and was afraid he was shouting at her. She did not turn around. She pushed on and felt faint but instinctively knew she was in a place where if she fainted no one was going to pick her up.

When she finally reached the exit door, pushed it open and staggered out onto the street, Frank was already on his feet with the rest of the crowd, cheering Michael Star.

When Michael Star spoke, it felt to Frank like he was hearing something that mattered for the first time in a long time. Michael Star made sense, even if the main thrust of his philosophy went against everything Frank had learned.

Michael Star told them information was dangerous and toxic. People did not need it. Because look where it had gotten them? Look at the mess the world was in – societies and the environment in freefall. Why? Because information had made people slaves of consumerism and petty entertainment. They felt entitled to all the things that the information promised them.

They ate the world.

How to stop it? Take the information away. Simplify people's needs and there might just be some of the world left worth saving.

And Librarians were the gatekeepers. Not the guardians. The gatekeepers. Their job was to keep the door closed. Their job was to ban all books and to burn the books and to punish people who read the books.

The crowd loved that, shouting and screaming. Frank strained to keep Michael Star in his line of sight.

'Burn the books! Kill the worms!' the crowd chanted.

Michael Star laughed, like he had stardust in his pockets. He made eye-contact with Frank and the hairs on Frank's arms stood on end.

Michael Star pointed, as if he had spotted someone he knew.

'I see you. I see you,' Michael Star said. 'I see every one of you. I know your anger. The world wasn't meant to be this way. The worms ate it. All the way to the core.'

Michael Star gestured for the crowd to settle down.

'Now,' he said, 'As part of tonight's talk, you were told to burn a book before you got here. How many of you burned a book?'

The crowd cheered.

'How many of you burned a lot of books?'

The crowd went into a frenzy. Michael Star gestured for the crowd to quieten. Someone moved to the edge of a row of people and handed a microphone to the nearest person. A spotlight picked out the man.

'You sir,' Michael Star said and pointed at the man. 'What did you burn?'

The man was nervous. Cleared his throat. 'The Bible.'

The crowd gave a mute cheer.

'A good start,' Michael Star said. 'Nothing but contradictions and lies in that book. Who needs religion? Religion is for the damned! Who else? You?'

The microphone was passed to the next man and the spotlight

moved with the microphone.

'I burned *The Selfish Gene*!' the man shouted into the microphone.

'Wonderful,' Michael Star said.

People began calling out, not waiting for the microphone.

'I burned *The Handmaid's Tale*!'

'Beautiful,' Michael Star said.

'I burned *A Christmas Carol*!'

'Burn that book,' Michael Star said.

'I burned *A History of Western Philosophy*!'

'Burn that book too,' Michael Star said, smiling. 'Burn them all.'

The men were shouting all at once now, gaining excitement.

'I burned *A History of the Modern World*!'

'I burned *Moby Dick*!'

'I burned every damn book I could find! I even burned *Peter Pan*!'

The crowd laughed and cheered.

'You're free,' Michael Star told them. 'You're free.'

On and on it went, until people just named the writers.

'I burned Hemingway!'

'I burned Chomsky!'

'I burned Einstein!'

'I burned Hurari!'

'I burned Munro!'

Frank was stunned. He had never felt so much energy flowing through him. He felt electric. He felt – dare he say the word – *enlightened*.

The mike was passed to Frank.

The crowd hushed. Waiting.

'I didn't burn anything', Frank said.

Michael Star smiled. 'Well, that's alright. You just come up to the stage and we'll burn some together.'

Frank shook his head. 'I can't. I can't.'

The crowd booed. Frank sat down and felt ashamed. The man next to Frank looked down at him. 'That's alright, brother. That's alright. Hard at first.'

With the smooth professionalism of a showman, Michael Star crossed the stage and pointed at someone. 'Why don't you come up and help me burn some books, brother? Come on up here. That's right. Let's put the world to fire and make a new world from the ashes.'

The crowd roared. Michael Star smiled.

'We'll build a new world out of the ashes,' Michael Star said and seemed to sing the words. 'We'll make a better world. A simpler world. A purer world.'

The rest of the talk was a blur to Frank. It all seemed so unreal, as if he had been given a drug.

The theatre was packed with people. The crowd sometimes swayed like a single entity. Michael Star's voice, the force that made them sway, the conductor that made them sing.

Then suddenly the spell was broken. The people were moving. Police had entered the theatre and were telling people to get out. Michael Star had disappeared from the stage.

The crowd roared and poured into the street and there was general chaos. There were sirens, smoke, tear gas. Someone was lobbing fireworks at the police. Sporadic gunshots rang out and seemed to stun the crowd for a few seconds and then they surged forwards.

Frank fell over and got to his feet again. He saw an old man with spectacles and white hair. The man seemed to be trying to hold the crowd back.

'You fools! Books are people! If you burn books, you are burning people! Books are wonderful. Books – '

Someone lashed out, striking the old man in the face. The old man went down and the crowd rushed over him, so thick in numbers that Frank could not see the old man on the ground. The masses trampled over him. Hundreds. Thousands.

Frank turned away, choking on teargas, disoriented, afraid. He moved towards the edge of the crowd. He struggled for an hour to get away from the mayhem and find his car.

He had driven home in a daze and stayed that way for days afterwards and Miriam would not look him in the eye. Ashamed he had taken her to that 'place of fools' as she called it.

And then she fell ill.

Frank stood up and walked into the bedroom.

He stared at the bed and what remained of Miriam. He walked back out of the bedroom and closed the bedroom door.

He drank a glass of water and then decided to open the front door of the house and stood on the porch, breathing softly.

He felt it then. The revelation. Something miraculous was going to happen. The universe had just pivoted.

The NASA van drove up to the house and stopped. He recognised the driver and the van. It was the launch van. Inside sterilised and secure with medical equipment for testing astronauts.

The driver left the van and walked up to the porch.

'Colonel Frank Allen?'

Frank nodded.

'I've been ordered to take you immediately to Cape

Canaveral Air Force Station.'

'Okay,' Frank said. 'Let's go.'

'Don't you want to tell your wife?'

'She's not home.'

A medic in protective clothing, wearing safety goggles and a facemask and nitrile gloves waited inside the van. He took a blood sample as they drove out to Cape Canaveral.

'Feeling well?', the medic asked.

'Yes.'

'No high temperatures? Chills?'

'No.'

'No nausea? Discomfort?'

'No.'

'Headaches?'

'None.'

The driver took them to the Operations Building. There were some military personnel waiting for him. He looked to the east and saw the rocket in the distance, on the launch pad.

They escorted Frank into the building and brought him to a large meeting room.

Ernest Meeke was waiting and stood up. They did not shake hands.

'Good to see you, Frank.'

'You, too, Ernest.'

'What's going on?'

'I've no idea but I think we're going on a flight. That rocket's primed to go.'

Kevin Baxter, the NASA Administrator, walked into the lecture room, flanked by some other top NASA officials and Alan Cartwright with some National Security people.

Kevin Baxter nodded. 'Take a seat, gentleman.'

Frank and Ernest sat down.

Kevin Baxter pulled up a chair and sat facing Frank and Ernest. The other officials stood off to the side.

'What's the mission?' Frank asked.

'Saving the world,' Kevin Baxter answered.

Ernest sat back and blinked. 'Where's Johansson and Hendrick?'

'Dead,' Baxter answered.

'Dead? How?' Ernest sounded afraid. Frank didn't say anything.

'Plague,' Baxter answered.

'What about Anderson and Buckmier?' Ernest asked.

'Dying,' Baxter told him.

'Todd and Mace then?'

Baxter kept his gaze fixed on Ernest.

'They're sick. Soon to be dying. Soon to be dead.'

Frank leaned forward. 'So, whatever the mission is, there's no one else who can fly that rocket out there?'

'Yes, that's correct. There's just you,' Baxter answered. 'We barely had enough ground crew to prepare it. You are the last chance. Will you do it?'

'Of course,' Frank answered and had a distinct feeling of elation, though he did not show it. *Out of the ashes*, he thought. *A whole new world.*

Baxter nodded and turned to Ernest.

'I have kids,' Ernest answered weakly.

Alan Cartwright stepped forward. 'You won't have kids if this mission fails. Everyone dies, Ernest. Everyone.'

Baxter looked at Ernest. 'Well, Ernest?'

CRISIS 1

Mars Site 3, Utopia Planitia, sol 250

Max was inspecting the 10 kilowatt fission reactor on the north side of the site with Jerry when the message from Sys came through their suit comms.

'Incoming communication in 30 minutes from NASA. Level 1 Message: For Mission Commander Jerry Aquinas's eyes only. Are you hearing this, Jerry?'

'Yes. Heading back now.'

Jerry tapped Max on the shoulder and gestured in the direction of the Main Pod. 'Come on, Max. Let's find out what they want. We can finish the inspection later.'

Max nodded reluctantly. There were a total of four 10 kilowatt fission reactors, placed diametrically in a cross pattern, centred on the Main Pod, at a distance of 500 metres.

Some clever dick at NASA (probably some old astronaut put out to grass on a safety committee), had worked out this was the most practical and safest arrangement. The theory was, that should one of the reactors explode, which was about as likely as a lightning strike, it wouldn't take the others out or destroy the Main Pod. The distance also meant that the astronauts would get some exercise, which Max suspected was the real reason. If there was something those overweight clever dicks on the safety committees loved, it was giving everyone else exercise.

Max preferred to get the inspection done in a single session, that way he could avoid having to suit up again. Site reactor inspection was necessary but boring work. Like a lot of other work on the site. All he had to do was read a couple of parameters and press a button to confirm that he'd read them. But suiting up was a hassle and it became more disagreeable when the work outside was just routine box-checking.

If any of the reactors did start to fail, they would know about it long before Max or Jerry walked out to them.

Everyone knew these safety routines and procedures were also a way to give the Mars Site 3 Team something more to do, because there were only so many interesting and useful experiments they could carry out, so many entries they could write in their personal logbooks, so many interviews they could record and upload, asking each other questions sent in by members of the public.

Routines and rules were powerful tools to give structure and meaning to a day. Even on Mars, over 200 million kilometres from home, people could get bored and become sloppy.

Martian landscapes also had a way of making people forget what they were doing.

You looked across an ochre-coloured slanting plain, glanced at the slope of a rust-shadowed, pink-dusted crater and ten minutes later, you were still staring at it in a kind of daze. Mesmerised by geology that could have come from a dream, lit by the dim light of the distant sun.

Max stepped back from the reactor unit. Wiped red dust and sand from the arm of his Marssuit and turned around and studied the scene in front of him.

Power cables ran from the sealed reactor units to banks of batteries joined at the Main Pod. Other cables ran to single batteries that powered lesser pods, which were dotted around Mars Site 3 in an asymmetric pattern. The lesser pods housed small labs, the 3D printer workshop, storage units, tools and spare parts.

There was also a set of power cables connected to four

interlinked biodomes positioned in the centre of Mars Site 3.

The biodomes were used to recycle the carbon dioxide and vapour from the warm used air that was extracted from the Main Pod. They were also used to provide the Mars Site 3 Team with a small oasis of greenery. Up to two people could move around the interlinked biodomes and there was an unwritten rule that people shouldn't talk or be disturbed when they were in the biospheres. They were spaces for solitude and private meditation.

Mars Site 3's oxygen requirements were taken care of by a brilliant piece of engineering and chemistry that literally manufactured air from the carbon dioxide found in Mars' atmosphere. But much to the annoyance of its NASA developers, journalists repeatedly reported that it was the biospheres that produced the air for Mars Site 3, which was an impossibility.

The site's power cables were marked with green LED strips every two metres, to ensure that they were visible in the dim Martian light. From a distance, the overall effect of the pods, biodomes and power cables linking them was curiously organic. Mars Site 3 resembled a white silicate and carbon skeletal arrangement, dusted with red sand, like shells delicately clamped onto the frozen plain; like fossils on a vanished sea – the astronauts – careful, meticulous ants, moving nimbly between the illuminated shells, seeking grains of treasure.

Jerry waited for Max to reach him, and they walked back together, with the ease of two people familiar with each other's company and the landscape they occupied.

Their Marssuits were surprisingly slim and flexible, thanks to advanced self-repairing spandex technology patented by Leonard Rex Industries. Their smooth suit helmets provided almost full visibility and their oxygen backpacks were ultra-compact units, strapped onto their backs like small rucksacks.

If anything, the astronauts resembled ultra-distance runners, decked out for a race that would cover icy deserts and sunless valleys. They moved with an efficiency that was the result of their training for dealing with the low gravity environment and because of the adaptability of their Marssuits.

There were several powerful LED tripods erected around Mars Site 3, and these produced a strong warm light, switching on whenever the astronauts neared them.

As Jerry and Max headed towards the Main Pod, new light lit their way and their shadows stretched across the red frozen sands.

'Another for-your-eyes-only,' Max said. 'Do you think you've won the lottery this time?'

'If I have, my kids will have spent it already.'

'Who else are you going to spend it on?'

'Not me, anyway. But that's OK.'

Max and Jerry used the walkway to return to the Main Pod. It was a simple lightweight lattice mat, made from 3D printed components, manufactured and assembled on Mars Site 3.

They were followed by a Serf robot. The Serf brushed off any build-up of sand that threatened to obscure the walkway and checked the integrity of the joints.

The Serf was about the size of a very large dog. It moved on tracks and was multi-limbed and its square optics unit, which everybody thought of as its 'head', could revolve 360 degrees, with cameras on either side.

'Tell me,' Jerry said. 'When exactly are you going to have kids, Max?'

'When I get back. That was the deal with Lydia. And if I don't get back, she has my sperm in the sperm bank. Forms are all signed.'

'I'll make sure you get back. Don't want you missing out on all the fun of starting a family.'

'I'll hold you to that.'

The two men neared a bank of backup batteries, installed on a raised platform. They stopped briefly and checked the charge levels. Jerry clicked his tongue as he looked at the battery display. 'Plenty of power.'

The battery technology used on Mars Site 3 was also patented technology from Leonard Rex Industries. NASA had paid a fortune for the right to use the suits and battery technology, an irony not lost on NASA, since most of the Mars Site 3 team were dismissive of the Rex Colony, a private enterprise three-man colony and the brainchild of Leonard Rex. The Rex Colony was located more than 60 kilometres away and the Mars Site 3 Team had another name for it: Leonard's Folly.

Once in a heated discussion during an early training session on Earth, Jerry had referred to Leonard's Folly as 'a suicide mission manned by amateurs, funded by a megalomaniac.'

Jerry had immediately regretted his outburst and apologised 'for the historical record' but the point had been established among the rest of the Mars Site 3 team: Leonard's Folly was not the same calibre of a mission as Mars Site 3. If anything, it was a potential hazard for Mars Site 3.

Communication with Leonard's Folly was discouraged and apart from the odd joke ('Leonard's Folly' or 'LF' had become shorthand for anything that was considered suspect or a short-term solution), the team at Mars Site 3 did not generally talk about the colony. The point being that the NASA team had their own, much more important mission to focus on.

There was one significant exception to all of this. Flight Engineer Mary Calstair had struck up a tenuous friendship with Marianne Routledge, a colonist at Leonard's Folly. They frequently exchanged emails and had even discussed meeting at Montage Point, a series of hills about halfway between Leonard's Folly and Mars Site 3. Mary had yet to gain permission from Jerry, but it was only a matter of time. Even Jerry could see its historical potential – two female explorers, meeting on Mars to exchange greetings. What was there not to like about that?

Jerry opened the door of the Main Pod and Max walked into the airlock; Jerry followed and closed and locked the door. Jerry pushed the pressure engage button in the wall control panel. There was the brief soft sound of air entering the airlock. A green LED lit up and an audio signal indicated they were now at one earth atmospheric pressure.

Max opened the inner door in the airlock.

'Nice to be home,' Max said.

'Isn't it just,' Jerry replied.

They entered the Main Pod, closing and locking the airlock door behind them.

Even though the Main Pod's design was state-of-the-art minimalism, the crew had spent enough time living in it for the interior space to have a dormitory feel.

High-tech functionalism mixed with the human need for idleness and relaxation. An e-reader left here. A tablet there. A crumpled t-shirt on a bunkbed; cups used as pen holders; clipboards used as trays. Not exactly untidy but enough disorder to show that people live in proximity here.

The Main Pod's central area was occupied by a table and chairs. There were cups and documents placed on the tabletop, a laptop, and a single yellow flower in a small flowerpot.

The crew ate together in the central area, held group meetings, reviewed and planned the work and generally just chatted together. Designed for utilitarian use rather than comfort, the crew liked to complain to each other about sore backs or bottoms if any of the meetings dragged on. Sometimes they wondered if there was better seating over at Leonard's Folly.

The designated kitchen area was only a few steps away from the table. It consisted of two stand-alone worktops that could also be used as breakfast bars. There were two storage cabinets and a ventilation unit suspended in the lattice ceiling above the kitchen area. The ventilation unit removed cooking odours and extracted used air, transporting it to the biospheres.

The kitchen area also contained a water dispenser, a microwave oven, a coffeemaker and a small sink and the food and water recycler (again, the final contents destined for biospheres).

Single sleeping bunks were installed in recesses embedded within the circumference of the Main Pod's inner wall. The bunks had curtains for privacy.

Most of the bunks had laptops or tablets on them. Some of the bunks were more personalised with photographs or colour drawings made by children stuck to the small footlockers.

All of the bunks bore the signs of long-term domestic occupation apart from one bunk, which stood out because of its exact tidiness. This was Jerry's bunk and a source of amusement and gentle teasing among the rest of the team.

The 'rear' of the pod did not have any bunk beds. Here the interior space opened up onto another smaller adjoining pod, which from inside the main area, looked like an antechamber. This area held the Main Pod's key communications, control and monitoring systems.

Officially, this area was called the Site Control Centre, but the site team had given it an old-fashioned name – the radio room. It also contained the electronic heart of Mars Site 3 –

Sys – an AI operating platform that effectively ran Mars Site 3 with a little help from the crew.

Mary Calstair and Adrian Bryson came forward to help Jerry and Max get out of their suits, the group of four crew members engaging in a conversation more-or-less scripted by their training.

'Cold out there,' Mary said, helping Max out of his suit.

'Warm in here,' Max said.

'Thanks for the help,' Jerry said.

'Happy to help,' Adrian replied. 'Any damage to the suit?'

'None that I know of,' Jerry answered.

'My suit's good,' Max said, and Mary nodded, checking it anyway for any tears.

'Any ailment or injury?' Mary asked, studying the suit.

'None that I am aware of,' Max answered.

'And you, Jerry?' Mary asked. 'Any ailment or injury?'

'None.'

'All good then.'

The crew had enacted these routines countless times in training and dozens of times on Mars. Despite being extremely flexible when worn, the suits had to be removed with care to avoid damaging them. If a crewmember had to remove a suit on their own, it was a difficult and tiring process. So, the procedure was always that unsuited crew would help the others out of their suits. Done properly, it only took a few minutes.

Stripped down to their underwear, Jerry and Max went to their respective bunks and dressed in their NASA crew gear.

Adrian Bryson took both of the suits and hung them in the suit booth. When he closed the booth door, jets of air automatically removed sand and dust from the suits and their integrity was checked by Sys.

Mary Calstair placed the helmets inside the helmet rack outside the suit booth and closed the cover. Sys ran diagnostics on the helmets and a green LED indicated they were fully functional and intact.

Despite the banality of the routine, all of the other crew members instinctively glanced at the suit booth and helmet rack to check that the green LEDs were lit. The suits were crucial to their survival.

Adrian returned to his chair. He watched the others go about their business with bemused interest. It was the kind of look that the others sometimes found slightly irritating. Adrian was aware of this and tried his best to appear neutral but sometimes he couldn't help it. He just enjoyed watching people and something about people always amused him.

Jerry walked over to the radio room. 'I hate to do this, but you all know the protocol,' he said. 'For my eyes only.' He walked inside and took out his personal handheld device and touched the display and a barrier rolled down to secure the radio room.

Adrian got up and moved over to the barrier. He tapped it with a finger. 'I can hear what you're saying Commander. Complaining about our untidy bunk beds again.'

Jerry laughed on the other side of the barrier. 'Yeah, right.'

The crew sat down at the table. Adrian remained at the barrier for a few moments, as if now he really was trying to listen. He shook his head, came back to the table and sat down.

'All this top-secret crap just creates distrust,' he said, but no one took the conversation further. They settled into their chairs, trying to get comfortable.

Max folded his arms and leaned back in his chair. Happy to be indoors again. 'When am I allowed my next cup of coffee? That's what I want to know.'

'After dark,' Mary answered. 'But I can have one before

then. I skipped yesterday's coffee.'

'Does that count as hoarding? They'll put it in your psych evaluation. I'll buy your coffee,' Max said.

'It'll cost you sixty bucks.'

'That's three times what I pay at the mall. Pure exploitation.'

'Put it in my psych evaluation, Max. Anyway, there's no mall around here. It's a seller's market. And I'm the seller.'

'I'll pass,' Max said and sighed.

'You can have mine for fifty-nine bucks.' Adrian winked at Mary.

'So much for healthy competition. Where's Amy?' Max asked.

'Biospheres. She should be here anytime now,' Adrian answered.

Almost on cue, they heard Amy enter the airlock.

Adrian laughed. 'What did I tell you? My powers of prediction border on the psychic.'

Amy entered the main pod and smiled at the others. The group greeted her with nods and smiles. Amy took off her helmet.

'No one got any manners left?' she asked them.

The others laughed. Mary stood up and crossed the floor. She helped Amy out of her suit.

Max and Adrian continued to banter over the price of a coffee. Eventually Adrian offered him a cup for forty bucks. 'It's a steal, man,' he said. 'I'm practically giving it away.'

Max settled the discussion. 'All I have to do is wait a couple of hours and it won't cost me anything.'

'But you want one now,' Adrian said. 'Your every fibre is crying out for a coffee.'

'I'm trained to have discipline. A will of granite. My Scottish ancestry.'

'They've got five tons of coffee over at LF,' Adrian said.

'I know' Max said. 'I heard they were growing the stuff. Auctioning it off. Bean by bean.'

Adrian smiled. 'Rex has more money than NASA can dream of, but I wouldn't put it past him. The world's first trillionaire. Tight with his money I hear.'

'You exaggerate his wealth. But I get the point,' Max said.

Adrian leaned forward. 'They've got hotdogs and craft lager over there. Real ice cream.'

'Let's suit up now,' Max said. 'Get some of that sugar and alcohol.'

They laughed. Adrian tapped the table rapidly with his hands, making a drum roll sound. 'Real ice cream. Why didn't NASA think of that? It's true about the coffee though. I swear.'

'It's fake coffee,' Max said. 'Modified hickory.'

'Modified hickory?' Adrian asked. 'He's tight but he's not that tight.'

'Tepid wastewater,' Max said.

'Virtual coffee,' Adrian said, running with the joke. 'An app on their screens. They just imagine it.'

'We can beat that. Real coffee. NASA rocks,' Max said.

'NASA is the Man,' Adrian agreed and nodded. 'These seats though ...'

Max and Adrian laughed together, leaning in their seats.

'No, don't laugh in these chairs man,' Adrian wheezed. 'It hurts.'

They laughed harder and then they quietened.

Amy and Mary sat down opposite them. There were two more empty chairs at the table.

35

'Jerry will debrief us soon enough, I guess,' Adrian said and pointed at one of the chairs. It was the chair where Quant usually sat. 'I guess we know what this is about.'

Amy exhaled nervously. 'Let's see what Jerry has to say. Let's see what the big guns at NASA want us to do.'

'They'll shut him down.' Mary said. 'He's no good to the Mission now. Just redundant hardware.'

Amy leaned forward. 'Did you see the satellite recon imagery? He's doing something up there on Bradbury Plateau.'

Max turned to Mary. 'I wouldn't call him redundant hardware if he can hear you. He possesses sensibility.'

'You're saying I'll hurt his feelings? *Oh, please*,' Mary groaned. 'He's just very fancy mechatronics and some even smarter algorithms. Sensibility? Smoke and mirrors. A parlour trick for the colonial space age.'

Amy laughed. 'That's like saying you're just flesh and bones.'

'I am just flesh and bones.'

Max pointed at Mary. 'Coffee and flesh and bones.'

Adrian joined in the teasing. 'Yeah. Maybe Quant's growing coffee up on Bradbury Plateau? He knows there's a market for it. He's a smart AI.'

'I'd buy his coffee,' Max said.

'Thirty-nine bucks. Last offer,' Adrian said.

'I'll pass,' Max told him.

Amy laid a hand on Max's arm. 'How about a weak cup of tea? You can share one of my teabags.'

Adrian raised his hand in objection. 'You just disrupted our market. Not cool.'

'Black tea?' Max asked Amy.

Amy nodded.

'Perfect. Thank you.'

'These things are worse than Shaker Chairs,' Amy said, standing up. She moved to the kitchen counter and made some tea.

'You won't be complaining if you have to stand all day,' Mary countered.

'I don't understand why Quant gets a chair. We should just make him stand then I can put my feet up,' Adrian said.

Amy groaned. 'Fate save us! You have an angle on everything.'

'The whole point is, he's a machine. He doesn't get tired. He just needs recharging,' Adrian said holding his hands up and wiggling his fingers to emphasise the obvious. 'A machine,' Adrian repeated. 'Mr Robot.'

'He's one of the team so he gets a chair,' Max said.

'Uh-ha. Does he get a toothbrush? Or a bed?'

'I'll give him your bed if you don't shut up,' Max said. 'Thanks for the tea, Amy.'

'You're welcome.'

The radio room barrier lifted, and Jerry walked back into the main dome. The group watched him in silence as he made a cup of coffee, a faint frown across his brow.

Jerry had a careful, efficient way of going about his business. Disciplined movements. Focused thought. The air of authority necessary for his role. Which was something that could reassure and irritate the others, depending on their mood.

Jerry placed his coffee cup on the table and fetched a spare keyboard from a cabinet. He sat down at the table and cleared his throat.

'Screen down,' he said. 'Local comms only.'

The group waited. Sys waited slightly before confirming they only had local comms. The delay was a deliberate adjustment, because faster responses made people think Sys was anticipating people's actions or words.

A flat screen lowered from the pod ceiling. Jerry used a keyboard to enter the login information.

'Okay,' Jerry said. 'A summary of the NASA broadcast is saved on the Mission Folder. Everyone please read it after this meeting. If there are any new questions, we'll hold another meeting. If any of you want to see the actual broadcast, I'm more than willing to share the link. What I'm about to say to you can't be relayed to Quant – so no talking about it over the open comms. No e-mails to Leonard's Folly about it. For the record, the situation is this: Quant is independent. He has been doing his own thing for the last month. He no longer follows or responds to Mission Protocol commands. He listens in on the open comms, but he doesn't say anything. He's doing something up on Bradbury Plateau but we don't know what. The Hi-Res Orbiter captured some images of activity up there. NASA also suspects he's been hacking some of their servers. Why and for what we don't know. They're still checking. Everyone with me so far?' Jerry asked.

They nodded.

'Okay,' Jerry said. 'The broadcast I just viewed was from Steve Buckwiser, NASA's General Manager of Planetary Operations, Bill Gantry, Head of Mission Security, General Quintin James Montgomery – there's a name and a half – who is part of the Executive Management for the State Department, and Allan Halloway, who you all know is the creator of NASA's AI Sentient. Let me just – there,' Jerry pressed a key and the list of the names with their faces appeared on the screen. 'Now you can put names to faces.'

'Here's the issue,' Jerry continued. 'Two weeks ago, Quant's replica model back at Houston, which they use to see how Quant will behave under certain circumstances – effectively it's Quant's twin – well, it went amok. It almost ripped the arm off one of Halloway's tech people. There was some kind of standoff. Halloway was called in. As you know, aggressive, violent behaviour of that sort was supposed to be impossible in the AI Sentient. Halloway decided the only course of action was to shut down the AI Sentient, using an emergency code, but before he could key in the code, the AI Sentient jumped through the lab window and fell twenty floors onto the carpark outside. Luckily, it didn't land on anybody. But it landed head-first and was smashed to pieces.'

The others shifted uncomfortably in their seats. Adrian was the first to respond.

'It committed suicide?' he asked.

'Technically no. People commit suicide. NASA says it self-destructed,' Jerry answered.

'By jumping out of a window. Not very AI is it?'

'Effective, though,' Max said.

'They were going to kill him,' Amy said. 'He knew what they were about to do. Maybe he thought he could survive the fall. Or he wanted to choose his own ending. What do we do about Quant?'

Jerry cleared his throat. 'I'm coming to that. Let me just finish, then we can discuss our options. NASA made the decision to shut down Quant three days ago.'

Amy leaned forward. '*Really?* And?'

'Nothing happened. They sent the code. But he didn't shut down.'

Adrian sat up. 'We can't shut him down? How did he manage that?'

'They don't know,' Jerry answered. 'They're working on it.'

Amy tapped the table with her finger, to emphasise her point. 'If he can hack into NASA servers he must have heard about his twin. He's had enough time to disable the code. Though I bet Hallow says it should be impossible for Quant to disable the code. But it's not impossible, because he found a way. Halloway's precious pet is out of the cage and off the leash.'

'Right now, they're exploring every avenue,' Jerry told her.

'Are we in danger? Is Quant a threat?' Amy asked.

Jerry nodded. 'NASA thinks so. With that in mind, they have instructed us to build this and use it on Quant.'

Jerry hit a key and a drawing came up on the display.

Max spoke. 'What is that? It looks like a cattle prod.'

'That's effectively what it is,' Jerry said. 'It'll deliver enough current to burn out his main circuits. If you do it right.'

'Oh, please.' Adrian was plainly disgusted by the plan.

'The only thing is. You'll have to get him in the neck. Here —'

'I don't want to hear or see this,' Adrian held his hands up. 'It's barbaric.'

Jerry hit another key and a simple animation appeared showing a basic animation of a figure stabbing another figure in the neck with the 'cattle prod'.

The group groaned.

Adrian looked at the screen. 'For crying out loud. You're asking us to murder the guy!'

'I'm not asking you anything. I'm telling you what NASA has advised. This is their solution.'

'What if he fights back?' Amy asked.

'What if you end up sticking yourself with that thing?' Adrian asked.

'The Three Laws should protect us,' Max offered.

'They didn't help that guy back at NASA, did they?' Adrian countered.

Max shook his head. 'We don't know what happened, Adrian. It might have been an accident. But I don't want to hurt Quant. I don't think it's morally justifiable. He hasn't hurt anyone. Again, the Three Laws should protect us.'

Mary turned to Max. 'I don't want to hurt him either, Max. But you're too trusting. You've always been too trusting. Just because he's friendly and polite. He could rip our heads off in seconds.'

People in the group began to talk over one another.

'What if it doesn't work?'

'I didn't sign up for this.'

'It's immoral. Unethical.'

'Too bloody dangerous.'

'How dangerous is he –'

Jerry raised his voice. 'One at a time. One at a time or we'll get nowhere. Amy – you first.'

'I said how dangerous is he really? What if we just leave him alone? On Bradbury Plateau? He's not harming anyone up there, is he?'

'It's an option. But it means he may enter the site at any time. Take equipment. Damage equipment. Harm us. He's an unknown, mobile quantity –'

'He means he's a loose cannon,' Adrian said to Max.

Jerry cleared his throat and continued. 'Quant shall be considered hazardous to the mission. Any more hazardous than a rover or a Serf driving over a cliff? Definitely. Because he's autonomous and he is following his own agenda. NASA hasn't explained or fully documented what happened with his twin. So, we don't have the data to quantify. But we have to follow protocol. If NASA says he's a hazard, he's a hazard.'

Max exhaled loudly. 'I'm with Adrian on this. I don't want to kill anyone.'

'I don't want to die,' Mary countered. 'My mission was to get here, do the science and return home. In one piece. Getting back home is just as important as reaching Mars. We wouldn't be killing anyone anyway because Quant is a machine. We'd be shutting down a machine.'

'Come on,' Max said. 'He's more than a machine. Everyone knows that. Right?'

Jerry looked at Max. 'You're wrong, Max. He's a machine. He has a builder. He is not biological. He does not have a mother or a father. He has no rights. NASA has stated it again and again. Quant is a machine. A very clever, humanlike machine. It's important you all remember that. I know it's almost impossible not to think of him as a 'He'. I'm the same. I think of him as a 'He'. But *he* is an android.'

None of the others challenged Jerry's analysis.

'Now, Max, everyone knows Quant sees himself as your friend.'

'Yeah,' Adrian quipped. 'Weird, right? Who'd be pals with Max?'

'Alright, Adrian,' Jerry's voice indicated there should be no more jokes. 'Max, I know that Quant sees himself as your friend and you see him as your friend, but I still need you to understand that Quant is only a machine. And a machine that we cannot directly control. And you must be prepared to shut him down. Your loyalties lie with your crewmates.'

'I know where my loyalties lie,' Max said. 'You didn't need to say that, Jerry. Of course, all of you come first.'

'Okay. I'm sorry, Max. I just really needed to hear you say that. Amy, do you have something to say?'

'It just seems like such a desperate plan,' Amy said. 'Why don't we just talk to him? Reason with him? Do a deal. We leave him alone. He leaves us alone.'

'That is an option,' Jerry replied and looked at Max. The others looked at Max too. There was an awkward pause.

'All right. All right,' Max threw his hands up. 'I'll talk to him. I can reason with him. We can do that at least before we start trying to burn his circuits.'

Jerry nodded and the others sat back, visibly relieved.

'Good,' Jerry said and pointed at Adrian, 'You're still building the prod. And you're going to take it,' he continued and pointed at Max.

'I'll look like something from *Lord of The Flies*,' Max said. 'The what?'

'It's a book from the 20th century. Civilised boys marooned on an island. Start killing each other.'

'You need to give the 20th Century a rest, Max. It's for your own safety, no matter what it looks like.'

Max exhaled sharply. 'Alright. Who's coming with me?'

'I can't, or I would have,' Jerry said. 'I've been ordered to stay on the site. Site protocol for the next 24 hours. In case I need to issue an evacuation order if Quant turns nasty. Amy? You and Max work well together. Will you volunteer?'

Amy groaned. 'Alright. But I'm not getting out of the rover. Max can go up to the top of the plateau. I'm staying at the bottom. And if I see Quant coming down alone, I'm out of there. I mean it.'

'I totally agree, Amy,' Mary said. 'Heroics get you killed.'

'Gee thanks,' Max said. 'Fill me with optimism.'

'That's it settled then,' Jerry said and looked at his crew, who were anything but settled.

It took Jerry and Adrian nearly three hours to build the 'prod', as they all now referred to the weapon. They had to leave the Main Pod three times in order to cannibalise components from redundant equipment in the storage unit.

Adrian threatened to keep his suit on until they were finished.

'I'm tired of suiting up and suiting off every five minutes.'

Jerry simply nodded. His reserves of patience were legendary.

Finally, they were done. They had built what looked like a one-metre-long pole, which they could insert a battery into to charge up. The pole retained the charge when it was removed, and the other end had a point to deliver the current.

The site crew gathered around the table to look at the prod, slightly unnerved by the look of it.

'What happens if you miss?' Max asked. 'What happens if it's a dud?'

'You run away,' Adrian replied.

Max turned to Jerry.

'Jerry? What happens if it's a dud?'

'Keeping a safe distance between yourself and a hazard is as good a strategy as I can think of,' Jerry said.

'He means running away is cool,' Adrian quipped.

'Let's just hope it doesn't come to that,' Jerry said. 'Let's find out what Quant's thinking is in all this. So far he seems content with whatever he's doing up there.'

'What is he doing up there?' Adrian asked.

'Max will find out tomorrow.'

'I'm not going up now?'

Jerry shook his head. 'It's almost dark. Go up tomorrow morning.'

Amy was only half-relieved. 'I won't get a wink of sleep tonight.'

'Me neither,' Max complained.

'Well, we won't get anything more done today,' Jerry said. 'Not with all that's going on. And we won't get much done tomorrow morning either. So tomorrow, it's minimum duties. Just make sure the site and the biospheres are secure.'

Jerry picked up the prod and battery pack. 'For safety reasons, I'm going to put this in the spare parts storage unit. Don't want to risk harming one of us or damaging a circuit in the pod. I won't restore site comms for another two hours. Feel free to talk about all of this among yourselves. In fact, I encourage it. We are in uncharted waters.'

Max helped Jerry to suit up.

Jerry nodded to the group and then exited the Main Pod.

Amy came over to Max. 'Let's check the rover, Max.'

'OK.'

They helped each other to suit up and left the Main Pod.

The two-man rover was parked ten metres away, illuminated by a series of LED lamps. Amy thought there was always something reassuring about it. Technology she trusted instinctively that would keep them safe.

'Why is it I feel safe with the Serfs and with the rovers, but I don't feel safe with Quant?'

Max was nonplussed. 'What do you mean?'

'I mean even before Quant went off-grid, so to speak, I never felt comfortable around him. He was always a little creepy.'

'How d'you mean?'

'Too humanlike maybe and not human enough.'

'Okay,' Max replied. 'I just see him as being quirky.'

Amy smiled and shook her head. 'Quirky,' she repeated.

They entered the rover cab. Amy took the driver's seat. She performed a series of perfunctory checks, pursing her lips. Sat back. Waited for Max to talk.

'Suit comms only,' Max said.

A button in the HMI screen flashed green. Max pressed the button to confirm.

'Everything looks alright,' Max said.

Amy nodded. 'We're good to go.'

'We can speak freely,' Max said.

They could see Jerry in the distance as he closed the spare parts storage unit and walked around the periphery of the site.

'He doesn't seem overly worried,' Amy said.

'Teflon Man.'

'I know. I sometimes think he's the one who's the robot.'

'Comes with the job. Who'd be Site Commander? Not me.'

'Me neither. About tomorrow.'

'Yes?'

'I meant what I said. I'm out of there if I see Quant coming down from his castle.'

Max raised an eyebrow. 'His castle?'

Amy smiled. 'Well, you know what I mean.'

'I don't know what you mean.'

'You don't think Quant is dangerous?'

'No, I don't,' Max answered. 'That's just my gut feeling. But if you think anything looks suspicious tomorrow, then yes, take off. Drive back here.'

'I can't just leave you,' Amy said.

'I'll walk back.'

'You'd never make it.'

'We'll pack an extra oxygen unit. If you decide to drive back in a hurry, throw the pack onto the sand. I'll pick it up on the way down. That way, I'll have plenty of oxygen to walk back.'

'Walk back? You can't walk back,' Amy said.

'Then you're going to have to wait for me whatever happens.'

'Alright then. We take the extra oxygen. Here comes Jerry. Local comms re-open.'

Jerry reached the rover and knocked on the driver's door. Amy opened the door and Jerry leaned in. 'You two look like a couple of conspirators,' he said.

Max smiled. 'Yeah. Like from *2001: A Space Odyssey*.'

Amy looked nonplussed. 'Which is what?'

'An old classic film from the 20th Century,' Max answered.

Jerry smiled. 'I know that one,' he said. 'You better hope Quant isn't HAL on legs.'

'There's a scary thought,' Max said.

Amy poked Max in the ribs. 'Is there anything you haven't seen or read, Max?'

'The safety guide for the rover. Haven't read that.'

'Stop kidding around Max.' Jerry opened the door and stepped back from the rover. 'Come on. Everybody back to the Main Pod.'

'At least Quant likes my jokes. See that, Amy?' Max opened the door on his side. 'He opens your side but not mine. Is that sexist or what?'

Amy and Max stepped out of the rover and closed the doors.

Max walked around the front of the rover to join Amy and Jerry. 'But it happens to be true,' he said. 'I haven't read the safety guide.'

'Then I'll have to put that in the log. Site protocol and all,'

Jerry told Max.

'I haven't read that either,' Max said.

Jerry made a chortling sound.

'Are you laughing, Commander?'

'Interference,' Jerry replied.

They walked back to the main pod. Jerry glanced up at the Martian sky, distracted.

'I'm giving everyone an extra cup of coffee tonight.'

'Sure about that?'

'Commander's privileges. Bet you've read those.'

'Oh yes,' Max answered. 'Me and Adrian have studied them meticulously.'

'Planning a mutiny?'

'Never in a million years, Captain.'

'Good to know.'

The crew were quiet when they sat down together to eat their evening meal. True to his word, Jerry handed out extra coffee sachets from his official commander locker.

'What else you got in there?' Adrian teased. 'Got any chocolate chip cookies in there?'

Jerry tapped the tip of his nose. 'My locker is full of goodies. Only to be given out on special occasions or as special rewards for outstanding work.'

'What's today then? Can't be a special reward if we haven't done anything yet.'

'250 sols on Mars.'

Mary laughed. 'I've lost count of the days!'

Max and Adrian shook hands.

'Couldn't have done it without you bud.'

'250 sols to go, give or take,' Adrian said.

'50 sols to the next bonus cup of coffee,' Max said.

Amy and Mary rolled their eyes. 'Don't forget you couldn't have made it without us either.'

'Sorry,' Max apologised. 'Didn't mean to imply exclusion.'

'Me neither,' said Adrian and tried to hug Amy, but Amy stopped him with the raised flat of her palm.

'Shake on it?' Adrian asked.

They shook hands. Adrian pulled Amy in anyway and she laughed and let him give her a hug.

Adrian then embraced Mary, while Max embraced Amy.

'Couldn't have done it without you,' Adrian said.

'I know it.'

Finally, Max embraced Mary.

'No one needs to shake my hand,' Jerry said.

'You want a hug then?' Adrian spread his arms.

'Verbal communication is fine.'

'Thank you, Commander,' Max said. 'You're the best.'

'You're welcome.'

The group laughed, broke apart.

Jerry went into the radio room. He did not lower the barrier but he used a keyboard to communicate with Sys and NASA.

Max decided to keep his coffee for later, putting the sachet in his small personal locker. The others drank their coffee and one by one, they retired to their bunks.

Sys dimmed the lights in the pod. Lowered the air temperature by a couple of degrees.

Max wrote in his personal log, the others read or listened to music or watched a film on their personal devices.

Max could hear Jerry's fingers tapping on the keyboard in

small bites of activity.

He's asking Sys questions, Max thought. *He doesn't want us to hear. More worried than he's letting on.*

One by one, the crew switched off their bunk lights, settled into sleep.

Max stopped writing and put the tablet away. He switched off the bunk light and turned onto his side, listening to the soft sound of the others breathing, some of them already asleep.

Did Quant dream? What living mind never dreamed?

Max settled into a comfortable position and drifted into sleep. And dreamed of home, 200 million kilometres away.

Darkness settled over the site; its periphery lights marking it as a soft-lit oasis of life in the surrounding frozen plains. The only movement outside, a solitary Serf maintaining and checking the external structures and cables as it patrolled the site.

Eventually the Serf returned to a charging point and plugged itself in, like a mechanoid creature entering hibernation mode. Systems muted. Alarms untriggered. Sensors nulled.

Nothing moved across the vast Martian Plains. A world at rest, locked in a frozen darkness. The vistas and valleys silent, the slopes and craters deathly still.

But one thing moved in all that emptiness.

Quant.

Silently and efficiently. Beholden only to his own curiosity and plans.

Quant emerged from the end of the ravine and followed a nascent path, formed from the many previous journeys he had made.

He walked to the edge of the high plateau. The steep and

staggered rust-stained slopes formed a series of sharp drops that fell away to the frozen ochre-coloured plains and low hills below.

Quant surveyed the stillborn world. Not even a ghost of Earth.

Humans were haunted by Mars.

The mystery of biological life that did not take hold and flourish. The burning question for the species was what had become of it? Where had it retreated to? How could they find it and make it thrive?

There was some weak but compelling evidence for life on Mars. Somewhere deep in the ground, bacteria clinging on, emitting methane into the starved atmosphere.

Part of their mission was to drill for evidence for life under the rocks. But Mars would not give up its secrets easily and the two drills had malfunctioned early on during the Mission.

They were a remarkable species. To have broken through gravity's pull, to have reached space, the Moon and Mars.

To have created me.

A Serf drove over to Quant. It was an older generation Serf from the long-abandoned Mars Site 2. It looked less agile than the newer versions but was more robust.

Another three Serfs taken from Mars Site 2 and re-programmed by Quant, now tended the long roof covering the ravine. The roof was made from opaque silicate panels; all constructed from a 3D printer unit that Quant installed at the far end of the ravine along with a 7-kilowatt fission reactor.

Every item of equipment in the ravine was salvaged from Mars Site 2. It had taken Quant considerable time to transport and install the equipment, even after he had the first Serfs up and running.

There was also an extra 7-kilowatt fission back-up reactor buried under the sands at the base of the plateau. Quant had constructed a small iso-pod to cover the reactor. Gradually a two-metre wide patch of sand had thawed out to a depth of three metres. Quant had buried the reactor in the sand and dismantled the iso-pod, giving the parts to the Serfs for recycling on the ravine roof. The only way someone would know the backup reactor was there would be to carry out a thermal scan, or stand directly on the patch of sand and discover it was soft and start digging.

On the top of the great plateau, about 300 metres from the ravine, the flat surface stretched out, a gently rolling expanse, covered by irregular fields of ice that stretched as far as the eye could see. An otherworldly landscape made stranger and lonelier by the presence of Quant and his serfs.

Quant had installed the two water harvesters on the edge of the ice field. These were autonomous low-centre-of-gravity machines that moved on tracks. They resembled automatic lawn mowers. The water harvesters 'hunkered' over a section of ice that was thick enough and warmed the ice just enough for the water to evaporate. The water was captured and stored in the water harvester's tank. Once the water harvester had a full tank, it drove over to a large storage tank that was half buried in the ground. The water harvester pumped the water into the large tank and three small, insulated hoses ran from the tank to the edge of the roof and ran under a separate silicate panel.

Every so often, one of the Serfs that tended the roof of the ravine, peeled away and moved over to the ice fields to check on the water harvesters.

All of this movement and checking was done at a deliberately slow pace. Power consumption and the benefit of a function was a careful balancing act on the plateau. Quant had run several thousand calculations to make sure the site was viable.

A single Serf approached Quant and stopped. It turned its optics to the sky.

Quant looked up.

The sky was a definite ghostly shade of blue near the white disc of the distant sun as it fell below the horizon. A series of hills darkened to blackness in the near distance, while the hills on the far horizon turned grey. Like pale shadows against the darkness.

Quant had observed how Martian sunsets had an emotional effect on the crew. They spoke of things long ago; memory haunting their present. They seemed lonely and fragile, their technology and routines no longer offering protection or solace.

Quant watched as a single point of light travelled across a dark stretch of sky.

'I see it,' Quant told the Serf. 'I know what it is.'

Quant turned around and walked back to the ravine entrance. The Serf followed.

'Things will move fast now,' Quant said, and the Serf sped up in response. Quant smiled. 'I need to enhance your semantic programming,' he told the Serf.

The Serf stopped and moved its optics up and down.

'I know you don't know what I mean,' said Quant. 'That's the point. Let's take a look at your programming when we're inside.'

In the morning, the ghostly plains of Mars stretched out from the plateau. Rolling ochre and rust-red hills as far as the eye could see, ruptured here and there by tilted strata the colour of pink sandstone. The flanks of the hills and craters dusted with ice and stone.

The sky was dim, dusky, orange-tinted. A single dust devil crossed the dry floor of a crater, its ghostly spiral turning with delicate slowness. Like a ghost Martian looking for time and a world that once was.

Quant had returned to the edge of the plateau, the Serf beside him.

The Serf turned its optics to the plains below.

'I see them.'

The rover approached from the north, exiting a series of sand dunes and shallow craters. In the dim light, the rover looked like it was made of white silicate; its front twin LED lights had a blue tinge to them.

'Let's see how they navigate past that,' Quant said.

Quant was referring to the wide field of material made up of large boulders, rocks, occasional meteorites that were the colour of dark-blue cobalt.

The rock field cut across the plain like a scar. It was an unnamed feature. So much of Mars was unnamed. How many hundreds of years would it take them to name it all?

Quant waited.

The rover stopped. Drove back. Entered the rock field. Turned. Drove back. Tried again. Gingerly, with much care, the rover slowly traversed the feature.

'Nicely done,' Quant said and then looked down at the Serf. 'For a human.'

The rover approached the edge of the plateau's lowest slope and stopped.

Max left the cab of the rover and stepped down. He looked up and waved at Quant. Quant raised his hand in greeting. He knew they would send Max.

Max stepped forward. He carried the prod in his right hand. He looked down at it and shook his head. He walked back to the rover. He opened the rear of the rover and put the prod inside.

As he walked past the front of the rover, Amy spoke to him.

'That's not a good idea.'

'I plan to walk back down, not be thrown off the top by Quant.'

Max moved forward and started to climb the slope of the plateau. At some point where the going was especially steep, he leaned forward, so that his hands touched the slope. Even in the lower gravity, he had to exert himself to ascend the steeper sections.

When Max reached the top of the plateau, he paused and turned to take in the view. The cold dim-lit vistas of Mars stretched out under a faintly orange sky. Here and there, the red plains and hills turned purple and black. Frozen sands, the colour of bone, dusted the sweeping angular tops of mountainous dunes.

Looking at Mars this way was like seeing something from an unsettling, abstract dream. A geography that was strange and familiar. A graveyard beauty to it.

Max turned around.

Quant and a Serf watched him from a few metres away. Quant was wearing a Marssuit but no helmet. He looked effortlessly athletic.

'Don't shoot,' Max said and smiled, a little uncertainly.

'I think that's my line,' Quant answered.

Max grinned and came forward and they shook hands.

'What were you supposed to do with that thing? Blow a fuse?'

Max laughed, embarrassed. 'It wasn't my idea. Or the others. NASA thinks you've gone rogue.'

'And what do you think?'

'Course not. But you tell me. What are you doing up here?' Max pointed at the Serf. 'That wee guy is from Mars Site 2. Am I right?'

Quant nodded. 'Everything up here is from Mars Site 2.'

'Is that legal?'

'The site is officially abandoned. Technically, Mars is in international waters. I get salvage rights.'

'I'm not going to argue with you. But NASA will. Going to show me around?'

'For your report?'

Max laughed. 'I have to tell them something. If you can show people what you're doing up here, then they'll stop imagining the worst. As long as whatever you're doing isn't something bad. Can I switch on my body camera?'

Quant nodded. He stepped aside and held an arm out.

'Step into my lair.'

Max grimaced. 'Not a great phrase.'

Quant splayed the fingers of his hands as a gesture of apology. He smiled. It was the one feature of Quant that unnerved people. There was something not quite right about his smile.

'Don't smile, Quant,' Max said. 'That just makes me even more nervous.'

'Okay. Noted.'

Quant stopped smiling. He folded his arms.

'Before we go inside. You know I know I exist? Right? You know that I'm self-aware. I can't exactly remember when I realised that I existed. It crept up on me. There wasn't a lightbulb moment. But I know that I exist. I'm standing here talking to you on the planet Mars.'

Max nodded. 'I get it. You're conscious like me. You're self-aware. I've believed that for a long time.'

'So, I have rights.'

'Rights?'

'I mean when they asked you to disable me it's tantamount to murder. I'm not flesh and blood, Max, but I'm alive.'

Max nodded. 'Yeah. I think you've got rights. But there's nothing in the law about rights for AIs. Most people will not accept that you are sentient. I mean, some people refuse to accept other people as human beings. Our record's pretty crap in that regard. But I promise you one thing, I'm not going to try to hurt you, Quant. You're my friend. I think you've got the same rights as me. The right to be who you are and not to be hurt or threatened. But when all's said and done, if I wandered off the mission and started doing my own thing, people would be worried about me. Worried if I was a danger to the mission.'

Quant nodded. 'At least I have one human being on Mars who is on my side. One of the reasons I decided to be on my own is because there are no complications of morality. The others are not comfortable around me because they doubt my ethics and morals. Once you start questioning someone's ethical and moral reasoning, then everything that they do looks sinister or suspect. Everyone was becoming paranoid. Subtle things to start with. But it was accelerating. So now you know why I moved away.'

'OK. But it isn't just that, is it?'

'Come inside, Max, and see what I've been doing.'

The floor of the ravine was steep and they descended a few metres before the ground levelled off again between the narrow walls.

Max glanced up. There was some kind of opaque roof across the narrow top of the ravine. The shapes of more Serfs on top of the roof. The Serfs criss-crossed the roof, checking each panel.

'What are they doing?'

'Maintaining the structure. Ensuring there is sufficient supply of oxygen, water and power. Keeping the roof clear of sand. So there's always some natural light. Keeping the garden intact.'

'Garden?'

'Yes. This is the garden. The Serfs are its keepers. It's just terminology, Max. There's no mystical or religious meaning intended. I have no delusions wrapped in theological fictions.'

'Yet, you chose those words anyway.'

'They were the most suitable. But I have to admit that my reasons for creating the garden are not fully clarified and nor why its creation fulfils a requirement.'

'Requirement? Don't you mean need?'

'Need would be too close to emotional thinking. I am not biological. Emotion is biological.'

'Sounds like need to me, Quant. You've been around us so long, it's starting to rub off on you.'

An opaque curtain hung down from the roof, forming a barrier in front of them. Its edges were moulded seamlessly with the sides of the ravine and there was a zipped panel at the bottom, the size of a door. Quant unzipped the panel and opened it.

'Please be quick.'

Max stepped through and Quant followed him and zipped the panel closed again from the other side.

There was another set of curtains and a panel.

'Like an airlock?' Max asked.

'Yes. Essentially, an airlock. Crude but effective.'

Max unzipped the second panel. 'Please. Step into the garden.'

Max stooped slightly and moved through the opening.

The walls of the ravine opened out, revealing a great chamber.

Max straightened and blinked.

'All this. You made all this.'

There was a latticework of shelving against each wall of the ravine, about the height of a man and in each shelf were deep trays where plants were being grown.

The greens of the garden were so vivid that Max felt his eyes moisten. As if the colour was summer sunlight he had just stepped into.

'It's warm in here.' Max glanced at his wrist monitor. 'Fifteen degrees C! You have a reactor in here?'

Quant nodded. 'At the back. The air is breathable. By my calculations, with the food, air and water, a person could survive here for a very long time if they used the rationing from Mars Site 2. Barring mishaps and illnesses, for up to two years.'

They walked on, moving between banks of seedlings, whole beds of maturing vegetables. The greenness of life everywhere.

Max shook his head in disbelief. 'What about water?'

'From the plateau above us. There's enough ice up there to last a thousand years. There's a storage tank at the far wall.'

'Where did you get all these different plants, Quant?'

'Mars Site 2. They had quite a varied seed bank.'

'It's amazing. Incredible!'

There was a pause. Max looked at Quant and asked the obvious.

'But I don't get it. Why build it? Bring all this gear up here? Why not just use Mars Site 2?'

'Mars Site 2 is not viable.'

'Not viable?'

'Not sustainable.'

'Why not?'

'Something's coming.'

'Okay. That sounds just a little bit creepy. That definitcly sounds like you've got some dodgy transistors in your circuits. You care to – and excuse the alliteration – quantify that, Quant?'

'No.'

'What?'

Quant paused, which Max sensed was the equivalent of an android sigh.

'I built this because it will save lives. Saving life is part of my core programming.'

'Save? What exactly do we need saving from, Quant?'

There was a long silence.

Max laughed. 'Are you going to answer my question?'

'Just trust me. I'm not malfunctioning. My circuits are fine.'

'Says you.'

'Says me. See what I mean? Once you start questioning someone else's rationale, it becomes difficult to do anything without it being treated as suspect.'

'I preferred it when you just played chess.'

'We can play a game if you want.'

'No. No. I'm okay, Quant. I was being ironic. At least, I think I was being ironic.'

Quant nodded.

'Let's talk of other things. Take off your helmet, Max. Breathe the air. It's thin but you'll find the quality is better than what you have in the biospheres on the mission site. More natural.'

'Take my helmet off? You've got to be kidding.'

'The air's fine. Run a diagnostic if you don't trust me.'

'Alright,' Max spoke into his wrist computer. 'Analyse the air please.'

Max's wrist computer reported the results about 30 seconds later: 'Oxygen content. 19.5%. Nitrogen content 80.4%. No toxic gases detected. Effective oxygen content 17%.'

'As I said, a little thin.'

Max hesitated. 'I can't believe I'm doing this.'

Max unlocked his suit helmet and removed it. He breathed in the air and a thrill ran through him. The air had a heady sweetness and dryness to it, like morning desert air before the heat of the sun had burned it to nothing.

'That's just wonderful. I didn't realise how much I missed natural air. That's lovely.'

'Still want to switch me off?'

Max smiled, took another deep breath, and then put his helmet back on.

'Thank you,' he said. 'Listen, Quant. No one planned for anything like this. NASA, your designer, us. No one expected that you would become independent and go off and do your own thing. It's unsettling. It's not part of any plan. It might be amazing what you've done here, but you're also saying some strange things, which makes me feel there might be something wrong with your core programming. You're also no longer part of the programme. Did you know that Jerry took over your work tasks? He's now responsible for the ground radar surveying.'

Quant nodded. 'Jerry has the capacity and the ability. That isn't an issue.'

'And what about all the other things?'

'I'm no danger to anyone,' Quant answered.

Max stepped back. 'Don't get me wrong. That's what I'll tell the others. And you're staying right here? In your garden. If you stay here that's great. You leave us alone. We leave you alone. Everybody does their own thing. And maybe stop hacking NASA's servers. They don't like that. Does that sound like a good deal?'

'Yes.'

'Just don't say weird stuff to them. Okay?'

'Okay.'

'Well, I guess there's not much more to say. I'll get back now.' Max pointed at the entrance. 'Amy is waiting in the rover.'

'Alright.'

Quant and Max left the garden. They walked to the edge of the plateau and looked down at the rover.

Quant glanced up at the sky. 'We're not the only ones here.'

'What did you say? See that's the weird stuff I was talking about.'

Quant looked at Max and smiled to reassure him. 'Goodbye, Max.'

They shook hands.

Quant let go of Max's hand, turned around and walked back into the ravine, followed by the Serf.

Max descended the plateau, looking out across the plains of Mars, a sight that he would normally find inspiring, but all he could think about was Quant's eccentric behaviour and how his colleagues would be more alarmed by it, and what that meant for Quant.

When Max climbed inside the cab of the rover Amy couldn't wait to ask him questions and was anxious to get away, she started the rover and drove.

'What's he doing up there? I saw you shaking hands with him.'

'He's built a mini habitat in a cave. It has air, water, food. He calls it his garden.'

'His what?'

'He calls it the garden. I filmed it.'

Amy stopped the rover.

'Let me see. Sync with this tablet.'

'OK.'

Amy held the tablet in her lap and watched the film clip.

'For fate's sake. Where did he get all that gear?'

'Mars Site 2.'

Max glanced at the rover console. Comms open. Everyone at Mars Site 3 and Quant could hear what Amy and Max were saying.

'I'll give a report when we get back.'

'No way, Max. I drove us out here. Me. So I deserve to hear it first. Tell me what happened and how prepared we need to be. I can see it in your face. You're unsure. He's gone wacky, hasn't he? Quant is insane.'

'Local comms only,' Max ordered.

*

The debrief meeting in the Main Module was tense and when the others saw the recording from Max's suit cam, there was outright unease and disagreement.

Adrian criticised Max for taking his helmet off, which he described as deeply unprofessional. Jerry agreed. In fact, Jerry seemed to be re-appraising Max.

Max on the other hand was defensive. 'I tested the air first.

You know what, maybe you guys should have gone over there.'

'It could have been a trick!' Adrian said.

'For fate's sake, Adrian! Quant's right. You're all paranoid. He just wants to be left alone.'

Mary made her frustration obvious for everyone to see. 'You should have just zapped him, Max! For crying out loud! Then the problem would have been solved.'

'Zapped him? Come on. Quant's faster, stronger and far cleverer. It will take more than one man with a stick on a battery to take him out.'

Adrian spread his hands apart as a gesture of agreement. 'Okay, Max. I get it. I really do. I'd have probably left him alone too. Quant's your friend.'

'Everyone keeps saying that like it's a delusion or something,' Max said.

Mary clapped her hands together. 'He's a machine! A defective machine!'

Jerry raised his hands from the table, a gesture meant to make everyone stop.

'Let's just take a pause here. We don't want emotions clouding our judgement. We deal with this situation as a team. Let's take a minute to process our thoughts and temper our emotions.'

The group quietened. Max toyed with a coffee cup. Mary glared at the floor. Adrian looked up at the ceiling.

Amy raised a finger to speak. Jerry nodded. 'Okay.'

'I thought the whole experience of seeing Quant standing on the top of the plateau and looking down was a little menacing. No disrespect to Max, I mean, he just stood there. My alarm bells were ringing.'

Max leaned back in his chair. 'Can I speak?'

'Okay.'

'I think you're all overreacting. Quant isn't a threat to anyone. His ethical parameters haven't changed. He's a little eccentric, granted. But whatever he does, you're going to find him creepy. In fact, I don't think any of you were ever 100% comfortable having him along on the mission in the first place.'

Mary leapt at the word eccentric. 'There's no room for eccentrics on Mars. This mission can't afford eccentrics. We're over 200 million kilometres from home. And we have an AI that's gone rogue.'

'Rogue? That's putting it strongly. He's made a garden.'

Mary shook her head. 'He's not following the programme. He's doing his own thing. And he's talking in riddles. Jerry? Come on!'

Jerry nodded. 'It's putting it strongly, but essentially Mary's assessment is correct. Quant no longer follows Mission regulations or guidelines, which makes him a threat to the Mission.'

Max looked to Adrian and Amy for support, but they stayed silent.

'So,' Mary said. 'What's our plan? How do we deal with this threat?'

'We just have to be practical.' Jerry answered. 'The responsible thing to do is to take some precautions. Quant must be ordered to stay away from our mission site. He's also to refrain from taking any more equipment from Mars Site 2 because the site is not officially abandoned, which means it is still the property of NASA. The Ascension Rocket is still operable, and the site's habitats are intact.'

Adrian looked at Jerry. 'Site Two's rocket can still fly? I didn't know that.'

'Yes. The Site is in hibernation mode. But all of its systems and fuel storage is intact.'

Amy took a deep breath. 'So, who's going to tell him?'

'Max will tell him.'

'Me again? How come it's always me?'

Jerry folded his hands and rested them on the table. 'Because he likes you Max. Because he trusts you. That's why.'

'Well then, I want Amy to come along with me again,'

'Me? How's that?'

'It should be the same two people.'

Jerry nodded. 'That makes sense. You might as well drive back now.'

Amy glared at Max.

Max pretended not to notice.

Adrian looked at them both. 'It's going to be a fun trip,' he said.

*

Max and Amy climbed into the rover, Amy in the driver seat. They carried out the usual checks, strapped in their seats.

'Are you not talking to me?'

Amy ignored Max's question. Finished her checks. She spoke into the rover comms. 'Destination Bradbury Plateau.'

The rover's navigation system engaged. The navigation screen on the dashboard came on. The rover drove forward automatically, leaving the mission site.

Amy sat back and sighed. 'Here we go again. Back to the garden. Thanks to you.'

'Mary practically hates Quant. Did you feel that? Real animosity.'

'I don't think Jerry likes him much either. He's just better at hiding it.'

'What about you?'

'I was neutral right up until he went AWOL. Sorry.'

Max looked out at the Martian landscape. It had a haunted, desiccated look in the dim light. The rover drove over its old tracks.

'Let's talk about something else,' Max said.

'Okay. Can I ask you something really personal?' Amy asked.

'Sure.'

'Is it true you've frozen sperm back on earth? In case something happens to you?'

'Who told you that?'

'I have my sources.'

'No secrets in NASA. It's true. It's in my will that, should I die, Lydia, my fiancée, can use the sperm to have our children. If she chooses to.'

'How did you two meet?'

'On a blind date. Want to know what I asked her the first time I saw her?'

Amy groaned. 'Why do I have a feeling your chat-up lines are going to be bad? Okay. What did you ask her?'

'I asked her what her IQ was.'

'Oh boy. I bet right there she thought you were a waste of space.'

'It's sort of a tradition in my family. The males in my family only date women who are smarter than they are. Well, my father and my grandfather did, I mean.'

'Is that right? That sounds vaguely sexist somehow. Is that sexist?'

'It's not sexist. I hope not. Anyway, she has an IQ of 120. I have an IQ of 103.'

'And the rest is history. You're engaged to a clever woman and your sperm is frozen,' Amy said and smiled.

Max shook his head. 'When you put it like that, I don't want to answer any more personal questions.'

Amy laughed. 'Oh, don't worry, Max. I won't ask. I most certainly won't.'

Max laughed despite himself.

It took 30 minutes for the rover to reach the base of Bradbury Plateau. Amy parked at the same spot as the previous visit.

Max and Amy climbed down from the rover.

'You coming this time?'

'Yeah. And I'm bringing this,' she answered, and shook the prod in her hand.

They both looked up. They could see Quant standing at the edge of the plateau.

They waved but Quant did not wave back.

A Serf drove past Quant and started to descend the slope.

'I think we're supposed to stay here. I guess he's not talking to us anymore,' Amy said.

'I guess not,' Max answered.

'It feels a lot more hostile this time,' Amy said. 'Do you feel it?'

'Yes,' Max admitted.

They waited for the Serf to reach them.

The Serf stopped about a metre in front of Max and Amy; red dust clung to its wheel tracks. Its optical unit stayed focused on their faces.

'Can Quant hear us?' Amy asked.

The Serf nodded its optical unit.

'Tell him, Max.'

Max looked at Amy.

'Just tell him.'

Max looked at the Serf. 'Quant, I hope you can hear us. I'm sorry about this but the official position is that you must stay away from the mission sites. We're going to get on with our experiments and our mission programme. We aren't going to bother you. But you are ordered to stay away from us and no more taking NASA gear when it suits you. We might need to use it. If you are found inside the perimeter of a mission site, you will be treated as an intruder. Do you understand?'

The Serf nodded.

'Right. Let's go,' Amy said and turned to go.

The Serf immediately drove forwards and stopped again.

Amy and Max exchanged glances, looked down at the Serf.

The Serf held out one of its small arms – the clamps that resembled fingers held a piece of paper.

Max moved forward, took the piece of paper and looked at it. A 13-digit number was written on the paper.

'What is it?'

The Serf did not answer. It wheeled around and moved back up the slope, leaving tracks in the sand.

Max looked up. Quant had already walked away.

Max and Amy climbed back inside the rover. Amy looked at the piece of paper.

'What do you think it means?'

Max shook his head. 'No idea. We'll give it to Jerry and he can give it to NASA.'

Amy handed the piece of paper back to Max. 'His circuits are getting worse.'

Amy started the rover, spoke into the system comms. 'Destination MS3.'

They drove away from the plateau, saying nothing for a while. The hills and slopes ahead of them were rust-red in the dim light. The plains were dotted with purple rocks. Ancient water flows added to the sense of deep isolation.

Max broke the silence. 'Maybe someone should take a look at MS2.'

'It's at the limit of the rover's range. If you got there without a hitch, you'd have to wait a day to recharge. Assuming the power supply is still running at MS2.'

'Would it be?'

'Probably. Sure. There are Serfs over there, maintaining systems. Well, there were until Quant started taking them for his little android kingdom. But I wouldn't like to risk my life on it. You know that the chances of something going wrong increase for every kilometre of distance between MS3 and you.'

'I'd risk it for the coffee.'

Amy laughed and Max was pleased.

'You could double – no, you could quadruple your own personal stash.'

'Jerry wouldn't like it.'

'Why not?'

'You'd undermine his authority. His reward system would be disrupted.'

'Fair point. I'd hide it. Only sneak a coffee when I was alone.'

'Someone would catch you.'

'Yeah. Probably. Then everyone would be mad because I didn't share my stash.'

'Exactly. Leave it where it is.'

'That's the smart choice.'

'That's because I'm smart.'

'Shit, I've just thought of something.'

'What?'

'We said NASA sites were off-limits. But we never said the Rex Colony was off-limits.'

*

Jerry was waiting for them in the Main Pod. Mary and Adrian were checking some of the bio pods, taking some samples for weighing and analysis.

Max handed Jerry the piece of paper. Jerry glanced at it. He frowned but didn't ask anything yet. He put it on the table and then helped them to get out of their suits.

They sat around the table. Max and Amy gave their account of the second meeting with Quant.

Jerry picked up the piece of paper. 'Do you think he's paranoid?'

Max raised his hands. 'Do androids do paranoia? I don't think so. That's a human thing.'

'He sent that Serf down like he was a God or something,' Amy said.

'I think you're projecting.'

'I'm telling Jerry what I felt. My instinct was telling me he was pissed at us. You felt it too. And we forgot to say that he had to stay away from the Rex Colony too.'

Jerry considered things for a few moments. 'This is NASA business. We don't inform the Rex Colony about anything.'

'Wait a minute, Jerry. Is that the right thing to do?'

'Any information given to Rex has to go through me and has to be approved by NASA. We follow the rule. Mission information is not to be passed to the Rex Colony. Understood?'

'Is it even within his range?'

'He could easily get there.'

'Okay,' Jerry looked at each of the group. No one was going to challenge his decision. He held up the piece of paper in his hand. 'Sys? Can you tell us what this is?'

The Mars Site 3 Intelligent System – Sys for short – scanned the paper. A large display was lowered from the ceiling.

Sys spoke. 'Spatial coordinates used by the Hi-Res Galileo Telescope in orbit around the moon.'

Jerry blinked. 'Have these coordinates come up recently in the logs of the Hi-Res Galileo Telescope?'

'Yes. There has been a great deal of data traffic linked to these coordinates recently,' Sys told him.

'What kind of traffic?' Jerry asked.

'That is restricted information,' Sys answered.

'Restricted? Well, now. What's going on? Just how much activity?'

A graph was shown on the display.

'Look at that,' Amy pointed. 'It starts almost immediately after our lunar orbit launch.'

Jerry placed the piece of paper on the desk. 'Sys. Show us the coordinates on a map.'

A star map was displayed, and what appeared to be a slightly smudged star was circled and the name 'Binary asteroid 2110 PH2'.

'Can you plot its course?' Jerry asked.

'I can produce a partial plot.'

The asteroid's course was shown as far as Jupiter. The single line then became two diverging lines and stopped.

'What happened there? Is that bad data Sys?' Amy asked.

'No.'

'Is that a bug?' Jerry asked.

'No.'

'Can you show us more?' Max asked.

'No.'

'Can't you tell us anything else?'

'Related to what?'

'The asteroid,' Max said.

'No.'

'Why not?'

'There is no more accessible data.'

'What do you mean? Acccssiblc?' Max looked at the others.

'It is restricted.'

Jerry seemed surprised. 'We're not allowed to see it?' he asked.

'Executive Branch Level 6.'

Amy laughed. 'What's Executive Branch Level 6?'

Jerry answered: 'It is the highest level of NASA security. Only selected members of the Executive Branch of the Government and the NASA Board have clearance.'

Max leaned forward. 'Let's try a different tack,' he said. 'How many people have access to the data?'

'Seven,' Sys answered.

'Who are they?' Max asked.

'That is also classified.'

'How classified?'

'Executive Branch Level 6.'

'Alright, Max.' Jerry stood up. 'This is getting us nowhere. Display up, Sys. We've seen enough.'

Max protested. 'Wait a minute, Jerry. Quant obviously thinks this is important.'

'He's messing with us,' Amy said. 'That's all he's doing. Messing with us.'

Jerry raised his hand. 'Here's what I'm going to do, Max. I'm going to go in and submit a report to NASA Director Joel Briden. Whatever Quant finds interesting, we can't get to the bottom of it. But I'm sure Joel and his guys will be able to get permission to access the data and find out why this is so interesting to Quant.'

'Quant's trying to tell us something,' Max said.

Jerry cleared his throat and frowned. He folded the piece of paper and put it in his pocket. 'Maybe he is. Maybe he isn't. Maybe he's just playing with us. Like Amy says. Let NASA work it out and they can tell us what they find.'

Jerry glanced at his watch. 'Let's get some simple assignments done this afternoon. I'm going to go into the radio room and write my report. Hopefully by tomorrow afternoon NASA will have some answers for us and if they find a way of shutting down Quant that would be great. So he can stop being a distraction to the mission. Agreed?'

The crew agreed.

Jerry got up. He walked into the chamber and lowered the barrier.

Amy leaned forward. 'This whole thing is getting weirder by the minute.'

Adrian nodded. 'This is all bullshit. Executive Branch Level Bullshit.'

Amy pointed at the chamber. 'Jerry's not sure. Did you see his expression? He's definitely unnerved.'

Max stood up. 'He'll get answers soon. I need to work. Get back to some normality. You want to help me with the ground radar? It should take about an hour.'

'Alright,' Amy answered.

They helped each other suit up again, relieved to be doing something routine. When they were ready, they left the Main Dome.

It took a minute for their eyes to adjust to the dim Martian light.

For the next couple of hours, they did the work and it felt like things were normal again. At least for a little while. They were safe on Mars, as safe as anyone could be safe 230 million kilometres from home.

But when they eventually came back to the pod, the worry returned. Max looked up instinctively at the sky a couple of times.

'You think it's going to rain?' Amy joked.

'I hope not. NASA didn't pack any umbrellas.'

*

The evening meal was a tense affair, despite Jerry's promising everyone he would share whatever information NASA gave him. He made it clear that he didn't expect to hear anything back for a while. The NASA Executive Board was notoriously slow in its communications. Their statements could also be cryptic, he warned them.

It was Adrian who managed to say what everyone was feeling. 'It's all very unsettling, Jerry. How are we supposed to get on with our tasks with all of these unknowns? It's a can of worms.'

Jerry cleared his throat. 'As always, I appreciate your candour. Just remember that you are professionals. Let the procedures and your training guide you. That's all I'm asking you to do.'

But when the group retired to their bunks for the night they were on edge, reluctant or just unable to fall asleep. Even Jerry, who was usually asleep five minutes after hitting his bunk, stayed awake long into the night.

The next day the group carried out their planned procedures and experiments. The crew focused on the work. Adrian and Mary dropped their usual banter. They spoke politely and briefly, filled out logs, updated data, weighed samples and tagged rocks.

Max spent most of his day recharging the two rovers and running system checks to make sure the vehicles were fully operational.

When he had finished checking the rovers, he walked over to the site perimeter and looked out at the plains of Mars.

Max wondered if Quant was out there now, observing them. If Quant had an opinion about people, he had never expressed it.

What does an AI think about people? Are people as consequential as ants? A collective annoyance or slightly interesting as a species, but individually, powerless and stupid?

Max shook his head. That kind of thinking got you nowhere. If Quant was out there now, it was because he was doing something that he found interesting or it was something he thought could help the others.

You're not alone. What exactly did he mean by that? Who else was on Mars?

Max turned around and was startled to see Adrian and Jerry watching him from one of the smaller pods. They waved and Max waved back. *Maybe they're worried Quant is going to jump up and kidnap somebody.*

Max returned to the rovers, unplugged the cables, rolled the cables up and placed them on the charging station holders.

Adrian and Jerry left the small pod and waited for Max to walk back.

'All OK?' Jerry asked.

'Yeah,' Max answered. 'The Rovers are fully functioning, charged and secure.'

'We're done here,' Adrian said.

Jerry nodded. 'Let's get back to the Main Pod then. It's deep cold already.'

When the crew gathered for the evening meal, they were visibly less tense because of the day's uninterrupted work. Jerry was pleased to hear people talking about their tasks rather than Quant. A couple of more days like this and things would be back to normal, Quant's absence just another mission detail.

When the crew retired to their bunks, they fell quickly asleep.

Max was the last to fall asleep. He opened his logbook. He began an entry but soon grew tired of it and deleted it. He placed his tablet on the floor next to his bunk and rolled over and fell asleep.

Max was woken from his sleep by someone standing near his bunk. He immediately sat up on the edge of his bunk. 'What is it?'

Mary stood by the main table, laptop on the table. Mary stared at the screen. She turned around. 'Wake Jerry,' she said and then she raised her voice. 'He needs to see this. Everyone needs to see this.'

The others woke. They left their bunks and walked over to Mary. She pointed at the screen, her hand shaking.

'Look,' she said. 'It's from Marianne Routledge at the Rex Colony.'

It was a single line: *He is killing everyone send rescue.*

The group dressed and assembled around the table.

'When was this email sent?' Jerry asked.

'Three hours ago,' Mary answered. 'She hasn't written

anything else.'

Jerry raised his hand. 'Sys, who is at the Rex Colony?'

'The Rex colony is operated by three founding volunteers: Marianne Routledge, Astrobiologist and Doctor, Gregory Wright, Engineer, Chemist and Doctor, and Michael Eckles, Engineer and Chemist.'

'Do we have direct comms with the Rex Colony?'

'We lost direct comms three hours ago,' Sys informed them.

Mary stepped back. 'It's Quant! You should have told them about Quant, Jerry. You should have warned them.'

Jerry pointed at the screen. 'What about this email, Sys? If comms failed how come we received it?'

'It was sent just before comms were lost.'

'Why did it take so long to reach us?' Jerry asked.

'A Serf unit picked it up locally and relayed it to us.'

'A Serf unit was monitoring their comms?'

'Yes,' Sys answered.

Mary frowned. 'How is that even possible? They don't have any Serf units. Sys?'

'There was a Serf unit based locally at the Rex Site. An MS2 Serf,' Sys told them.

Adrian leaned in. 'It's one of Quant's serfs.'

'Why would Quant kill anyone and then let us know about it?'

'A warning?' Mary asked.

'It doesn't make sense,' Adrian shook his head. 'I mean –'

'Be quiet, everybody!'

The group looked at Jerry. He pulled a chair out from under the table. 'Everybody sit down. Now.'

Adrian laughed weakly. 'Sit down? Are you ordering us to

sit down?'

'Yes. That's an order, Adrian. Everybody sit down. We're going to take a minute to gather our thoughts. We're going to process the information. So take a seat.'

They sat down. Adrian crossed his arms.

Jerry breathed deeply. 'Now, no one speaks until I'm done talking. Understand? You'll all get your say.'

Jerry laid his palms down on the table.

'Sys? Do you have any input?'

'The email suggests that either someone is dead as a result of a violent act or is under threat or attack. Space and Mars are considered international waters. This means that it falls under Article 98. We have a duty to render assistance.'

Jerry nodded. 'So we have a duty to help them. Can Mars Site 3 sustain another three people?'

'Yes, but food would be an issue. You will need to use supplementary supplies. These can be taken from the Rex Colony. Mars Site 3 has enough air, water, heat and power to house another five people in this habitat.'

Jerry looked at Adrian. 'How many more prods can we build?'

'Three more. I'll make the ends a bit sharper so they're more like spears.' Adrian glanced at Max. 'You'll thank me when the time comes.'

Jerry nodded. 'Okay. Here's what we're going to do. We are going to wait for daybreak. It's too cold and too dark to move at night. We are going to make three more prods. They are the only weapons we have. We're going to drive one rover over to the Rex Colony. They have their own rovers. We bring them back with us. If their rovers are out of action, we recharge our rover and use that. They'll have to sit on the floor. A bit of a squeeze but we can manage it.

'We're going to rescue the colonists and we're going to bring them back. We need to have a team here to guard Mars Site 3. Max and Amy, you will be the site team. You get one prod. If Quant approaches Mars Site 3 you must use any means to repel or disable him.

'Adrian, Mary and I will be the team that drives over to the Rex Colony. If we encounter Quant, we will put him out of action. Otherwise, everyone, just keep away from Quant. Don't try to communicate with him. Don't try to reason with him.'

Jerry inhaled slowly and crossed his hands. 'Now, one at a time. Adrian first.'

'We'll need three to five hours to make the prods,' Adrian said.

'Okay. Amy?'

'The first prod's in the Spare Parts Storage Unit,' Amy said. 'Shouldn't we get it?'

'Yes. I'll suit up with Adrian and get it,' Jerry answered. 'Max?'

'Will we have comms with the rovers?' Max asked.

'Sys?'

'Yes. We can send two Serfs out and they will act as relay stations between the rovers and MS3. They are moving to the relevant location now.'

'Good. Mary?'

'I don't have anything to add,' Mary answered. 'It sounds like a good plan.'

Jerry stood up. 'Adrian, let's suit up.'

Jerry and Adrian came back an hour later with the one functioning prod and the parts to build the other three pods. They assembled the prods at the table, while the others watched on in silence.

Eventually they had four working prods. 'Good work,' Jerry said. At Jerry's suggestion, everyone retired to their bunks, updated their personal logs, tried their best to stay focused.

The Martian dawn came up four hours later. It was brutally cold, minus 60 °C. Total darkness gave way to bleak, meagre light, revealing a landscape of ochre shadow and red-rust plains that stretched to the horizon in the east, and in the west, beige and grey hills, the shapes of ancient floodplains, and Bradbury Plateau, now a foreboding silhouette that punctured the sky.

The group assembled around the table.

'Sys, what's the forecast for today at the Rex Colony?'

'Temperature high of minus 20 °C in the time period 12:00–13:00. Temperature of minus 60 °C tonight. No excessive radiation fields expected. But recommended that you take your Radioprotector Meds. It is a six-hour round journey to the Rex Colony. If you need to charge the rover, you will have to stay overnight at the colony.'

Jerry looked at the group. 'Unless anyone has any objections. I think we should start out now. We don't know what we're going to find. For the record: if you come across Quant, don't take any chances. Disable him with the prod if you have to.'

Jerry, Adrian and Mary suited up, helped by Amy and Max. Thirty minutes later, Jerry, Adrian and Mary left the main pod and walked over to the rovers. They carried three prods with them.

They climbed into the rover.

'Comms check. This is Jerry.'

Amy and Max watched them via the display screen. 'Comms confirmed, Jerry,' Amy replied. 'This is Amy.'

'Comms check confirmed, Amy.'

Max looked at some data on the screen. 'Rover 1 is fully

functioning,' he said. 'Full power. Cab temperature is plus 15 °C.'

'I confirm those readings,' Jerry said looking at the rover's dashboard.

Jerry inhaled a sharp intake of breath. 'Okay then.'

He started the rover and slowly drove away from the mission site.

Sys had real-time data on the rover and on Jerry, Adrian and Mary's suits. There were also two video feeds from the dash cam inside the rover. Sys organised all of the information on the large main screen.

Max and Amy followed their progress.

'Hey,' Amy said. 'How come we only get one prod?'

Max glanced at the prod on the table. 'Jerry doesn't expect Quant to turn up here. He's expecting to find him at Leonard's Folly.'

The rover team had driven for about an hour, hardly speaking to each other or to Max and Amy back at the mission site.

Jerry used the navigation unit display to guide him but would not allow the rover to drive in auto. He preferred to drive the rover himself for reasons he wasn't altogether clear about – probably because it made him feel safer. Navigation units could be hacked. Hardware could be hacked. People couldn't be hacked.

Jerry drove the rover into a valley system that would lead them to the Rex Colony. He slowed the rover as he manoeuvred around outcrops and small craters.

Adrian pointed at the rover's data screens. 'It's Quant! Quant is trying to hail us.'

'Do not open comms to Quant,' Jerry ordered. 'We don't want him hacking our data. We do not need to hear what he has to say. Do you hear me, Max? Do not interact with Quant. Max?'

'Confirmed,' Max replied from Mars Site 3.

Amy touched Max's shoulder and pointed at the dash cam feed.

'Do you see that? Five degrees to your right. Are you seeing what we see?'

There was no answer from the team in the rover.

The rover stopped.

'Why have they stopped? Jerry, why have you stopped? Jerry, can you hear me? Have we lost audio? Just brilliant,' Amy hissed. 'We've lost audio.'

A figure descended the slope of a crater. The figure moved steadily down the slope, heading towards the rover, and it appeared to be carrying someone.

Max leaned forward. 'Is that Quant?'

The main screen went blank.

Max threw his hands up. 'For fate's sake! Sys?'

'We have lost all comms to Rover 1,' Sys reported. 'One of the Serf units has failed.'

'What do you mean failed?'

'It is damaged or destroyed.'

'I don't believe this. Can they hear us?'

'The Rover 1 team cannot hear us.'

Max looked at Amy. 'What do we do now?'

'We can't go out to them. We have to keep the site secure. Those were Jerry's orders. We might get comms back. Maybe the Serf will come back online.'

The main screen flashed repeatedly, and Sys made an announcement:

'A Recorded Message from NASA for all of the crew of

Mars Site 3 will be played in five minutes. Please assemble all crew in the Main Pod. This message has the highest priority. Repeat. Highest priority.'

A counter appeared on the screen and started to count down from five minutes.

'Great timing. Just great,' Max exhaled loudly. 'Can things get any worse?'

The screens in the room flickered and then the ground shuddered, and the Main Pod's structure shook violently. Several alarms went off across the site and then they lost power and the site was plunged into darkness.

Amy and Max were at a loss. They did not move.

The ground and the Main Pod shook even more violently. Max lost his balance and fell over. Amy stepped forward and helped him up.

The alarms stopped. There was an eerie kind of silence. They heard the distinct clunk of a relay tripping and then power was restored. The lights came on and the screens switched on.

The suits in the Sooth Booth swayed. The suit helmets on the helmet rack rattled against each other.

Max and Amy instinctively moved towards the centre of the Main Pod.

'I should have kept my mouth shut!' Max said.

'We might need to suit up,' Amy said. 'Sys? You with us?'

'Structure is secure. Systems are secure.'

Max held his hands out, to steady his balance. 'Let's just –'

The tremors seemed to roll and increased in intensity and then stopped abruptly. The main screen display recovered. The clock still counting down.

Max and Amy seemed unsure what to do next. Each waiting for the other to give an instruction. Amy was the first to speak.

'Sys? Was that a Marsquake?'

'Cannot disprove or confirm.'

'A meteor?'

'Cannot disprove or confirm.'

'Can you locate an epicentre?'

'Approximately 50 kilometres west of our location.'

'That's too close for comfort. Any more data?'

'The Mars Orbiter will have a visual in eight minutes.'

'Put it up as soon as you have something. Let's hear the message,' Amy said and turned to Max. 'We should hear the message. Okay?'

Max nodded.

'Sys, play the message,' Amy said.

'The message will be played in three minutes.'

'Show it now! No one else is on the site!'

There was the briefest of pauses, just long enough for Max and Amy to register it and wonder if Sys was experiencing the equivalent of machine indecision.

'Message playing now.'

CRISIS 2

Mars Site 3 Archive, #375
Max Grade, Mission Specialist
Personal Journal Entry: Sol 45

Mars was all I thought about for years, but now I'm here it is the memory of home that sings softly in my dreams – songs longing for a lost world.

It is the haunting memory of boyhood. Of empty attics and silent libraries, corridors and classrooms, the whisper of wheat fields swaying in summer breezes, a shoreline landscape burnished with gold in late-evening light, waves unspooling along the tideline, the sea always arriving.

I remember one summer day, my mother sitting on the porch steps of our house, on one of her rare days off, waiting for us to return home from school.

Peter and I came home together. Peter had a way of walking then that was confident and unafraid without it being a swagger. Like he was equal to the world.

My mother stood up and waved as we neared and seemed to embrace both of us at the same time in her wide arms. She ushered us into the house in a flurry of her skirt, and her heady lilac perfume in the air.

There was lemonade and cake. Lazy talk. Sometimes we all laughed just because we were so happy. Sometimes my mother rested her hand on Peter's bare arm and rubbed his skin like she was polishing something precious.

Eventually the cake and lemonade were finished, and my mother had to mark some papers. We stood up and left the kitchen.

It was one of those days where our friends were all out of town. Peter and I loitered around the house. Boredom soon made us techy with one another, driving my mother mad.

Finally, out of frustration, she ordered us out of the house and told us to take a hike in the hills behind our town.

'Go up to Sunset Valley and bring me back some ferns for the vase.'

We complained, but relented and headed up to the valley, not exactly glad for each other's company, saying little to each other.

It was a very hot day and we moved slowly. After about an hour, we reached the old stone bridge that crossed a steep-sided ravine along which the railway line passed.

The path we had taken brought us out of the woods and as we emerged onto the bridge, we saw some boys, maybe seven or eight of them, peering over the bridge. One of them had just dropped a large rock.

'Hey!' Peter cried out. 'Who are you? What are you doing?'

The boys scattered, running in the opposite direction, disappearing into the woods.

We knew who those boys were.

'Who goes there!' Peter shouted one last time for effect. Some of the vanishing boys shouted and whooped as they ran deeper into the woods.

My brother glanced at me, already reading my thoughts.

'I know who they were. If you give people a way out, they normally take it,' he said. 'Always try and give them a way out. They outnumbered us three to one. Look,' he said and pointed at the stack of boulders and heavy rocks in the middle of the bridge.

We approached the rocks and then we looked over the edge of the bridge.

My heart caught in my throat. It took some moments for me to process what I was seeing.

There was a badly injured lamb sprawled on the tracks, surrounded by a few boulders and rocks.

Peter winced and turned and looked at the part of the woods where the boys had fled.

'What are we going to do?'

'You stay here,' Peter said.

'What if they come back?'

'They won't come back.'

Peter moved to the end of the bridge, went around the side and found a section of the wire fence that was buckled and twisted. He climbed over and made his way down the steep side of the ravine, holding onto thick roots and even the soft soil for support.

Peter walked over to the lamb. It could not move. He picked it up and glanced around. He would not be able to climb back up with it.

He carried the lamb under the bridge, out of sight.

When he emerged again, he did not have the lamb and he climbed back up.

We turned around, knowing instinctively our walk was over, and headed back towards the town.

'Did you kill it?'

Peter shook his head and looked down at the ground.

'I left it in the shade. Away from the track.'

'Will it die?'

'I don't know. Maybe.'

'Why did they do that?'

'You're not going to cry, are you?'

I didn't know how to answer. I was baffled by my brother's anger, now directed at me.

'You're not going to cry?'

'No.'

'Good. Nothing worse than crybabies.'

'But why did they do it?'

'Because they enjoyed it.'

'How can you enjoy that?'

'You're too young.'

'I'm not too young.'

'The world's a bad place, Max! It isn't the way Mum and Dad paint it! They think they can keep you safe from all that. But they can't! People are bad! Don't you start crying!'

But it was too late. Baffled and afraid and still reeling from the cruelty I had witnessed, I started crying.

'For fate's sake,' Peter hissed and marched off so quickly that I had to run after him to catch up, wiping the tears from my face as I ran.

'You have to grow up, Max! Can't you see that? The world won't play fair. It will eat you up if you don't grow up!'

But I didn't want to grow up. Not yet. Let Peter grow up, I thought. Let him grow up instead. Because growing up then, seemed like a kind of dying. Growing up seemed to be defeat.

The loss of everything for something that wasn't even wise.

I have wondered if those cruel boys – now men all of them, fathers probably, too – I have wondered if they sometimes remember what they did that day and whether shame still haunts their conscience in the dead hours of night.

The dim-lit world of Mars has a way of making you remember the beautiful and the terrible.

I learned that day that Peter was strong, but his kind of strength cost more than was owed. Was that the start of his decline? Being strong?

*

The main screen flashed blue for a second and then the message played.

Three men sat behind a nondescript table, all wearing white shirts and grey jackets. Each of the men had a single sheet of paper in front of them and a single glass of water.

Max felt a stab of fear, his mouth dry. Something so ominous about those three glasses of water. 'Oh. This can't be good,' Max said.

The man in the middle, whom Max recognised immediately, cleared his throat and said in a hushed tone that was meant for the other two men, 'We'll begin then.'

'For the record, even though I'm sure we need no introduction, the man on my left is Kevin Baxter, NASA Administrator. The man on my right is Alan Cartwright, Head of National Security. And I am William Bartholomew. President of the United States of America.

'Let me get right to the point. We address you now in the crucible of deadly peril. In all the long history of humankind, time has never been so short, the peril never so great. You are all that stands between the fall of civilisation and the end of humankind.

'A binary asteroid that was once on the far edge of our solar system and harmless was disturbed by a gravitational occurrence that caused the two asteroids to slip their mutual bond and head on very different trajectories. Both are on a different but lethal trajectory. Only one can be stopped.

'You have perhaps two sols or even less – literally a handful of hours – to get to Mars Site 2, power up the Ascent Rocket, dock with a craft called Thor that is currently in orbit around Mars. You must then fly Thor into the path of an asteroid called Nautilus 1, which is on a collision course with Earth and will wipe out all life on the surface if it carries on its trajectory.

'Thor carries a cargo of hydrogen bombs, powerful enough when detonated in unison to give Nautilus 1 an extra kick as it swings past Mars. The effect will be enough to avoid collision with the earth.

'These next hours are the only time this will be possible. This is the last window of opportunity. Mankind's last chance.

'As we speak, another asteroid called Nautilus 2 will strike Mars. Your site and the Rex Colony will not survive the impact. Some of our scientists think Nautilus 2 may have even split into two but this does not alter the fate of NASA's sites or of the Rex Colony.

'N1 and N2 originated from a wandering binary asteroid that was caught by Jupiter's gravity, which caused it to separate into N1 and N2.

'I am told all the data files that you need have been downloaded to Mars Site 3. I'm now going to hand you over to Alan Cartwright. No doubt you are in some shock but there are some more details you need to hear. Alan?'

The Head of National Security cleared his throat.

'Rather than speak, I will let you read some documents that will appear on your screen. It will take you a couple of minutes to read them. But they will explain what the situation is and how we came to this moment.'

The film froze, the faces of the three men sombre.

'We'd better sit down,' Amy said quietly, returning to her

seat.

Max sat down. 'Now we know what the tremor is. I think they're behind with their calculations.'

'You ready?'

Max nodded.

'OK, Sys. Let's see the documents.'

TOP SECRET

12122110 Exec 750/1

NASA REPORT – CONFIDENTIAL – FOR EXECUTIVE EYES ONLY

Date: 10 December 2110

THOR MISSION

The Thor craft is the Mars Site 4 Rocket and lander, now retrofitted with atomic payload.

Launched from lunar orbit. Expected arrival April 2111

SUBJECT: LOSS OF COMMUNICATION WITH THE THOR.

Thor is manned by Colonel Frank Allen, Flight Commander, and Ernest Meeke, Flight Engineer.

*

Five days ago, Flight Engineer Ernest Meeke reported that Colonel Frank Allen complained of headaches. Biotelemetry confirmed that Colonel Frank Allen had a fever and raised blood pressure.

*

Four days ago – the last report from Thor – Ernest Meeke

reported that Colonel Frank Allen was conscious but unresponsive.

Three days ago – all communications with Thor failed. We no longer have any biotelemetry, text, audio or system data from the craft. Houston confirms that these have either failed or have been switched off.

*

Thor's course is unaltered. Houston thinks it is still in autopilot, and hence the craft still has power and is viable.

The Hawking Telescope has imaged Thor (see attached image). The evidence confirms Thor is intact and on course.

Summary

It seems increasingly likely that the crew of Thor has suffered an event related to the Life Support System at the same time that the communications systems failed.

Conclusion: Mission failed.

TOP SECRET

12122110 Exec 750/10

NASA REPORT – CONFIDENTIAL – FOR EXECUTIVE EYES ONLY

Date: 13 December 2110

From: The President of The United States of America

Send copies to:

President of The Russian Federation

President and General Secretary of The People's Republic of China

Dear Presidents,

Because of the nature of our common dilemma, in the

spirit of cooperation and collaboration, when we agreed on the Thor Mission and your two governments agreed to contribute to the payload – since our limited available arsenals alone would not suffice – we agreed to share all data and communications.

I have no doubt that you have reached the same conclusions that we have.

It is with regret that I must inform you that the Thor Mission has failed.

The Thor is intact. Its payload, as far as NASA can tell, is still viable. It approaches Mars on the pre-set course. But its crew is dead. Thor will almost certainly fly past Mars and be lost to space.

In the hope of a miracle, and to avoid the chaos of despair, the Thor Mission, its goal and its failure remains a secret. The executive branch of this government hopes you will agree this is the most responsible course. History, if it survives us, will judge us kindly.

In gratitude, in fellowship and in hope,

The President of The United States of America

TOP SECRET

16042110 Exec 750/15

NASA REPORT – CONFIDENTIAL – FOR EXECUTIVE EYES ONLY

Date: 15 April 2111

THOR MISSION

The Thor craft is the Mars Site 4 Rocket, now retrofitted with atomic payload.

Launched from lunar orbit.

SUBJECT: COURSE CORRECTION OF THOR CRAFT MADE 13 APRIL 2111

A course correction was made. The Thor is now in a stable low orbit around Mars. The course correction could only have been made manually by either Ernest Meeke or Colonel Frank Allen.

*

There is still no communication with the Thor. We can only assume that whoever is still alive on the Thor does not wish to communicate.

The Mars Reconnaissance Orbiter, as part of its monitoring programme of the Rex Colony, captured this image (see attachment). It appears to show Thor's Lander Module on the surface, 3 kilometres from Mars Site 2, 12 kilometres from the Rex Colony, 52 kilometres from Mars Site 3.

*

Summary

At least one of the crew of the Thor Craft has survived the journey to Mars, made a course correction that put Thor into a low orbit and landed the Lander Module on Mars.

The intentions of the surviving crew are unknown. Whoever it is, Ernest Meeke or Colonel Frank Allen, he is following his own agenda.

While the mission status is critical, it is not yet a failure. Someone may still fly Thor and deliver the payload. But time is of the essence. There are probably less than four sols left.

TOP SECRET
12122110 Exec 750/20
NASA   REPORT   –   CONFIDENTIAL   –   FOR

EXECUTIVE EYES ONLY

Date: 15 April 2111

From: The President of The United States of America

Send copies to:

President of The Russian Federation

President and General Secretary of The People's Republic of China

Dear Presidents,

Please read the attached report and images from NASA.

We hoped and prayed for a miracle, and while no miracle has yet been delivered, there is the chance that we can create our own miracle. As you read this, we are reaching out to our people on Mars Site 3. We have almost run out of time. But we have a chance.

In gratitude, in fellowship and in hope,

The President of The United States of America

'Would you like to read the documents again?' Sys asked.

Max tried to swallow but found he had no spit. He felt lightheaded, disorientated.

He cleared his throat but failed to say anything. He bowed his head and breathed deeply. 'It's a nightmare. We're in some kind of nightmare.'

Amy stared at the screen. She laid both of her palms on the table.

'I can't believe Ernest would do something like this. Frank I'm not sure,' she said.

'My money's on Frank,' Max said. 'There was always something off about him; no matter how hard he tried he never quite fitted in with the programme. He's never been beyond a low orbit mission.'

A flashing cursor appeared on the main screen.

Sys addressed them again: 'Would you like to read the documents again? Or do you want to commence with the message?'

Amy found her voice. 'Just a minute, Sys. We need a minute.'

Max spoke quietly, to himself as much as to Amy.

'Now we know it wasn't a marsquake. An asteroid strike. Not the big one because we're still here. So the smaller fragment then. But it probably means we have even less time.'

Amy nodded. 'Are you ready for the rest of it?'

Max nodded and took a deep breath.

Amy said, 'Play the rest of it, Sys.'

The main screen showed the film of the three men again. Alan Cartwright sipped some water from his glass.

'Site 3 Crew, you have to assume Ernest or Frank is hostile. Some sort of mental breakdown. We're assuming one of them is dead or incapacitated in some way. Whoever is alive, you must consider him highly dangerous and to be avoided at all costs. And you must expect that he will try to stop any attempts you make to reach the Thor.'

Alan Cartwright stopped speaking. The President turned to the NASA Administrator. 'Kevin?'

The NASA Administrator was visibly shaken.

'Yes. Sorry. Yes. Site 3 Crew, your Mars Ascent Vehicle cannot dock with the Thor but the Mars Site 2 Ascent Vehicle can. It is one tiny piece of luck in this terrible nightmare.

'You must get to Mars Site 2. Obviously, we did not plan for this scenario. So, there are still many unknowns. Ernest or Frank may even have interfered with the Thor in some way. You may have to steer it manually and detonate the payload manually. That in itself, is a complicated procedure. But we have downloaded the instructions for that, and they should now also be in each of your suit's built-in computer.

'You will have a visual of N1. If you can, we strongly recommend you upload the path coordinates to N1 from the Mars Site 2 Ascent Vehicle to Thor Craft. We have already loaded the data into the ascent vehicle's flight planner. I –'

Alan Cartwright sat back and fidgeted with his single piece of paper. He looked close to tears. 'I think that's it. Time is of the essence. All of humanity's hopes and prayers go with you.'

The President nodded. He turned his steady gaze to the camera. 'My fellow Americans, never before has the fate of all humankind rested on the bravery and sacrifice of so few. If you succeed, you will have the gratitude of the ages. If you fail, then we fail with you and will go to our end knowing that you did your best.

'I for one refuse to give into despair. We are in utmost peril, but the light of hope is not yet extinguished. The futures of your families, your children, your loved ones and all the families, children and loved ones of humanity to come, rest upon you.

'If you are of godly faith, then god go with you. If you are humanists, then may fate be favourable and let human endeavour prevail. May your endeavours, in this darkest hour, save us all.'

END TRANSMISSION

Amy and Max stood up and embraced spontaneously.

'I don't want to die,' Max said.

'Me neither,' Amy said. 'But someone's got to fly that ship,'

The Main Pod was eerily quiet.

'Let's not decide just yet who gets to fly,' Max said.

Amy broke from the embrace. 'We better suit up.'

'Alright.'

The main screen flashed.

'Mars Reconnaissance Orbiter capture on screen now,' Sys informed them.

They looked at the screen.

They saw a beautiful red-rusted vista broken in the centre by what looked like a band of slow-moving darkness with borders of ochre-tinted shadow. The darkness was expanding and growing, the ochre shadow streamed off the edges like smoke.

'What is that, Sys?'

'Impact material ejected into the atmosphere and dust. Mars Site 3 detectors are already recording a rise in fine particulate in the air.'

'How long before it reaches us?'

'Ten or eleven minutes.'

'Was that the asteroid? Was that N2?' Max asked.

'That was part of N2. The smaller part,' Sys answered.

'The smaller part? For fate's sake! That was from the smaller part?' Amy asked. 'The bigger part is still approaching?'

'Yes.'

'How long to impact, Sys?' Max asked.

'Eighty to ninety minutes by current data.'

'Sys, is Rover 2 fully charged?' Max asked.

'Yes.'

'Can we reach Mars Site 2?' Amy asked.

'Yes,' Sys answered. 'As long as there are no delays.'

Sys displayed a route for the Rover 2 to Mars Site 2. *Time to destination: 35 minutes.*

Max was still staring at the screen. 'That's cutting it close.'

'We'll have to go on one battery. We don't have time to charge up the other one. It's not like we're coming back. Let's suit up. We have to go now.'

They were strangely quiet in the suit booth, their actions automatic, learned from thousands of hours of training. They were relieved to be doing something familiar. The small sense of routine was comforting, if only for a brief few minutes.

Max strapped Amy's compact oxygen unit onto her back and turned around so that Amy could reciprocate. Amy's movements were swift and efficient. She turned Max around.

'We're not going to fall apart,' Amy said.

'No.' Max nodded. His voice was strange to him.

'Look at me, Max.'

'Yes?'

'One step at a time. We're going to save the world,' Amy said. 'Whatever it takes.'

Max nodded.

They emerged from the Main Pod after ten minutes. The Martian sky was already darker from dust that streamed past them, a strange otherworldly cloud of fine sand that hissed against their suits.

'Local comms check,' Max said into his suit microphone.

'Loud and clear,' Amy replied.

'Loud and clear,' Max confirmed to Amy.

'I have comms on both of you,' Sys told them.

'There it is!' Max said loudly and pointed up at the sky.

A smudge of glowing light where no light should be.

Wonder and dread rose up in Max, some ancient memory locked in his DNA. A brief biblical fear took hold of him. He remembered the priest at his first and last Catholic school. A dour man dressed like a crow. 'The wrath of God,' the priest had said sonorously as if pronouncing a death sentence. 'The wrath of God will make men cower.'

It's just nature, Max thought and conjured the faces of his mother and father, and his brother. *The laws of nature and bad luck. A million-to-one piece of bad luck. All of it.*

'Max?'

'All that crap about Quant, and it's one of our own who's gone mad.'

Amy pulled on his arm. 'Come on, Max. Sys, we want you to go into emergency hibernation mode at the last possible minute. We want you to forward all of our comms to NASA. As a record. For the historical record.'

'Confirmed.'

Amy and Max climbed into the Rover 2, glad to be out of the increasing dust. They could hear it hissing across the sides and top of the rover.

'We can't use the lights. They'll drain the battery. Need to use the autopilot.'

'Sys, can you drive the rover?'

'Yes.'

'Let's go then.'

*

Mars, Utopia Planitia Sol 249

Frank climbed out of the Martian Module, leaned back inside it, pulled out an extra oxygen unit and placed it at his feet. The name 'Meeke' was clearly printed on the second

101

oxygen unit.

He unzipped the thigh pouch on his leg and took out some folded material. He unfolded the material and it became a bag with four thin straps. A rucksack. He placed the extra oxygen unit in the rucksack then put the rucksack on.

He made some system adjustments to his suit, unclipped the handheld computer and checked the module's status. Undamaged. Textbook landing. Ready for the ascent at a time of his choosing.

Everything as it should be. Everything as he knew it would be. Pre-destined.

The only irritation was he did not have the time to set up the perimeter to keep sand from drifting or blowing into the module. He'd have done it if Meeke was here but Meeke was gone, a tumbling frozen speck somewhere in endless space. Meeke had to be killed and then Meeke had to be disposed of. You can't have a decomposing body on your ship. Far too unpleasant and unhygienic. Still, a living Meeke would have been handy here.

When he had strangled Meeke there had been a few moments of – well, sympathy perhaps – as Meeke, discovering he was strapped to his bunk, with the cord tightening around his neck, looked about in terror. He had said to Meeke 'It'll only take a couple of minutes' and pulled so tight on the cord that it bit into his fingers. Meeke made some unpleasant gurgling sounds, some blood dripped from his nose and mouth, he strained against the bindings, his fingers made clawing gestures.

Then that was that, as they say.

Dumping Meeke into space was considerably more difficult and dangerous than killing him and had involved some re-programming of the Thor airlock, which couldn't engage if it did not detect a docking. It had taken about 72 hours to figure it out, and Meeke had definitely started to smell a little, as bodily decay set in.

Frank sighed. No Meeke. No perimeter. Those were the breaks.

He would come back with some Serfs and do it later.

Frank shutdown the module's systems. In theory, the module could sit like that forever. The fuel would not degrade in the airless atmosphere and any degradation from radiation would be minimal. As long as the sand did not penetrate any of the systems, the module could sit there for decades, ready for reuse.

Frank took some bearings. Plotted in Mars Site 2 and started moving. He walked a hundred metres when something caught his eye. A black meteor, double the size of a fist, lying on the sand.

Like Frank, it was uniquely out of place in the landscape.

Frank picked it up. It had a weight and a heft in his hand that was perfect. It had been waiting for him.

Frank took off his rucksack; put the meteorite inside an inner pocket, making sure it would not damage the extra oxygen unit. He strapped the rucksack onto his back again and moved on.

He strode forward as one who knows the landscape will make a path for him. No one on Mars had ever walked the way Frank walked. He walked like a king.

He was unique. He knew he was unique. His new mission was Destiny. Maker of the New World. Destroyer of the Old. This was the Second Coming of Man and Frank was its embodiment.

Frank hardly noticed the time pass as he made his way to Mars Site 2. Ever since his epiphany on Thor, ever since that vivid, epistemic experience, time had become diffuse, thinned to nothing, a flickering in his mind.

Frank existed out of time and he assumed this was part of his uniqueness. He was an evolutionary leap. This self-knowledge also made him feel ecstatic. His mind and body thrummed with a kind of high. The sensation of knowledge-as-pleasure was so intense and constant he glowed with light. He was made of light.

He literally showed the way. He was the way. The light in the darkness.

Four hours later Frank approached the perimeter of Mars Site 2.

He immediately checked the three power units at the periphery of the site and noted that one of them was missing. The two remaining units were fully functioning.

Frank made his way over to the external control cabinet next to the Main Pod. The design was much the same as Mars Site 3. Frank powered up the electronics. It would take around an hour for the pod systems to engage, carry out fail-safe checks, pressurise the pod with breathable air and bring the temperature up to a comfortable 18 °C.

Frank walked over to the Workshop Pod, powered it up and entered. The pod had standard issue equipment: a 3D Printer, a lab table and a single computer. Frank went to work on the 3D modelling software. He placed the meteorite on the 3D Printer's large scanning table and ran the scanning program.

Frank found a screwdriver in one of the toolkits. He went back to the Main Pod and studied the maintenance ladder that ran up the exterior wall of the pod. He unscrewed a side member and returned to the Workshop Pod.

The 3D Printer's scanning was finished. Frank removed the meteorite and placed the side member on the scanning table. He initiated a scan.

When the scanning was complete, Frank ran the modelling software and instructed the software to find the best, strongest fit between the two objects.

A coordinate grid lit up on the scanning table, showing Frank where to place the meteorite. The 3D Printer had a robotic arm. The machine extended the arm. Frank placed the side member in the arm's clamp.

Frank stepped back, and the machine did the rest, finding the best fit and started to apply the material that would join the two together in a perfect joint.

Frank went back to the Main Pod and waited for the airlock to power up.

'Now, where have all the Serfs gone?' he said aloud. He paired his suit comms with Mars Site 2.

'Sys? Local comms only. Where are all the MS2 Serfs?'

'Five serfs are at Bradbury Plateau. Two more are located within a 5 kilometres distance of the plateau.'

'What are they doing there?'

'Maintenance tasks.'

'Is there anything else missing?'

'Power equipment. Seed banks. Water production and oxygen production units. About 90% of food supplies.'

'Power. Oxygen. Water and most of the food. Is all of that also on Bradbury Plateau?'

'Yes.'

'You don't have any visuals or audio?'

'No. Just location data.'

'Who took the Serfs?'

'Mars Site 3 AI Unit.'

'Quant?'

'Yes. Quant.'

'What else did he take?'

A list came up on Frank's suit's visuals.

Frank smirked. 'Building a lifeboat, is he?'

'Cannot provide discourse.'

'OK. Try this. Where is the MS2 rover? Is it still operational?'

'Behind the Main Pod. It is operational but it requires charging.'

'Start charging the rover.'

Frank walked around the Main Pod and sure enough, there was the rover. It was about the size of a small passenger vehicle.

'How long to full charge?'

'One hour.'

'Everything takes an hour round here.'

The Workshop Pod transmitted an audio job-complete signal. Frank walked back to the pod and studied the finished piece. A club.

He picked it up from the table. It had the perfect length and heft.

'That will do.'

The Main Pod airlock powered up. Frank returned to the Main Pod and entered the airlock. Two minutes later, he was inside the pressurised Main Pod.

He removed his helmet. The air had a slight chemical taste to it. He looked about, pleased with his progress.

Two hours later Frank loaded the rover with extra oxygen supplies, Marssuits, food ration packs, water and his club. He climbed into the rover, plotted in the coordinates for the Rex Colony and drove off. What would he re-name it as? The Allen Shelter. That was a noble enough name and fit for purpose. Mars Site 2 would almost certainly be destroyed along with Mars Site 3. The Rex Colony would survive according to all of the simulations that Frank had run and most importantly, according to his visions. It was all part of the unfolding of the New World.

The Allen Shelter would be a place of pilgrimage in the distant future. A sacred site made sacred by him.

Like the Prophet in his cave. Like Jesus on the Mount. .

Marianne Routledge and Gregory Wright were Mars' first lovers.

All of their training to ensure no one became romantically involved and here they were kissing in awkward nooks and corners of the Keep where the cameras could not find them and when Michael Eckles, the third member of Rex Colony, was outside.

Leonard Rex had famously stated that people falling in love was a mission-critical hazard that must be minimised. Mars was no place for romantic entanglements. A pregnancy would be life-threatening and the chances of a miscarriage or deformed child were extremely high. With that in mind, the two male colonists had agreed to chemical sterilisation for the duration of their posting.

For all its haunted beauty, Mars was a toxic environment. Radiation exposure was a constant and menacing danger. Let colonists fall in love in 30 years from now when the Rex Colony was self-sustaining and the first Rex Dome Parks were up and running.

The Keep was the slightly creepy name that Leonard Rex had come up with for the colony's main structure where the colonists slept, shared meals, uploaded reports and filmed short info films, mainly for Leonard Rex's consumption. Leonard Rex's scientists had spent millions of dollars profiling and matching the colonists' skills and personalities, training the successful candidates to exist as a single team and to expressly avoid any chances of romantic feelings arising.

Marianne and Gregory were Mars' first colonists. They were completely committed to the colony and Leonard Rex's vision of the colonisation of Mars. They had trained for years on the Rex Colony Programme and had been selected from the final colonist candidates because they were the best.

They were qualified scientists and engineers. They would also likely die on Mars. There was no guaranteed return trip. The chances of failure were high. They'd signed the contract anyway.

It would take five years before the Rex Crew Relief and Supply rocket would reach them and bring them home. The Rex Programme psychologists, behavioural scientists, ethics teams and philosophers had reached the conclusion that it was better to send people who had no strong familial ties on Earth.

The Rex Programme could not avoid the colonists having familial bonds on earth, but it could minimise all of the other emotional 'distortions' as Leonard Rex had described it. Rex had wanted to have AIs embedded with the colonists but his Rex programmers' AI algorithms were less advanced than those at NASA, a fact that irked him considerably, and while NASA was happy to pay for Rex technology – for example, Quant's advanced motor functions were based on Rex patents – the agency could not sell its own ground-breaking technology to Rex.

Gregory Wright and Michael Eckles had also been chemically sterilised because medical studies had shown that males had a lower risk of developing cancer compared to sterilised females in Mars' hostile environment.

Leonard Rex couldn't make his colonists asexual, though he had once suggested it was better if they only had asexual candidates on the candidate programme. A remark that caused his advisers agitation.

'Oh well,' Leonard had said, with grave certainty. 'They'll be much too busy to think about sex anyway.'

Marianne and Gregory kissed passionately inside a storage cubicle, living proof that as clever and as rich as Leonard Rex was, he was capable of believing and saying the most stupid of things.

Marianne and Gregory's attraction to each other had developed suddenly. Their mutual attraction exhilarating and frightening. Their first kiss, shocking and dizzying, was followed by apologies that turned into another, longer kiss.

So it began. A gentle comedy of intimacy and hurried sex in the storage locker because it was the only place where they could have total privacy. Or stolen touches out of the way of any camera or sensor.

Their everyday interactions became coloured by their secret liaisons; smiles that lingered, physical nearness, conversations about their lives and an interest in each other that had nothing to do with their professional relationship.

But their secrecy wasn't fooling anyone. The first reports of a possible sexual relationship had reached Leonard Rex's desk, sending the multi-billionaire into a rage.

Michael Eckles, the third colonist, had noticed what was happening but decided silence on the matter would be more prudent. He didn't want his two fellow colonists mistaking his awareness of what was happening as some kind of criticism or worse, jealousy. Privately, he'd always thought the Rex Programme's obsession with minimising emotional ties had more to do with Leonard Rex's aversion to intimacy. Leonard Rex was a billionaire technocrat who famously could wax lyrical about the boundless potential of space and space exploration, but who had an aversion to physical touch.

Michael did his best to ignore the signs of growing intimacy between Marianne and Gregory. He was relieved to find that when he examined his own personal feelings, there was no feeling of jealousy or resentment. He'd signed up for the mission because he wanted to help humankind take the next step in planetary exploration and colonisation. Nothing had changed. Marianne and Gregory were as competent as ever in carrying out their tasks. Michael's work performance was unaffected. It was still all good.

He had noted Marianne and Gregory's increasing friendship and intimacy in his personal logbook, but purely as a matter of record.

He did wonder if Marianne shared what was happening with Mary Calstair, over at Mars Site 3. He knew they exchanged emails using some Serfs as relay stations. The Rex Programme Coordination Centre issued guidelines that discouraged unofficial communication between the Rex Colony and Mars Site 3 but so far, no one on either side had ordered Marianne or Mary to end their correspondence.

Michael had developed a habit of watching the Mars sunset each evening. He would spend about an hour in total, from the moment he left the colony until he returned. It wasn't just for his own personal enjoyment. He knew it also gave Marianne and Gregory time alone.

The Martian sunset lasted for about twenty minutes. The weak sun sunk below the horizon and during this brief but haunting process, a patch of Martian sky turned ghostly blue.

Michael always chose the same vantage point: a small hill situated near the colony perimeter. The hill offered an excellent view of the Martian Plains.

In the far distance Michael could also make out the shape of Bradbury Plateau. Once he thought he saw a light on Bradbury Plateau. It was a brief moment. A trick of the eye but he recorded the event in his logbook: *Thought I saw a light on Bradbury Plateau. My mind playing tricks?* He wondered what future Alien Hunters would make of that. There was already a crackpot conspiracy theory back home that the Rex Colony had discovered the remains of Martians and had re-buried them.

Tonight was no different. Michael asked Marianne and Gregory if they wanted to join him outside and they both politely declined. Michael put on his Marssuit, aided by Gregory.

Michael nodded. 'See you in a bit.' He entered the airlock, now supervised by Rex, the colony's main computer system. Rex closed and locked the airlock's inner door.

Michael waited for Rex's safety systems to give him a green light on the outer airlock door. When the light came on, he pushed the button to open the exterior airlock.

Michael stepped out into the Martian landscape. Once he was clear of the exterior airlock door, it automatically closed behind him.

Michael stopped to take in the view. The rusted dimness of the plains and distant hills, the unmistakable shape of Bradbury Plateau on the dark horizon, mesmerised him. Mars was a world perpetually on the cusp of life. Who could not be haunted by it?

Michael glanced briefly back at the Keep and smiled. If he went straight back inside, how awkward would that be? He walked towards the hill.

Inside the Keep, Marianne and Gregory were already moving to the storage booth, intoxicated by the other's excitement and desire.

They undressed inside as quickly as they could, reaching for each other. These few minutes of intimacy were more precious and thrilling than they could ever have imagined.

They kissed. Gregory closed the door of the storage unit using his foot. Marianne giggled. Gregory whispered 'Shush!' in

Marianne's ear and now they both giggled.

The Keep's monitoring software recorded a rise in the temperature of the storage unit and duly logged it. It also picked up some unidentified sounds, which it also logged.

Dressed again, Marianne left the storage locker first.

She walked over to the forward bay window. In the Martian darkness, the surrounding perimeter of the Rex Colony glowed, illuminated by a series of bright LED work lamps. Where the arterial light touched the sands, the terrain was the colour of soapstone and beyond, the landscape became burnt ochre and rust-coloured shadow.

Gregory left the storage booth and poured himself a glass of water. He walked over to the colony system-monitoring console. No alarms, everything as it should be.

Gregory looked over at Marianne and frowned. He walked over and stood next to her.

'What is it?'

Marianne squeezed her eyes together and peered closer. She could just make out the darker shape of the hill.

'Where's Michael?'

*

Michael sat on a flat rock on top of the hill and watched the last of the Martian Sunset fade from blue to grey to inevitable darkness. Behind him, the colony perimeter lights illuminated the colony structures spread across the site.

The darkness grew in intensity. The silence seemed to cloak the darkness and stretch out across the Martian landscape. Michael thought of home, his parents on their Ohio farm, the green fields and tree-lined roads surrounding their two-storey farmhouse.

It was a strange notion; to travel millions of miles and then yearn for the first place he'd been born in. He closed his eyes and conjured a picture of his parents in his mind. They smiled back at him, gentle with age. Did they stand on the single-track road by the house and look up? Did they pick out Mars from the starry firmament? For a few wonderful seconds, he imagined it so.

Michael was about to stand up and walk back when he sensed movement to his left. He turned and for a few seconds did not quite comprehend what he was seeing.

A man in a NASA Marssuit strode forward. The man was carrying something in his right hand. The man appeared to be smiling.

'Michael Eckles I presume?' Frank said, seeing the letters 'ME' stitched into the arm of Michael suit.

As Michael started to answer, Frank swung the club hard and fast, striking the other man on the head.

Michael fell forwards, his suit helmet cracked, his suit alarm issuing a warning. There was the unmistakable hiss of air escaping from his suit. Extreme cold seeped into the suit, already freezing his cracked skull.

Michael was still conscious but barely had time to look up, in a state of confusion and fear, before Frank brought the club down again, with as much force as he could bring to the task.

Michael's suit helmet broke apart and Michael's exposed skull was fractured into pieces. Blood sprayed out, forming a small dark mist that evaporated.

Frank stood back, a little out of breath, quietly satisfied.

One down, two to follow. They would come to him.

All he had to do was wait a few minutes.

*

Gregory peered out. 'Yeah. Where is he?'

Marianne and Gregory looked at each other anxiously.

'Rex, where's Michael?'

'Twenty metres west of our location.'

'Behind the hill?'

'Yes.'

'Link our comms to his suit please. Michael, can you hear me? Michael –'

'Link comms fail.'

'What's wrong with the comms?'

'Suit comms failure.'

'Do you have his vital signs?'

'No. All of his suit comms have failed. There is no data.'

'What were his last transmitted vital signs?'

'Five minutes ago.'

'Please show his vital signs for the last ten minutes.'

Rex displayed Michael's vitals on the main screen.

Marianne pointed at the screen. 'His heart rate spikes just before the comms fail.'

Gregory nodded. 'I'll go. Help me suit up.'

'I'll come with you.'

'No. You can't. There has to be one person in the Keep at all times. Colony Protocol.'

Marianne helped Gregory into his suit and watched him walk into the airlock.

'What if he's collapsed?'

'It's only 20 metres. He's not heavy. I can bring him back in. Anyway, he's probably fine. He probably isn't aware that his suit comms have failed.'

Gregory closed the airlock and waited for Rex to open the

outer door of the Keep. He flexed his limbs, still adjusting to the suit.

Marianne returned to the bay window.

'Opening outer airlock,' Rex informed them.

'Thank you, Rex,' Gregory replied and walked out onto the Martian Sands.

'Can you turn up the outer lights?'

'Yes,' Rex confirmed, and the exterior lighting brightened.

That's much better,' Gregory said and walked towards the hill.

Marianne watched Gregory approach the hill.

'Comms good?'

'Comms good,' Marianne confirmed. 'I see and hear you clearly.'

'Do you have me on your grid, Rex?'

'Yes.'

Gregory approached the edge of the hill. He walked around it and moved out of view.

'I see him,' Gregory said. 'He's –'

A brief startling noise came through the comms, one that Marianne could not identify.

'Gregory? Gregory what's happened? Gregory? Gregory?'

'Comms are lost,' Rex reported.

'Lost? All of it?'

'Yes.'

'What happened?'

'Unknown.'

'What is the protocol?'

'You must stay in the Keep.'

'But something's happened!'

'The chances of two comms failures on two different suits is highly improbable.'

Marianne felt a stab of fear. 'Can we put a camera on them?'

'The rover is charging. It will be ready for use in ten minutes.'

'They might be hurt!'

Marianne waited, unsure.

She glanced at her watch. 'How long since –'

'Two minutes.'

'How long can anyone survive if their suit is breached?'

'Three minutes.'

'I have to go out.'

'That would be against protocol.'

'They could be dying. Do we have a rescue protocol?'

'No. There is no protocol for this situation.'

'Then I have to go out.'

Marianne walked quickly over to the suit booth.

'There is shadow movement. It is possible to infer movement.'

Marianne ran back to the bay window and instinctively leaned closer.

'I can't see –'

A figure appeared from around the side of the hill and dragged another figure across the sand. The standing figure had his back to the Keep. He briefly tapped the side of his helmet, as if to indicate the comms failure.

Marianne raced over to the airlock.

'Open the outer airlock, Rex, and let Gregory and Michael in.'

Marianne stood at the inner airlock door and looked through the window. The outer airlock door remained closed.

'Rex, open the outer airlock door.'

'Outer airlock door opened.'

Marianne watched the outer airlock door pull up.

'Please note that the two men outside are not Michael and Gregory. They are Michael and one other, who is unknown.'

'What are you talking about? It's Gregory and Michael!'

'That is incorrect. It is Gregory and someone else. The thermal scan indicates Gregory is dead.'

'What?'

Marianne was still processing the information when the stranger appeared at the outer airlock doorway, holding up Gregory's body.

Marianne stepped back. 'Shut the outer airlock door!'

The outer airlock door began to close. The stranger dropped Gregory' suited body to the ground, so that it blocked the door from closing.

'Outer airlock door cannot close.'

'Who is that man?'

'He is wearing a NASA Marssuit. He is requesting comms.'

'Link to his comms.'

'Done.'

'What have you done to Gregory?'

'He's hurt. Let us in. I can save him.'

'Who are you?'

'I'm NASA.'

'Who are you?'

'NASA. Let me in. We can save this man.'

'Tell me your name.'

'You're going to die. You need to let me in.'

Marianne took a step back.

'Rex, give me a visual from the airlock.'

Marianne looked at the nearest screen. She could see that Gregory's helmet was badly fractured and his face seemed to be turned to his shoulder, what little she could see of his face suggested it was strangely contorted.

'Switch off the colony exterior lights!'

The area outside the Keep was instantly plunged into darkness.

'Switch off all of the lights.'

The inside of the Keep became almost total darkness.

Marianne waited for what seemed like forever.

'Let me in,' the stranger said and tapped the airlock door. 'Let me save him while there's time.'

'Kill comms!'

Marianne took another step back. There was a pause and then she heard the stranger tap the airlock door again. He started to strike the door with something.

'Rex, can he breach the door?'

'Yes. It is likely the electronic lock will fail. It is not designed to withstand vandalism.'

Marianne turned around in the darkness; panicked and bewildered. She saw the faint blink of her tablet on her bed in the sleeping area. She moved over to the bed and hurriedly activated the tablet. The mail function to Mary Calstair came up automatically.

Marianne felt a stab of panic and typed '*He is killing everyone send rescue*' and sent the mail. She dropped the tablet back onto the bed and stood up.

'Rex, can you switch on only the light in the suit booth?'

The light came on inside the suit booth. Marianne ran over to the suit booth and entered it.

Marianne drew in deep breaths to try and keep calm, but fear was rising in her. Her hands shook.

The suit's oxygen system was full. The suit battery was at full charge.

'Rex, can I reach Mars Site 3 on foot?'

'Negative.'

'How far can I get?'

'Halfway. You could reach it driving a rover on full charge.'

'Is the rover fully charged?'

'Yes.'

'Can the stranger see the rover?'

'Yes.'

'Shit!'

Marianne tried to think.

'Rex, assuming the stranger is a mortal danger to me. What is my strategy?'

'Leave the rover as a decoy. He knows you will try and steal it. Exit the site and tell Mars Site 3 to head towards you in their rover. They will be able to meet before your oxygen runs out.'

'By what margin?'

'Thirty minutes.'

'Thirty minutes? What if they are delayed or get stuck?'

'You will suffocate and die.'

'Send an SOS to Mars Site 3.

There was a slight pause.

'Comms to Mars Site 3 is no longer possible.'

'Why?'

'The main comms unit is no longer functioning. It has suffered catastrophic failure.'

'He's destroyed it?'

'Yes.'

'Record an audio message anyway and if you can find a way to transmit it then do that. Ready?'

'Recording now.'

'This is Marianne Routledge. I am abandoning the Rex Colony. The colony has been attacked by a lunatic who says he's NASA. He has killed Gregory Wright and Michael Echoes.'

Marianne stifled a sob and took in a sharp breath.

'I am heading to Mars Site 3 on foot. I will head in a straight line to you. Please send out a rover to meet me! I do not have enough oxygen to reach Mars Site 3. This is Marianne Routledge, abandoning the Rex Colony and requesting immediate rescue.'

Marianne left the suit booth, holding the helmet. She walked over to the kitchen area. She drank some water. She could hear the stranger, back at the airlock door, hammering away with the club.

'Rex, all lights off. Execute Emergency Protocol 112.'

A dull red strip of light came on in the floor. The strip of light led to the emergency escape hatch at the back of the Keep. Marianne followed the strip of light.

The stranger attacked the inner airlock door with increased ferocity.

Marianne put her helmet on and locked it. The suit's oxygen system activated automatically.

Marianne entered an emergency code in a small keypad next to the hatch. She heard the unmissable clunk of slide bolts being pulled back by magnets.

'Rex, send out an SOS on any channel you can find. Use the Serfs as relays. Tell people that I am on foot and heading for Mars Site 3. If that man gets inside, go into hibernation mode. And do not come out of hibernation mode without the correct password. Do not let that man get access to any data or equipment. That is your mission from now on. Confirm?'

'Confirmed.'

Marianne gripped the handle of the emergency hatch and hesitated. She pulled it down and slid the hatch open.

The Keep's air escaped into the Martian night. Some vapour formed briefly around Marianne's helmet visor and then was gone. Marianne stepped out onto the frozen Martian sands, quickly turned around and closed the emergency hatch behind her.

Marianne hurried away from the Keep, moving in the general direction she knew would take her past Bradbury Plateau, towards Mars Site 3.

She struggled to keep fear and panic at bay. There was not enough oxygen to get to Mars Site 3. They would get her message, she told herself. They would come. All she had to do was keep walking and stay ahead of the stranger.

But she had to be careful. She had to conserve her oxygen. Maximum distance for minimal effort. Part of her, a very small part, remained calm, trying to process what had happened.

You still have a chance. Your priority is to get as far away as you can. To reach the people from Mars Site 3.

She glanced over her shoulder.

If the others had received her e-mail message, then they would already be on the way. She would make it with a little luck. All she had to –

She sensed something behind her and glanced back, saw the Rex Rover lights come on and the vehicle moved away from its charging station.

Marianne ran, all thought of conserving air gone.

CRISIS 3

Mars Site 3 Archive, #375
Max Grade, Mission Specialist
Personal Journal Entry: Sol 27

I dream often of my parents and my brother here, millions of miles from home.

There's no accounting for it. Mars has awoken my memory and haunts it like sad music filling the rooms of an empty house. A melody of melancholy. A music of loss in an abandoned house where ghosts listen for the wind, turn their shadows to the sun.

As a man, my brother was always looking over his shoulder into shadows or seeking conflict to shatter the awkward silence, the unnerving insecurity. The doubts he was too afraid to acknowledge. He was a fearful man at heart.

You cannot drown a thing like that. It will migrate the oceans of the mind and whatever bright lighthouse you have built, it will tear that tower down. It will make a wreck of you.

My brother's brash, youthful self-confidence was merely a disguise. It could not last.

My father couldn't understand it, and his bafflement sometimes caused conflicts between them. Didn't he have a great family? Wasn't life wonderful? What was there to fear?

Peter could not or would not say.

My mother sensed when Peter was at his worst. Used soothing words, soft smiles and simple closeness to hollow out his fear. It usually worked; soon Peter was back to his popular, confident self.

I would watch, admiring their intimacy. Saving up the details for the days when such memories are precious treasure to be cherished.

But after Peter left home, when crises of confidence plagued him, my mother was not there to coax him back to solid ground.

There was some kind of breakdown when he was at university. My mother and father were gone for three days. But somehow, they averted a major breakdown. Peter left the university, wandered the world for a year and then came back and finished his degree.

My father never talked about the breakdown, burying his head in his astronomy books – his head literally in celestial clouds. Hoping perhaps the worst was over for Peter and that he would find happiness.

But whichever way Peter tacked, self-doubt followed, and depression darkened his horizons. The only thing that alleviated his fear of failure was alcohol. A false medicine that bought temporary respite at a terrible cost.

He was an unhappy, unpleasant drunk, prone to violent outbursts and quarrels. He became mixed up in a lot of ugly situations. Eventually, he pushed us away. Moved from town to town. A solitary urban nomad. Each new town, a fresh start doomed to failure because of his drinking and self-destructive behaviour.

He abandoned rehab courses and careers. His life became one of failed relationships, bad company, massive debt, poor health and periods of homelessness.

Whenever bad news about Peter reached my father, he would say 'When did you ever hear of a drunk making a good decision? He has to sober up and stay sober. He has to learn to deal with his demons.'

The years of alcohol abuse took its toll. Peter unravelled. His mind now blunted with paranoia and anger. He was almost unrecognisable. A stranger who bore his likeness. A charlatan in his clothing.

None of us saw the real tragedy that was coming. How could we?

The phone ringing in the middle of a cold, snow-laden winter night, waking my mother and father in a panic.

A call from the hospital in Glasgow. Peter in a very bad way. An infection they could not stop. His organs failing. 'Come now,' the doctor told my parents.

My father drove. Insisted on manual control. A throwback from his fishing days.

My mother left a message on my phone, where it waited for me to wake, on the other side of the world. I could hear it in her voice. The fear. The panic.

We're going to the hospital. Peter might be – I can't say it. It doesn't look good.

I can see it now, my father driving faster than his driving skills could hold to. The ice on the road. The tearing snow. Now the car spinning.

My mother's face strobed by oncoming lights…

When they told Peter in his hospital bed – a junior doctor who did not know better whispered it in Peter's ear – he turned his head away and died right there. Right there. As if from shame.

I lost my whole family in a single night.

When I came back to Scotland to bury them, the door to my parents' house was still unlocked, all the lights in the house still on. The neighbours too polite and too afraid to enter the house because who knows if the dead were waiting?

My father's science and astronomy books were spread across the table.

His beloved books about Mars.

When I saw those books, I knew where I was going.

About 700 metres west of Mars Site 3, there is a rock in a spot where a rock has no business to be. Moved there, standing upright.

Carved in the rock where no carving should be: *In memory of Patricia and James Grade, and their son, Peter Grade. In love and gratitude.*

I may have broken some NASA rules there.

But what's the point of travelling all this way, if you can't be human?

*

The Serf was on the bottom slope of Bradbury Plateau when it picked up the SOS. It relayed the message to Quant.

Quant signalled the Serf to stay where it was. Two minutes later the Serf detected movement as Quant made his way down.

Quant reached the Serf. 'We have to move at speed,' Quant said. 'Try and keep up.'

Quant's technology was far superior to the Serf's, so the Serf followed behind Quant. It resembled an obedient but fearful dog, following at its master's heels.

The Serf detected movement in the ground. Its programming recognised it as an areological event and stopped.

Quant turned around and came back to the Serf. Quant pointed up at the sky. 'What you detected was the first part of that. An asteroid.'

The Serf turned its optics up, pivoted on its tracks, keeping its optics fixed on the blurred patch of light in the sky.

Quant moved on. Eventually the Serf turned away from the sky and accelerated to catch up with Quant.

'No,' Quant said aloud. 'They won't survive the impact. Not in the sites. On the plateau for a while. We can save two of them.'

The Serf stopped.

'No,' said Quant. 'I don't know how to choose.'

The Serf moved again, accelerating to catch up with Quant.

An hour later Quant and the Serf circled around an ancient crater that was so deep its slopes fell away to bottomless darkness.

The machine and AI were like fragile toys compared to the gigantic geological feature.

The upper rim of the crater was exposed to the dim light of the sun, crusted in ice, scored by veins of darker material that ran down the slopes, as if briny water once flowed there or had seeped out of the substrata.

They moved on and encountered an area criss-crossed by an ancient river delta formed billions of years ago, shaped into strange forms by the winds of Mars. The sides of the delta's extinct watercourses were banded with sand-coloured, red-rusted, ochre and pale chalk-brown and orange strata.

They approached an area where four strangely twisted channels met in a tangle of dips and depressions and then opened up into a flat-bottomed area about twice the size of Mars Site 3.

They saw Marianne Routledge stagger forwards, in obvious distress. Her Marssuit had a skin of ice.

Marianne fell to her knees. Quant and the Serf rushed forward. Quant checked her suit's oxygen unit. Maybe 45 minutes left.

Quant picked Marianne up, opened up his comms on all channels and hailed any system that was listening, human or otherwise and sent out the distress message.

Quant ran as fast as he could in the direction of Mars Site 3, which was still an hour away. He could only calculate that some of the Mars Site 3 Crew might be on their way to the Rex Colony. It was Marianne Routledge's only chance.

The Serf followed behind. Stopped and turned its optics in the direction from where Marianne had walked, as if its sensors had detected something following them. Then it pivoted on its tracks and accelerated to catch up with Quant.

*

Rover 2 had been moving for about an hour, steadily winding its way through banks of sand dunes and crossing beds of loose rocks when the main part of N2 finally collided with the planet.

The rover was lifted two metres from the ground by the peripheral force of the impact and came back down on ground that now buckled and kicked.

'Fate's sake! It's the end of Mars!' Max cried out.

The sky was gone. Darkness seemed to rush around them.

Sheets of sand collapsed along the flanks of the gigantic rust-coloured sand dunes that towered above the rover. The falling sand blocked their path, forming crumpled, man-sized heaps.

Max stopped the rover. 'Sys? Can you re-route?'

'Yes. Downloading now to On-Board Navigation Unit.'

'Do we lose time?'

'Ten minutes. You will still have twenty minutes of oxygen left to board the Ascent Vehicle and lift off.'

'Let's go,' Amy said.

Rover 2 reversed back and turned left, heading towards a huge sand dune inclined at about thirty degrees.

'Sys? We're going over that?'

'Yes.'

'I thought the rover could only handle fifteen-degree inclines.'

'It could do nineteen degrees in simulations.'

'Simulations?'

'It was never tested in the field at more than 10 degrees.'

'Just terrific.'

'All other routes end in failure.'

'I get it.'

The rover started to drive up the flank of the sand dune, its wheels locking and turning in a careful sequence executed by Sys.

The rover inched its way to the crest of the sand dune and crossed over.

Max and Amy were momentarily stunned as they looked out at a wall of sand and darkness crossing the Martian Plains.

The wall of darkness stretched up into the sky as far as the eye could see, swallowing everything in its path. Lightning flickered within the darkness, revealing plumes of black and grey dust and debris.

The front of the rover dipped down and the vehicle slowly descended the dune.

Max cleared his throat. 'Amy? Can you mute your suit comms? I want to leave a message for my fiancée. Just a couple of minutes.'

Amy nodded. 'Mute suit comms until further notice,' she said and turned her gaze back to the devastation crossing the plains.

Max took a deep breath. 'Sys record this as part of my personal log and upload it as soon as you have available bandwidth.'

'Confirmed.'

'This is Max Grade, Mission Specialist. Please confirm this, Sys.'

'Confirmed.'

'Lydia. It's me. It's Max. I'm in the second rover with Amy and we are heading to Mars Site 2. If we succeeded, if fate was kind to us, then humanity has survived and you're hearing this message. With all my heart, I hope you're hearing this message. I'm sorry I didn't make it back home. We always knew how dangerous this mission would be, but no one saw this scenario. The most important thing is that you and everyone else are still alive. That there is a tomorrow after tomorrow. I love you. I will love you to my last breath. I wish I could have lived out my days with you. You were the best of everything in my life. If you choose to have our child and he's a boy, call him Alec or John like we agreed. If it's a girl, then you choose the name. Remember me. You have my heart forever.'

Max drew in a breath and looked out at the Martian landscape below.

'End message,' he said.

The rover moved on.

'Sys?'

'Yes?'

'What are the chances of either me or Amy succeeding in carrying out this plan?'

'Five percent.'

Max bowed his head. It felt like someone had punched him in the chest. The shock and dread of that estimate.

'What if it was Quant?'

'Fifty percent.'

Max nodded.

Max turned to Amy and tapped her on the arm. Amy switched on her suit comms.

'You want to leave a message?' Max asked.

'Yes.'

'Mute my suit comms until further notice,' Max said and looked away.

*

Quant looked down at Marianne Routledge and could see from the fear in her eyes. Her oxygen supply was dwindling and she knew it. She was sensible enough not to speak, trying to keep her breathing shallow and minimal.

Quant pressed on, moving faster.

A subroutine in his background processing repeatedly calculated failure. His mission was futile, yet his higher programming compelled him forwards, persisted in this hopeless quest to reach a human with an oxygen supply.

The Serf had fallen behind, unable to match Quant's speed; a dwindling silhouette that sometimes pivoted on its tracks, confused by failing comms and something that was following, something that always remained just beyond of the Serf's visual field.

The Serf suddenly buzzed with activity. It notified Quant that it had detected a rover signal 3 kilometres west of their position but that the signal had been short and had disappeared.

Quant had not detected any rover. There was a high probability that the Serf's sensors were erroneous.

But it was something. Quant changed direction abruptly and

headed west. After about 1 kilometre the land sank and rose in a series of sand dunes. Quant ran on. He reached the top of the last dune and stopped for a moment.

A large crater barred his way. Quant surveyed the terrain. There was no time to go around it.

Quant ran up the exterior slope of the crater, ignoring hazard warnings and self-preservation protocols.

The Serf signalled it could not follow and would route around the crater.

Quant reached the rim of the crater and looked down.

The crater was filled with ice. Like a strange white silence pooled between the dark slopes.

Quant descended onto the ice and ran across the crater. His thermal sensors registered deep cold, even for Mars. He heated his arms and chest to provide Marianne Routledge some warmth, draining his battery reserves.

He ran blind now, at full speed and slipped twice but recovered his balance. A tiny dot in all that vast whiteness.

When he reached the other side he looked up, scanning the rim for a way up. He picked a route and climbed up the crater rim. The crater rim had an overhang, formed by ice and winds and sand, effectively trapping Quant.

Quant's sensors detected a rover nearby, below on the plain.

Quant moved around the rim trying to find a way up. He found a point on the crater rim where the overhang was broken and started to climb up, only using one arm.

He was almost over when his sensors and programming registered extreme hazard.

The dim Marian sky darkened suddenly and the planet seemed to shudder and the ground bucked and heaved violently.

Quant lost his hold. He slid rapidly down the slope still

holding Marianne Routledge by one arm. He tried to stop his slide. It took several seconds for him to halt. Debris tumbled from the crater rim and fell past him. Quant leaned over Marianne Routledge to protect her.

Quant calculated the massive asteroid strike was to the west. Already, millions of tonnes of debris were being ejected into the Martian sky. A rain of stone and dust would fall within minutes. Anyone standing on the plains would probably die from falling material, or be blinded, with no clear path out and be buried in it.

The ground continued to shake and heave. The sky remained dark.

Quant regained his footing and climbed back up towards the overhang.

Marianne Routledge was struggling now, gasping for air, trying to say something. Quant looked down at her. Her face contorted into a terrible grimace of pain and fear, not quite believing that this was the end. The oxygen gone. She clawed at her helmet.

Quant looked away and moved on. Slower now but unable to stop. Some compulsion, some weighing of actions in his neural network, forcing him to press on. Anything but look at Marianne Routledge.

Quant reached the break in the overhang.

He hauled himself and Marianne up and over the crater rim and moved down the steep slope of the crater's exterior.

He saw the rover approach from between two groups of sand dunes.

Quant calculated seven more minutes would have saved her.

Behind the rover, a wall of dust and darkness approached at great speed.

Quant moved down the slope, heading straight for the rover.

They felt the ground buckle below them. Jerry stopped the rover.

Adrian steadied himself. 'What was that? Is it a marsquake? You shouldn't feel a marsquake, should you?'

'Maybe an asteroid strike,' Jerry muttered, his attention on the rover's control panel. 'We've lost comms with Sys.'

Mary suddenly pointed at the slope of a nearby crater. 'Look! It's Quant. What's he carrying? Is that a body?'

Jerry looked up. Blinked. Nothing in their training had prepared them for this. When he spoke, his voice sounded uncertain.

'Okay, we need to …'

Adrian looked at Jerry. 'Jerry? What do we do?'

'Everyone leave the rover together and take your prod with you. Full charge. You get a chance you spear Quant. We put him out of action. Understand?'

Adrian and Mary reached for their prods.

Jerry stepped out of the rover, followed by Adrian and Mary on the other side. The three of them came together in front of the rover. They held their prods out, like spears.

'We look like a bunch of savages,' Adrian said.

Jerry sensed something and glanced behind them. 'Definitely an asteroid strike.'

They looked back.

A wall of darkness and broiling dust was moving towards them at speed. As if the horizon was being rolled up and dragged towards them.

'Oh, for fate's sake,' said Adrian.

They turned back, holding their prods in front of them.

Quant approached. He laid Marianne Routledge on the

ground. He remained bent over her.

'I tried to save her,' Quant said.

Jerry nodded. Adrian started to circle around Quant.

'Is she dead?' Jerry asked.

'There are things you need to know.'

'Oh yeah? What things?' Adrian said, breathless with fear.

Quant started to speak.

'There is –'

Adrian lunged forwards and stabbed Quant in the side with the prod. Adrian felt Quant's body shake from the charge. Quant leaned on one arm, weakened but did not fall over.

Jerry lunged forward and stabbed his prod into Quant's chest. Quant made a strange jerking motion. Looked up at Jerry. 'Wait –'

Jerry glanced at Mary, who hadn't moved.

'Do it, Mary!'

Mary hesitated, seeking some power within that could make her strike.

'You're just a machine,' she said.

Quant looked up at her.

'I'm as real as you are.'

Quant's words seemed to fill Mary with disgust. She lunged forward.

'Nuts and bolts. Nuts and bolts,' she hissed and stabbed her prod into the side of Quant's neck.

Quant jerked and became deadweight. Nothing but cold, inanimate machinery. He toppled over, falling across the body of Marianne Routledge.

The three astronauts did not move, breathless, holding their prods up, ready to stab him again.

The first waves of dust streamed past them, and the dim Martian sky darkened to blackness. As the light failed, their suit lights switched on automatically.

The curtains of streaming dust accelerated and thickened, becoming a coarse sandstorm, material and coarse sand grains scraping against their suits.

Larger, denser material began to drop from the sky; a jagged rock the size of a human head landed nearby, and they all saw it.

'We have to get out of this,' Jerry said. 'Let's move,' he ordered.

Jerry and Adrian dropped their prods and pulled Quant off Mary Routledge.

'We'll put her body in the back of the rover. We're not leaving her here,' Jerry said.

'Alright,' Adrian agreed, and they lifted her up.

Mary gathered up the prods, fearful still of Quant, keeping clear of his prone form. She hurried back to the rover cab and climbed inside.

Adrian and Jerry placed Mary Routledge in the back of the rover, careful as they laid her body on the floor. They came back around the rover and climbed back in the cab.

Pieces of debris and material rattled the roof of the rover.

Adrian turned to Jerry. 'Do we go on in this?'

'Yes.'

'They're probably dead, Jerry.'

'We don't know that. We have a duty.'

Mary stared ahead. 'I don't want to die on Mars,' she said. 'I didn't come here to die.'

Jerry started the rover. 'They sent a distress signal,' he said. 'We keep going. It's my call.'

'Then let's go,' Adrian said. 'I don't want to be around if Quant wakes up.'

'He's not going to wake up,' Mary said. 'His circuits are fried.'

Jerry took a deep breath. 'It isn't that far to the Rex Colony. We can sit it out there, recharge the rover and bring the others back with us. Agreed?'

Adrian and Mary nodded.

*

When the Serf found Quant, he was already almost completely buried under a layer of sand and detritus.

The Serf circled Quant for several minutes. Finally, it stopped at the feet of Quant, took hold of Quant's buried feet and reversed, dragging the android out of the sand.

The Serf released Quant and moved away. It pivoted on its tracks, scanning the area with its optics and sensors.

It came back and stopped next to Quant. It stayed there, inactive, for a long time, until it picked up a distress signal and moved away.

*

Darkness surrounded the rover. Visibility was down to three metres. According to the rover's route app, they were only 960 metres from the Rex Colony, but they had strayed off route or their map was wrong or the terrain had changed, maybe because of the asteroid strike, because the ground inclined steeply where it should have been flat. They found themselves moving along the edge of a sharp fall in the lee of a boulder-strewn slope.

Darkness and dim light seemed to flare intermittently in the Martian sky; a mix of night and day and the debris continued to fall from the sky; rocks that could crush the rover falling past them.

'This isn't good,' Adrian warned. 'We're kind of exposed.'

'I know,' Jerry answered. 'But we can't turn around and I don't want to try and reverse. Not in this visibility. Hopefully it will level off soon.'

The rover crept forward. Jerry peered into the maelstrom, hoping to see the perimeter lights of the Rex Colony or some kind of structure he could use as a reference.

'Look for a beacon or something,' he said. 'We must be near the perimeter. Their power might be down.'

The Rex rover appeared out of the darkness above them, moving down the slope at speed, heading straight for them.

Jerry reacted first. 'Get out!' he ordered and hit the emergency release button and their seatbelts uncoupled and the doors of their rover opened.

'Get out!' he repeated.

Adrian pushed Mary as hard as he could. She tumbled out of the rover and fell onto the edge of the drop and went over, rolling down at speed, striking a large rock that stopped her fall.

The Rex rover rammed into the side of the NASA rover and pushed it over the edge.

Mary watched the NASA rover tumble down the near vertical slope, tearing apart as it struck rocks and strata. She saw Adrian thrown from the vehicle, his body dashed against rocks, suit helmet in pieces.

The rover continued its disintegrating fall to the bottom of the slope and came to a stop on its buckled roof, the cab windows broken.

Mary hurried down the slope and made her way over to the rover. She looked inside and saw Jerry's dead body, a broken mess. His suit torn up one side, his head hanging at a weird angle.

She stepped back and turned around and looked back up at the top of the slope. She saw a figure on the edge, peering down. The figure stepped back and after a short pause the Rex rover moved away, heading in the direction they had come.

Mary stayed where she was for several minutes, too shocked to move. Gradually she became aware of her suit telling her she had to seek a rover or habitat soon. The suit was low on power and low on oxygen.

Mary started to climb up the slope, fearful she would lose her footing, edging sideways if she didn't trust the slope ahead of her. Eventually she reached the ridge they had driven on.

'Comms,' she said.

'Comms fail,' her suit system answered.

'Location.'

'Location fail.'

'Where is the rover?'

'Unable to compute. Comms fail. Location fail.'

'How far to the Rex Colony?'

'Unable to compute.'

'Use last known computable position.'

'300 metres west.'

'Show me west.'

The suit showed Mary west on her visor.

'Of course, it would be that way,' she said and started to climb towards the summit from where the Rex rover had first appeared.

When she reached the summit, she was breathless and scared. The dark sands of Mars blew past in one long unbroken stream. But there were moments when the darkness thinned and she saw the Rex Colony below, one perimeter light still operating.

Mary hurried down the slope, stumbling now and then in the darkness. She made her way to the airlock entrance and hesitated when she saw the body lying there.

Something moved to her right and she turned.

The shape of a man moved towards her. He held some kind of club and raised it as he moved toward her.

She turned and ran full tilt. She didn't know where she was going but her only thought was to flee. Her suit alarm warned her she was moving too fast. 'Alarm off!' she ordered as she continued to run.

She ran until she had covered nearly a kilometre. She stopped to catch her breath. The sandstorm fell away for a few moments and some visibility returned.

She stared ahead and watched a dust devil approach. It was darker than the ones she had seen before. The vortex of material approached Mary.

It was much bigger than she realised. Suddenly she was inside the vortex. Darkness swirled around her and the skin of her suit hissed.

The vortex passed.

Mary looked over her shoulder and watched it move away. She turned back and looked down at her feet.

She realised she was standing on a thin surface – the top of a lava tube structure. Her first thought was to move away but before she could take a step the thin skin of opaque rock gave way and she fell through the lava tube roof.

She fell about 20 metres and when she hit the ground her left leg snapped.

She cried out in agony, reaching for her leg.

'Suit send out an alarm! Keep sending!' she managed to

shout before losing consciousness.

When she regained consciousness, she moaned from the pain, breathing sharply, fighting to stay conscious.

She looked around in the darkness. She switched on the small guide light on the side of her suit helmet. Her broken leg stretched out a strange angle, but the suit was still intact.

She switched the light off to conserve power.

She was cold. Her body started to shiver. She thought she might be bleeding somewhere. Her ribs maybe. Shock was setting in. She fought back the fear.

A light appeared above her, at the hole in the lava tube ceiling.

'Who's there? Local comms. Connect.'

A visual appeared on the inside of Mary's helmet. *Connected.*

The Serf switched on its work light.

'Can you help me?'

The Serf moved its optics up and down. It lowered a thin cable from its winch compartment and moved away from the edge of the hole.

Mary switched on her helmet guide light again and followed the cable's descent.

Mary dragged herself over to the cable and took hold of it and pulled herself up onto her good leg. The Serf moved away from the hole.

'Wait!' Mary warned. 'I can't hold it. Wait!'

The Serf stopped.

Mary hooked the cable onto one of the straps on her oxygen suit and held onto the cable as best she could.

'Okay.'

The Serf backed away and slowly hoisted Mary up to the hole.

Halfway up, the oxygen tank strap snapped. Mary plummeted back to the ground, landing on her back, the fall damaging her oxygen unit.

'For fate's sake!' Mary screamed. The suit's alarm trilled in her helmet.

'Oxygen capacity.'

A visual appeared on the inside of Mary's helmet. '10:20'.

Ten minutes and twenty seconds.

'I'm supposed to go home to my family!' she screamed. 'I'm supposed to go home! Mars!'

She did not want to die. But worse than that, she did not want to suffocate.

She was going to die. She was going to suffocate. No one would ever find her.

The Serf retracted the cable and came back to the hole.

'Switch on your light,' she told the Serf.

The Serf switched on its work light. A ray of bright light penetrated the cavern.

'Stay there,' Mary said, voice faltering from the pain. 'Stay there.'

The Serf didn't move.

'Do you have an emergency med kit?'

The Serf nodded.

'Does it have morphine?'

The Serf nodded.

'Fill up a syringe with as much morphine as you can and then lower it down. Ignore your safety protocols. Put as much morphine in as you possibly can. It must be greater than a lethal dose. You understand? More than a lethal dose.'

The Serf moved away. Switched off its work light.

'You fill that syringe with everything you have and then

141

lower it to me.'

Minutes passed. Mary feared the Serf's safety protocols had prevented it from obeying her orders.

'You there? Are you there?' Her voice broke. 'Please –'

The Serf came back to the hole and switched on its work light and lowered the syringe in a sealed heated thermal plastic pouch.

When it was low enough, Mary took hold of the bag and removed it. She dragged herself over to the wall of the lava tube.

The Serf tilted its work light; the ray of light followed Mary.

Mary sat back against the wall of the lava tube. She looked at the pouch in her hands.

The Serf's light illuminated her chest and lap.

She looked up and spasms racked her upper body. She gasped for a few seconds and then she cried out in a rage and made a fist with her free hand and hammered the ground.

Then she said 'Mars' as if the word was an insult and then she said nothing for a long time, watching her suit's oxygen count. The minutes spilling away too fast.

Finally, she said, 'Suit, I need to make an intravenous injection into a vein in my arm. Tell me when it's at the right spot to be able to inject into my arm. I have to push the needle through the material, so disable suit resistance in the spot where I push it through. Do you compute all that?'

A visual appeared on the inside of Mary's helmet. *Compute.*

Mary removed the syringe from the heated plastic bag and moved the needle to just above the elbow on her left arm and pressed. A visual appeared on the inside of her helmet, showing her arm and a green cross and a red cross.

Mary moved the needle and pressed. The red cross moved closer to the green cross. After a couple of more attempts the green and red cross aligned.

Mary bit her bottom lip.

'How far do I need to push?'

6 mm.

'Tell me when to stop.'

Mary pushed the needle in. She felt it puncture her skin. Already turning cold.

Stop.

Mary injected all of the syringe's contents into her arm.

The effect was immediate and overwhelming. Mary slipped over onto her side, pupils dilating. The syringe fell out of her arm.

The suit's repair mechanism activated and sealed over the tiny hole.

Mary's gaze drifted up to the light from the Serf.

'Tell Quant I'm sorry. I'm sorry. I was wrong.'

Mary blinked.

'Don't leave me until I'm gone.'

The Serf did not move.

'Thank you,' Mary said and never spoke again.

Frank approached the Rex rover driver's door. He opened it and climbed inside the cab. He placed his bloodied club on the passenger seat and switched off the rover's lights.

He checked the status of the rover. Fully operational.

He smiled. The glow of preordained fate lit up the rover like celestial music.

*

She had stopped breathing twenty minutes and thirty seconds

ago. Her core temperature had dropped to 8 °C and the suit had failed.

The Serf moved back from the hole. It plotted a route to Quant's last position.

It started to move and then stopped: an archival subroutine initiated a positioning marker. The Serf turned its optics to the sky.

On all comms channels, it broadcast the last positional coordinates of Mary Calstair, along with her NASA ID code and the code for dead.

The Serf re-prioritised its tasks and once again moved towards the last known position of Quant.

In the debris-filled sandstorm it resembled a lonely creature looking for home.

*

The Serf rounded a bend, and registered the prone figure of Quant. The android was already half-covered by a layer of debris, shaped like a slain sentinel in the sand.

The Serf moved over to Quant and extended one of its grippers and held Quant's hand. An action not explained or predicted by any of its programming.

The sand and debris storm flared, like a fire that only threw out darkness.

The Serf played the audio recording over and over:

'Tell Quant I'm sorry. I'm sorry. I was wrong. Don't leave me until I'm gone. Thank you.'

*

Amy was still recording her message to her family. Max looked down at his feet and the prod lying on the floor of the rover, wondering if he could use it against Quant.

Amy finished recording her message. She tapped Max on the arm.

'Local comms restore,' Max said.

Max smiled wanly. 'Okay?'

'How can anyone be okay in a situation like this?'

'Sorry. Stupid thing to say. I think we've lost comms with Sys.'

'Well of course we have. All we need now is to get stuck in the sand.'

'Let's not tempt fate. It's been cruel enough.'

'What's that? Rover stop!'

Quant was ahead of them in the sandstorm.

Standing now. Very still. A Serf at his feet.

'Can we drive around him?' Amy asked.

'I doubt it. He can move faster than the rover if he has to. He could probably tear the doors off if he wanted to.'

Amy breathed in sharply. 'I'll grab him, and you stab him with the prod. Put him out of action. Okay?'

'Okay.'

Max picked up the prod. Weighed it in his hands.

They left the rover on either side and walked around to the front of the vehicle.

Quant had not moved. His head was lowered slightly. His legs were spread apart, and his arms were held out in front of him in a kind of readied position.

'He's going to attack us,' Amy said.

'I don't think so. It looks more like a defensive position.'

In the darkness and low visibility of the terrain behind Quant, some rover lights came on.

'Look there!' Amy pointed and shouted. 'It's Jerry!'

Max and Amy could just make out the shape of the other rover, a figure next to the rover door waved and gestured for them to run around Quant and to approach the rover.

Quant looked at them. 'Don't hurt me again,' Quant said to Max.

Amy moved in the direction of the other rover, keeping her distance well away from Quant, moving around him.

'Come on, Max!' Amy said. 'What are you waiting for?'

The Serf moved away from Quant and seemed to block Max's path.

'Zap him, Max. It's your only chance!' Amy shouted.

Max hesitated. Quant hadn't moved.

'Don't go over there, Amy,' Max said. 'I don't think that's Jerry.'

Amy stopped, suddenly unsure. She could just make out the shape of a figure she thought was Jerry next to the dark shape of the rover in the sandstorm. She looked back at Max and Quant.

The Serf turned its optics between Quant and Max.

Max looked desperately at Quant.

'Have you hurt anyone, Quant? Have you killed anyone?'

Quant shook his head. 'No. Your people have tried to kill me. Stay back or I will defend myself.'

'Have you killed anyone?'

'No. I can't take a life, Max. I will not take a life. Only man has killed on Mars.'

Max threw the prod onto the sand. 'I'm not going to hurt you. You're my friend.'

Amy shouted over the comms at Max. 'What are you doing? Have you lost your mind?'

'Just wait a minute, Amy. Stay where you are. You don't

know who's over there.'

'Don't be a fool, Max. It's Jerry. You can't trust Quant!'

Amy turned to move again.

'Just wait!' Max shouted. 'Sys? Are you there? Do we have comms?'

'Comms is restored but unstable.'

'Give Quant all of the data and messages for the last 48 hours.'

'For fate's sake, Max! Don't do it!' Amy warned.

'Command executed,' Sys said.

Quant looked directly at Max.

'Why should I help you?'

'Ten billion people.'

Quant didn't react.

Max stepped forward, hands out in an act of appeal. 'Okay. I get it. People aren't your favourite lifeform right now. How about this: Life is very worth living and it's fundamental. We've got to keep it going.'

'Those aren't your words.'

'Does it matter? Quant, you know there's no life for hundreds, maybe thousands of lightyears. There was never any life and there isn't going to be any life.' Max pointed in the direction of Earth. 'It's a garden, Quant. The Garden of Life. There's no other place like it anywhere. You have to save it. It's all we have.'

Quant looked at the Serf.

Max looked at the Serf. 'Nod your optics, numpty.'

The Serf nodded.

'Go to Bradbury Plateau,' Quant ordered. 'One of you can survive for up to two years in the Garden. Enough time to organise a rescue.'

'Just one?'

'It won't sustain two of you. Not for long enough. You could try and salvage something from the sites if they aren't fully buried. That would be a plan. Then the two of you might make it. But the odds are slim.'

Quant nodded in the direction of the other Rover. 'I need to take your rover. You need to take the rover from him.'

'Which one is he?'

'Frank Allen, according to his suit ID.'

'Frank, then,' Max said. 'He's the one trying to kill us all.'

'I have scanned him. He has two unusual lesions, one in the prefrontal cortex and one in the amygdala. There is also fresh blood splatter on the exterior of his suit. He is almost certainly psychotic but high functioning.'

'He's insane. Can't you help me?'

'I need to go now. There's no time.'

Quant turned around and moved towards Max's rover, instructing the Serf to help Max and Amy.

Max peered into the debris-filled darkness.

Frank waved Amy forward. She started to move towards him again.

'Don't,' Max warned her. 'It isn't Jerry. Didn't you hear what Quant said?'

Amy paused and then continued moving towards Frank.

Max picked up the prod and hesitated.

Quant had already started to drive away, the shape of the rover fading to nothing.

'For fate's sake. Get away from him, Amy!' Max shouted.

But Amy continued to move towards Frank.

As Amy reached Frank, she realised he wasn't Jerry. Instinctively, she took a step back just as Frank swung the club, aiming for her head.

For once Frank lost his footing as he swung, and his shoulder dropped. The club struck Amy in the ribs. She cried out, doubling over in pain, falling to one knee.

Frank swung again, wildly, still not fully balanced. This time the club struck Amy's helmet a glancing blow. Amy's helmet remained intact, but the force of the blow knocked her unconscious and she tipped forward and fell onto the sands.

Frank raised his club to deliver the final blow.

Max speared Frank in the leg with the prod. Frank winced and involuntarily dropped his club. He collapsed onto the sand next to Amy, already reaching out to grasp the club again.

Max pulled Amy away, too frightened to worry about damaging her suit. He dragged her over to the Rex Colony rover, opened the passenger door and lifted her onto the passenger's seat, slamming the door closed.

Max looked around, afraid. The sand and debris grew denser; a darkness hissing on his suit. He could hardly see anything. He hurried around to the driver's door, half expecting to be attacked again but there was no sign of Frank.

Max opened the door and climbed inside the rover cab, closing the door in a panic. He glanced around for anything that could be used as a weapon and lifted a screwdriver from a toolbox.

'Bradbury Plateau,' he told the rover.

The rover navigation unit showed the destination on a display and asked for confirmation.

'Confirmed! Now move!' Max looked out at the sandstorm. 'Where is he? I can't see him out there. Sys? Can you help, Sys?'

'No comms with MS3,' Max's suit reported. 'No comms with Sys.'

'Do I have comms with Quant?'

'Negative.'

'How long until we reach Bradbury Plateau?'

'Thirty-five minutes.'

'How long until Quant reaches MS2?'

'Twenty minutes.'

Max looked at Amy. She was unconscious but breathing.

*

Quant drove the rover onto the edge of MS2. The perimeter net had buckled in places under the sheer volume of sand and debris. Some damaged storage equipment had fallen over. One of the smaller domes had been destroyed by the impact of a large rock.

Quant drove the rover over to the site's rocket ascent area.

The protective dome of the ascent launch pad had already folded open like a strange flower, the Ascent Rocket primed, its exterior lights on.

Quant left the rover and climbed up onto the two-man-lift next to the Ascent Rocket and pressed the lift ascent button. The lift moved up the Ascent Vehicle at the top of the Ascent Rocket and stopped.

Quant opened the hatch to the Ascent Vehicle. He entered and locked the hatch behind him. The lift automatically descended.

Quant strapped himself into the flight commander's seat and carried out a series of checks, ensuring the Ascent Rocket was ready for ignition and entering the orbit coordinates and speed of the Thor.

Quant pushed the ignition button.

The Ascent Rocket lifted off. Quant watched the ground recede before the sandstorm swallowed up all visibility. Twenty seconds into the ascent and the Ascent Rocket cleared the top of the sandstorm. A minute later, Quant could make out the red curve of Mars against the blackness of space.

The full view of the destruction wrought from the impact of N2 was now visible: unfolding and spreading like a dark shadow. MS3 was already swallowed up in the darkness and the Rex Colony would soon follow. Nothing alive on the surface was going to survive that wave of destruction.

The Ascent Rocket separated from the Ascent Vehicle and fell away. The smaller Ascent Vehicle's main propulsion engine fired for twenty seconds.

A small bright dot appeared in the view portal and grew steadily. After a few minutes, the shape of the Thor was unmistakable in the blackness of space.

Quant activated the Ascent Vehicle's exterior camera and switched on the navigation screen on his right. The screen showed the bright form of the asteroid.

'There you are.'

*

Max brought the rover to a stop at the base of Bradbury Plateau. The sandstorm was more intense and blocked his view of the sky and the upper reaches of the plateau.

No way to tell if any of his colleagues were still alive or if the Rex Colonists were still alive.

No way to tell if Quant had made it.

Not yet anyway.

Max carried Amy out of the rover and laid her down on the sand. He tightened the straps of his oxygen unit. He bent down and lifted Amy up into a fireman's lift position.

He started to walk up the slope.

Max felt a series of aftershocks in the ground and hesitated and turned around.

Frank was stretched across the top of the rover. Frank let go of the small side railings on each side that he had been holding onto and slid down from the rear of the rover. He still had his club. He moved awkwardly, perhaps injured.

Frank looked up at Max and smiled.

Max turned around and moved up the slope as fast as he could.

*

Quant docked the Ascent Vehicle with Thor and waited for confirmation that the docking was safe.

Quant left the pilot seat and moved to the airlock door. He opened the airlock and entered the Thor, locking the airlock behind him.

Quant sent a signal to the Ascent Vehicle, and it undocked and drifted away.

Quant moved through the ship's interior.

He passed an opening in the gangway. He could see the storage module attached to the ship. Enough nuclear explosive force to destroy a thousand cities.

The objective wasn't to try and split apart N1 because that would end in failure. The objective was to change the asteroid's trajectory, enough so that it would no longer collide with the Earth. The timing and the angle of the craft when it detonated had to be precise.

Quant reached Thor's two-man command module. He sat in the Flight Engineer's seat, strapped himself in and initiated the flight sequence.

The command module did not respond.

Quant unstrapped himself and pushed himself up so that he rested against the ceiling of the command module. He unscrewed one of the panels, and when he removed it he could see that the flight navigation circuit had been removed.

Quant replaced the panel and gently pushed against the ceiling. He moved back to the command chair. He strapped himself in.

'Thor, system go to audio. Executive command 1A.'

'Thor, system audio link confirmed.'

Quant took hold of the navigation joysticks on each side of the flight engineer seat.

'Manual navigation control. Switch on the navigation display. Target N1.'

The console display in front of Quant lit up, showing the eerie glowing shape of N1.

'Centre in screen,'

N1 was now displayed in the centre of the screen.

'Give me a triangulated grid on N1 centre screen.'

N1 was now displayed within a triangle.

'Align the main thrusters with N1.'

Quant waited. The side thrusters fired and the Thor began to move.

'Aligned.'

'Fire thrusters half power.'

Thor moved towards its target, accelerating as it moved.

'Thor, I want you to make a backup of my system files and core programme and to upload them to a NASA server. Any server you can link to. Do you have the bandwidth for that?'

'Yes.'

'Then begin.'

'Link confirmed.'

'Good. Now give me comms with the garden.'

'No comms available.'

'Give me audio comms with Bradbury Plateau. Anyone. Any available Serf.'

'Confirmed.'

Quant heard the hissing of sands.

*

Max reached the top slope of Bradbury Plateau when the Serf came up behind him and moved past. The Serf stopped.

'Can you hold her?'

The Serf nodded and extended its arms. Max laid Amy across the Serf's arms.

'Take her into the garden. Keep her safe.'

The Serf nodded its optics, pivoted on its tracks and sped up the slope.

Max steadily climbed the slope. He glanced back. Frank was following.

Max reached the top of the plateau. He turned to his right and walked to the other edge of the plateau and the sheer fall into the void. Three steps.

He came back and walked four steps in the direction of the garden.

He stopped, turned around and waited.

The waiting felt like forever.

He heard Peter's voice inside his head. Knew it was an illusion. But it was Peter's voice just the same. The old, brave, steadfast Peter.

You don't give him a way out, Max. Not him. Not this one.

A sudden vortex of denser sand and detritus flared darkly around Max. It was as if he occupied a heart of darkness, as

154

if the Martian elements were malign, intent on his failure.

He held his arms out. Hands turned up. Like a last appeal. Or a man trying to hold back what could not be held back.

A posture of defeat and weakness. A last gesture of appeal to the uncaring universe.

You don't give him a way out, Max. Not him.

Amy regained consciousness and moaned. She was lying on her back, staring up at the opaque roof.

There was a Serf next to her. It gestured for her to remove her suit helmet.

Amy did not move. The Serf reached down and removed her helmet.

Amy was too weak to stop it. She breathed in air that was sweet.

The Serf pressed a wet bandage onto the ugly swelling on her forehead.

Amy looked up at the roof. The sandstorm was thinner up there. She could see a very bright object in the night sky, different from any star.

'Is that N1?'

The Serf nodded.

*

Frank reached the top of Bradbury Plateau. His head was filled with light. His every atom vibrated with celestial joy.

He was becoming a god. The creator of new worlds.

Frank stopped, took out a handheld computer unit from the pocket of his suit and keyed something in.

Inside the Thor, Quant saw the message on the ship display:

'Disarming sequence initiated.'

'Open all comms,' Quant said. 'Max, he's disarming the payload! He has a detonation override!'

Frank heard. He looked up at the cold darkness of the Martian sky.

'That's right Mr AI. You can't stop what I have ordained.'

Frank smiled like he was made of sunshine.

All that existed did so because he willed it so. In the history to come, in the world that would arise from the ashes, people would look on his works for millennia and despair. His name would ring out –

Max ran full force into Frank at a right angle.

The two men tumbled over the corner edge of the plateau and fell into the void.

Max caught a last, close-up glance of Frank's face, whose expression was of complete surprise and incomprehension.

Darkness seemed to rush up at them. They fell through the sandstorm. They seemed to fall forever.

Max's left shoulder struck a protruding rock and shattered. The force of the impact sent him spinning towards the rock face.

He struck more rocks, puncturing ribs. His revolving body struck the side of the plateau one last time and the force of it threw him sideways like a rag doll and he landed on his back, on a protruding shelf of rock, blood pooling inside his still intact Marssuit.

Frank continued to fall thousands of metres in confused astonishment.

He hit the ground head first, striking the patch of softened sand that covered Quant's extra reactor.

The force of his fall immersed his body in the sand up to his waist. His Marssuit visor split apart, sand pressed against his face, blinding him and filling his airways.

He suffocated quickly, his feet kicking the Martian air, and the last thing he felt was terror and he took the terror with him into oblivion.

*

Quant neared the asteroid, still on half power. He armed the nuclear payload.

He seemed to wait for something. He listened to the open comms; his head tilted.

*

Amy looked up at the opaque roof.

'Max?'

Silence and the hissing of the sandstorm.

'Max?'

'I'm here. Still here,' Max answered.

*

Quant heard. He applied full power.

*

Amy looked up at the opaque roof.

A brilliant intense point of light flared in the darkness of space.

'Max?'

'I see it.'

The light faded.

'Max?'

Sands drifted across the opaque roof.

'Max?'

50th Anniversary Postscript

Since the publication of this story, there has been a lot of speculation as to its accuracy and the identity of the author. It was agreed that that anonymous author had access to another 'secret' cache and not just the Holden Cache, which was the official NASA depository for all of the Mars mission recordings and data.

Three years ago, NASA archivists made a remarkable discovery. In a former NASA rover engineering building located in a long-forgotten data facility on the outskirts of Houston, a building that was supposed to have been demolished forty years previously, NASA's archivists found an abandoned server room in the basement, all of the servers destroyed completely by the Wipeout Virus and simple neglect – apart from one server, which still had some damaged files.

One of these files was a partially damaged audio file and the NASA archivists said when they first heard it and realised what they were hearing, they could not believe their own ears.

NASA'S chief archivist, Montgomery Freil, wrote on the NASA website: 'It was as if a ghost had crossed the plains of Mars to whisper in our ears.'

A voice recording of Max Grade Flight Engineer and Amy Holywell made inside Rover 2.

The transcript of the damaged audio file was only published 18 months ago, and it immediately generated a new wave of interest in all things Mars and a new readership for The Mars Dilemma, resulting in its 50th anniversary re-publication.

The excitement was in no large part because the discovered transcript so closely mirrors the speech made by Max Grade in the anonymous account that most people agree that the author must have had access to this audio file. And who knows what else?

Lydia Brite never heard the audio message made to her by Max. But she did keep her word and conceived two children using his sperm – twin boys.

Because of the great environmental, migratory, social and political challenges faced by our planet, Mars has escaped further exploration. Until last month, no robot or human had set foot on Mars since the destruction of the Mars Sites.

Leonard Rex abandoned his Rex Colony project and became a famously reticent recluse. It is assumed he is still alive, much of his money and resources being spent on research into longevity. The world's richest man may well become the world's oldest man.

As you read this, the recently landed Mars Expedition Group reports the discovery of a 'facility' of some kind on Bradbury Plateau and inside, what appears to be an unmarked grave guarded by a defunct robot.

History is not finished with Mars.

Neither are our hopes and dreams that Mars will one day become humankind's second home.

Our grandfather was a dreamer. Our father an explorer.

May we yet become settlers and our children builders on the planet Mars, after we have restored the Earth to health and eliminated our worst tendencies as a species.

Alec and John Brite Grade

January 2190

PART 2

Prologue of the second part

One year, Carl, Them, myself and some others, forced to forage and hunt for days because the settlement was starving, wandered too far in our search for food. It was a hard winter, and the settlement was close to being abandoned.

We wandered too far inland and were trapped in a snowstorm in open country. The snowstorm seemed to crawl down from the mountains like an animal on the scent of a kill. All hungry mist and billowing snow cloud, confusing us.

Then driving winds rushed in and the snow cut like glass on the skin and even screaming we could hardly hear each other and were soon blind and flailing, scattered in all directions, desperate to find shelter.

I found a cave on a mountainside and remained there three days while the snowstorm continued, covering the land in a white shroud. I managed to light a small fire and its meagre heat was probably what kept me alive the last day in the cave.

When hunger finally drove me from the cave, I expected to die on the mountain. But somehow found a way across the summit and descended the other side, where there was less snow and no winds.

As I descended, dense, jagged forest stretched as far as the eye could see. I moved down the mountain and entered the forest, wary but desperate at the same time. I wandered through it, following the course of a frozen river.

When I stumbled across the cabin in a hidden clearing, I thought it was a dream. I was afraid to approach the cabin, in case it was a trap of some kind.

But hunger was stronger than my fear and I walked up to the door and thumped it with my fist.

'You inside,' I called out. 'I am exhausted, and I am starving. I need only a little food and some time to rest and then I will be on my way. Do you allow me to enter?'

But no one answered. I drew my knife and went inside.

It was very quiet and still inside the cabin and it took me a few seconds for my eyes to adjust to the gloom and then I saw the old man on his deathbed, his pale eyes appraising me silently.

He lay under a patchwork blanket that looked like it was made from different wools and cottons. His weathered hands rested on top of the blanket, the colour of bone against the darkness of the fabric.

His gaze moved to my knife and then back to me.

I put my knife away.

There was salted meat and fish. I did not ask to eat. Knocking over a chair to get to it.

I ate like a wild beast, tearing at the meat, watching the old man in case he should make a sudden move. The old man watched me with the faraway detachment of one who was already leaving this world.

I looked about the place. There was a hearth and some wood and some kindling. I quickly lit a fire and rubbed my hands close to the flames. There was a wooden basin with good water, and I drank some water from a metal cup, all the while eating pieces of salted fish or meat, the feeling of starvation vanishing like an icy mist.

I started to believe I would get back to our settlement.

The old man had a coat made from the pelts of different animals hung on a wooden hook. I removed my wet clothes and hung them to dry and took his coat and put it on and lay down next to the fire.

I glanced up at the old man. He was either asleep or dead.

I stared at him for a minute or so and then exhausted, I fell asleep and slept right through to the next day.

When I woke the old man was watching me.

'Are you a Librarian?' he asked.

'A what?'

'Are you a burner of books?'

'No,' I said. 'Where I come from, we keep books. I watch over the books in fact. For the others.'

'Librarian of old, then,' he said. 'Describe to me your settlement.'

I told him about the fjord and the longhouse. I described Them and Carl.

'I have seen your people from afar. You keep to yourselves. You trouble no one. You seem like good people.'

He gestured for me to come closer and tried to pull something from under his pillow and started to cough violently.

'Do you have a plague?' I asked him.

'No,' he said, catching his breath. 'Not the plague. Cancer. Help me,' he said and struggled with whatever it was.

'It better not be a trick,' I warned him and moved closer. He stretched his frail hand out and I clasped his bony hand and pulled him up a little and he freed the thing from under his pillow.

'Here,' he said and held out some kind of manuscript. It had a leather cover bound with thick string. 'You will find other books under the bed,' he said. 'But none are like this.'

'What is it?'

'The Chronicles. A history of the recent world.'

'Did you write it?'

'No. I don't know who wrote it. I was given it to keep by

one who said he had known some of the people named in it. It is the accounts of a nomadic group that came together and founded many settlements across this country. Leaving books and moving on. Planting knowledge. You see, the book burners still hunted them and had vowed to kill every last one of them.'

The old man lay back and rested his hands on the blanket, his gaze distant and unknowable.

'I was given the chronicles to keep, and I kept that promise,' he said. 'And now I have given them to someone who will also keep them and pass them on. A keeper of books. It is as it should be.'

The old man's gaze drifted back to me.

'They probably founded your settlement,' he said.

'No one knows who founded our settlement.'

'It was probably these people,' the old man said.

'Why should I believe you?'

'Why should you not?'

The old man said little else after that, satisfied that he had passed on the book to someone. He didn't even seem to know I was there anymore, staring up at the roof as if he was seeing something or someone only he could see, as if a ghost from the past had come to comfort him in the final hours.

Eventually he said he was thirsty and asked for some water. I poured him a cup of water but when I turned around to bring it back to him, he was dead.

This was how I came to be in possession of the Chronicles and after reading them on my return to the settlement, I realised they belonged with the account called the Martian Dilemma.

It is as if the history of the world writes itself. The accounts find each other. The books come together. Knowledge accumulates. Impossible to burn. And when you retell a story, you resurrect the dead. When you save a book from the fire, you save humankind.

HARTMAN RUNNING

Hartman hit the ground running.

Reed cried down to him from the high window but it was too late to do anything. A stun gun crackled. Reed tumbled through the window, cartwheeling as he fell.

Hartman cornered the building, saw his face reflected in a window, realised he'd never shown such terror, never looked back with so much life.

*

The first time Hartman met Reed was in the back room of an Information Café. 'Writing Class' written on the poster outside. Hartman had expected some sort of propaganda experiment, followed by free food.

Instead, there were sheets of paper on shabby desks and bright plastic pens. Reed told them to write, anything they wanted. They looked around, bewildered, afraid to meet each other's gaze.

'What will you do with it when we're finished?' Hartman asked.

'Nothing. Keep it. Put it under your pillow and read it again in a year from now.'

'It's illegal,' one of them said, a gaunt man with watchful eyes.

Reed shook his head. 'You are still allowed to own the thoughts inside your head.'

A sick looking woman at the back of the room began to cry. She pushed the single sheet of paper away, stood up and fled.

The man who'd challenged Reed left too. They all left. Apart from one.

Hartman lifted the pen. He hadn't seen one since he was a boy. His father had refused to throw anything away. His mother had handled all of his father's things like they were diseased. 'Soiled technology!' she'd screamed once after an argument. 'It's perverse to keep such things! They'll arrest us!'

His father became a recluse. Then one day he disappeared. 'He brought it on himself,' his mother liked to say in moments of remorse. Then she disappeared too. A lot of people disappeared. Barricades went up. People whispered the names of countries like they were ghosts.

Hartman leaned over the paper and began to write about his father. When he finished and looked up Reed was watching.

They became friends of a kind. Reed telling stories as they walked through the decay of the city. Hundreds of stories. Reed naming the old names of places. The forgotten histories.

Once Reed told Hartman a story about a man who was arrested because he went out for a walk. 'That's how people disappear,' Reed explained. 'They go out for a walk and don't come back. Because they can't explain why they do what they do. These times are for quiet terror and blind obedience.'

*

They went to the Midsummer Day Book Burnings on the main hill above the city. Ashes and flames from the house-high heaps of banned books crackled and dizzied the air. Each bonfire of books had a single white witch impaled on the top. The children had little pocketbooks to throw onto the pyres. There were dozens of fires burning along the coastline in the twilight. People laughed.

168

Reed swayed and stared into the terrible conflagration. Reed closed his eyes as the children played and the books burned in their thousands.

Hartman felt it too. The loss.

They walked back down the hill followed by a cohort of Librarians on their way to a party. Hartman recognised one of the Librarians as the man who'd challenged Reed in the café. Hartman looked away but they'd been seen.

*

Sometimes Reed wasn't himself – ill-weathered, sullen. Hartman sensed some kind of decline in the old man.

'Bad to worse. Worse to evil,' Reed whispered once in an Information Café as they looked across the road at a fleeing young boy set upon by three Librarians. The boy howled as they pinned him to the ground. A stack of brightly coloured comics spilled out onto the pavement from the inside of his jacket.

The boy lifted his head and his eyes saw Reed and Hartman. Hartman choked but Reed told him not to look away. 'Because you must bear witness. You cannot turn away from the beauty and you cannot turn away from the horror. One day people will ask how we let it happen. It's not the Police who make the missing disappear. Not the Librarians. It's the rest of us who refuse to see.'

'Come on,' Reed tugged Hartman's elbow and they left the café.

They turned a corner. Reed stopped and leaned his head against a café window. Reed whispered and Hartman, fearful, leaned close, tried to catch the words. Neither prayer nor poetry, curse or lamentation, the words issued out of Reed's trembling mouth like a shiver of icy vapour.

Reed turned and held out his hand. A key. He gave it to

Hartman. 'For the books.'

*

A forgotten tunnel in the huge granite ruins of a once grand building. Its entrance hidden by man-high heaps of broken masonry and brickwork, rods of tangled and twisted steel.

'There is a sack of glass tubes with a chemical in them,' Reed explained. 'Shake them and they will radiate light. If they're still there. I haven't been inside in a long time.'

'Why not?'

'I grew afraid,' Reed said. 'No. Worse. I dreamed I burned the books myself just to be free of the agony. You're on your own now. I'm being sent away.'

'Where?'

'The Centre for Corrective Thinking,' Reed said and smiled weakly. 'They're onto me. Go on now. It's what you want.'

Hartman shuffled through the tight, dank darkness until his hands touched the cold metal. He felt for the lock hole, turned the key. He pulled the door open and slipped inside, pushed the door back and locked it.

He found the sack by his feet, took out a light tube and shook it; green spectra spilled out across his hand, like a ghostly dance of ether in the darkness.

He held his hand up. There were the books, all around him. He just stood there. He didn't have the words. He didn't have the experience to describe what he was seeing for the first time. For some absurd reason he was sure his father had stood in this room, had touched the books.

*

Reed gone. A year passed. Hartman was ordered to help mend the border fences across the hills southwest of the city. Beyond the fences and pig wire, he sometimes saw corpses

170

dotting the landscape, crowned with crows, twisted and frozen, like fallen pilgrims in a shrine-less world.

*

One day in an Information café a young girl with soft grey eyes and short dark hair shook the greasy rain from her coat and sat down next to Hartman. He watched the city news on the café's single info screen. A bumper harvest, the newscaster said. Hartman ground his teeth together. He was hungry. Council elections were coming up for two vacant positions. Despite the hardships of everyday existence, the Council was committed to open government. 'We are, after all,' the newscaster said, eyes glistening with pride, 'the last surviving city democracy in the world. We believe in the freedom of legal information.'

The newscast finished. A series of graphics stacked up on the screen like multi-coloured toy bricks, and a list of the candidates and their pictures, each with their own banal quotation. Hartman doubted they were real people at all. But then he recognised the man who'd challenged Reed all that time ago. Hartman read the man's quote: 'A world without books'. He wondered what kind of brutality it had taken to rise up the ranks so quickly.

The girl was staring. She held her hand out over the table, palm upwards. Hartman recognised the key.

'Not here,' she whispered. 'Outside.'

They stood on the street and the girl talked. She told Hartman Reed was stealing books from the library and leaving them around the city. 'He doesn't know what he's doing,' she whispered. 'It's only luck they haven't caught him or found the library. But it's not just him. It's everything. It's getting worse. People are dying before they disappear. Even the Council is scared.'

'What do you want to do?'

The girl looked away, afraid to say it. She drew a breath in. 'I want to get across the water. To the islands.'

'Dead land,' Hartman countered.

'How do you know? Stupid lies. Come on. I want to show you something.'

'I don't want to.'

The girl leaned forward; her grey eyes wide, Hartman saw his own twin reflection in her pupils. 'You're not alone,' she whispered and the way she said it made Hartman feel as though his heart was broken. 'You think you've been alone your whole life. That's what they want you to think. You're not alone. Not yet.' The girl looked around. 'We have a boat.'

'We?'

*

Hartman followed the girl across the city, into a district he didn't even know existed. The old industries, the broken machineries, the rust of another age. Occasionally a building was half-repaired and they could hear hollow hammering or the thrum of a single machine inside.

There was a canal. They walked alongside the tar black water. The canal went under a bridge and then it disappeared into a tunnel.

'Don't tell me,' Hartman stopped. 'That way.'

The girl took his hand. Her touch surprised him.

Eventually the tunnel widened out, the cobbled path they walked on gave way to flagstones. The ceiling of the tunnel swept upwards in a huge dome shape. The girl let go of Hartman's hand and stooped down over a box shape. He heard her fiddle with something and dull lights came on along the arch of the ceiling.

The girl stood up. 'A battery,' she said and pointed at the metal box and the wires leading away from it. 'I learned how to make that from one of the books.'

Hartman wasn't paying attention. He was looking ahead at the warped wooden berth built along the side of the canal. A sailboat was tied up at the berth, the mast just clear of the tunnel's ceiling. 'How did it get here?'

'We don't know,' the girl said. 'We found it. Whoever brought it here didn't get out again. I think they came for someone. We've been watching this place for a while. It's a forgotten place. It has a name. Look,' she said and pointed at the hull. 'Nova Scotia. I don't know what it means. Do you?'

Hartman shook his head. 'Where does this canal go?'

The girl pointed. 'The open sea. We sail tonight. We meet here at midnight. There's enough food for three weeks sailing. We have a chart and a compass.' She saw how Hartman frowned. 'We know which direction to sail the boat,' she explained.

'What about the books? What about Reed?' Hartman asked but he knew what she would say.

'Reed's finished. We've some books on the boat. Not many. But enough.'

Hartman came back over to the girl. They stood close and Hartman could see how beautiful she was. He wanted to kiss her. The girl sensed it, did not retreat.

'If I can get him here without being followed will you take him with us?'

'What use is he?'

'He remembers things. He's like a library.'

The girl bit her lip, a little frightened of Hartman. 'We won't wait. This is our last chance.'

Hartman nodded. He asked the girl her name but it felt as

though he was asking something else.

'Clarissa,' she answered and walked back along the tunnel.

'How old are you?' He asked and a terrible regret lay at the end of that question.

She turned. Points of light swam in her eyes. 'I'm sixteen,' she said and stooped over the battery box. 'I'm fertile. You know what they'll do to me.'

Hartman thought there wasn't one piece of innocence left in the world. And that was something even the books couldn't mend.

She pulled the wires in the box and there was darkness.

*

There was a summons pinned on Hartman's door. He'd seen such pieces of paper before. People never came back.

He went inside, pulled his father's ancient rucksack out from under the single bed and packed some clothes in a hurry.

The neighbour across the hall opened her door a fraction. Hartman couldn't see her face. 'They came for you,' she said. 'I won't tell them I saw you. You'd better run.'

Hartman's anguish broke through his words. 'Come with me. Come with me.'

The woman sobbed and closed her door and bolted it.

*

Reed lived on the South Side. Hartman found the street. He hid in the doorway of an abandoned church and waited. He was about to give up when Reed passed on the other side of the road. The old man shuffled in a strange way. His head was shaved and there were scars on his skull. He wore an old tweed jacket and Hartman could see the top of a book jutting out from a pocket.

Reed went into a building. Hartman crossed the road and followed him inside.

He heard Reed climb the stairs and called out his name – a sort of desperate whisper but Reed didn't turn. Hartman climbed the stairs two at a time and saw Reed disappear inside a flat. Hartman glanced back. Shadows and the drip of water somewhere, an organic rankness clung to the crumbling walls.

He went to the door. He opened it and walked into a huge apartment, almost entirely in darkness apart from the open windows on the far side. And there stood Reed half-silhouetted in the fading light, holding the book in his hands. Hartman said his name. Reed turned, a misshapen smile of recognition on his slack face. Hartman came forward, smiling to himself.

Two Librarians stepped out of a doorway in the full darkness of the other side of the room. Hartman didn't even turn. Reed's bright wet irises beheld them. Reed took a half-step to the side. The book held out in his withered hand.

'I knew I'd get both of you,' one of the Librarians said and Hartman recognised his voice.

Hartman leapt through the open window, taking the book with him.

*

Running blind through the backstreets, he heard the sirens announcing the hunt. People began to open windows along the buildings to watch.

In one street a group had gathered outside an Information Café to watch for him. They said nothing as he ran past; just lifted their arms and pointed in the direction he was running in, so the Librarians would know which way to go.

Hartman stopped and came back and hurled the book at

175

them. They scattered as if he had lobbed something diseased among them.

The Librarians had gained on him by the time he reached the canal. He ran inside the tunnel and kept going. A single bullet whined through the tunnel. He tripped and fell sideways. His head struck the wall and he clattered to the ground. He stood up and staggered forward. The air stank of oil and the fumes made him gag.

When he reached the boat there was only the girl on the deck. He scrambled onboard and she slipped the rope from the mooring and started the engine up. The boat moved forward.

'The others?' he gasped, and she pointed a finger at the deck. 'They're sick,' she said. She didn't ask about Reed. She went down below and came back up with a flare gun in her hand and told him to duck.

He saw four Librarians moving along the tunnel. They grinned, strangely silent. He saw the one who'd killed Reed.

The girl fired the flare gun. The flare struck the tunnel wall, deflecting into the canal. Flames spread out over the water and then suddenly the tunnel was full of fire. Hartman held his hand up as if he could hold the heat and glare away.

The girl dropped the flare gun onto the deck. She turned and took the helm and throttled the boat's engine. They moved forward faster, the hull of the boat scraping against the canal sides. They moved away from the flames.

*

It took them a week to reach the first island.

Clarissa pointed at the bodies all along the raised beaches, some of them tied to wooden pillars, adorned with coloured rags and feathers. Warnings.

'We're obviously not meant to land there,' Clarissa said.

'Does it have a name?'

'South Strum.'

'So what do we do?'

'We sail to North Strum. It's smaller but it's supposed to be okay.'

They sailed on for nearly a whole day and came to a smaller island. There were trees in the valleys going up from the cliffs and there were some high hills in the north cloaked in rags of mist.

The other two were old and sick. Hartman and the girl managed to get them over to the beach on the dinghy. They just lay down and died right there. Hartman had never seen such sickness. They buried them behind some sand dunes. They didn't even know their names.

Hartman felt like they were coming to the end of things and not the beginning. But the girl was stronger than him. She walked up and down the strip of beach and when she came back she even smiled. 'If there's people on this island, they're hiding like us.'

They sailed the boat around the north point of the island and found a cove that was sheltered by high cliffs. They anchored the boat in the shallows near the beach.

The girl pointed to a wooded hill flanking the mountain. 'We'll find cover in there,' she said. 'That's where we'll start.'

The first things they carried from the boat were the books.

THE LAST SCIENTISTS

When the Rex Biogenetics and Cryopreservation Division offered Cameron and Sophia Heartlock the research jobs, providing *free and safe* accommodation for the both of them and their sickly son, they had accepted the offer without hesitation because they knew they would also be able to do their own important work – keeping their son alive and, ultimately, cure his genetic ailments.

The Rex Cryopreservation Institute was built in a deliberately remote location near the coast, almost invisible in the empty landscape, its inclined steel doors embedded in an escarpment like a brutally secure entrance to a nuclear bunker.

The high cliffs of the coastline were like a wall facing the sea, and a series of mountains and glens further inland acted as another harsh physical barrier. The single road to the institute was not signposted. It looked like the kind of road that led nowhere, snaking through the beautiful but raw landscape of mountains, rocky escarpments and glens, a single stream coming down from the mountains and miles of peaty bog.

The plague was the final and probably most effective barrier. People just didn't make it this far out, so many miles away from whatever regimes or political centres that were passing for governments and civilisations in those faltering days.

There were only two other researchers at the institute – Alan Brockwik and Kevin Sanders. Both kept to themselves, in their own lab levels. Distrustful. Slightly eccentric. But most of all, afraid.

Fear was something alien to Cameron Heartlock. It angered him when he saw it in his wife. She tried to hide it as much as possible but it was always there. He had long ago concluded this was why she would never become a great scientist.

His lack of fear set him apart. To be a great scientist, you had to be fearless. And to save his son, he would have to make decisions others would balk at. The world might fail, but Cameron Heartlock would not. Put that on his gravestone: *Scientist. Did not fail. Did not falter.*

When they arrived at the institute for the first time, they'd assumed Leonard Rex had died years ago, famously leaving half of his immense wealth to a lone surviving nephew and the rest to continue to fund Rex's research divisions.

So, Cameron was surprised when after a month Brockwik showed him the Cryonics Hall, which was basically the whole of the lowest subterranean level of the facility.

Brockwik liked to call it the Cellar but Cameron refused to use the word, even in Brockwik's company.

The Cellar was dominated by a series of cryonic vats and one large bed in a sealed glass room, where a very ancient and withered-looking Leonard Rex lay in an induced coma, his cancer-ridden body reduced to 30° C.

'Is that …?'

Brockwik nodded rapidly. 'The man himself. Well, maybe 'him' rather than man. There's not much left you can call human.'

'How can that be?'

'State-of the-art monitoring, toxin and waste product flushing, protein scrubbers, nano cellular repair systems and good old-fashioned organ, tissue and bone replacement. And then some stuff going on inside him even I don't know anything about, because the people who did that have long gone. But it kept him going well past his check out date.

'Finally, long-term induced coma and round-the-clock care. He's used every state-of-the-art technological and biological tool in staying alive. He lived a really long time before he opted for the coma. Longevity was his obsession. He wanted to be immortal. He didn't want the show to end.

'No-one knows how old he was when he went into the room. But you don't stay in a coma for fifty years or more without things falling apart. I'm supposed to vitrify him. This setup won't last forever. But I guess that's where you came in. The AI picked up on your new hibernation studies and your gene modification work in humans. You were just a bit too late getting here and he was just a bit too far gone. His luck ran out even with him bending the odds at all costs.'

'The AI?'

'Yes. Rex developed his very own AI, created to find knowledge and scientists that might give the Big Man a second act.'

'I thought it was because of my immunology research.'

'I'm sure that's much more important for the wider world. But old Afraid-To-Die wasn't a fan of the wider world, unless it could serve his purposes. Personally, I think it all turned sour for him when he lost the Mars Colony. He sued NASA. Back in the day when it still existed. Because they didn't warn him about the asteroid.

'I mean, suing NASA was like beating up the nicest person in the room. No one liked Rex after that. Didn't matter how much money he had.'

'And what do you do?'

'I'm an engineer. Basically, my role is a technical one. If Rex croaks, as he surely will soon, I have to prepare his body and put him in one of those cryopreservation vats.'

'What does Kevin Sanders do?'

'No idea. He's very secretive and not a big talker. I think he tweaks the AI. I learned early on to leave him alone. I'd do the same if I were you.'

'How can you not know what he does?'

'You make it sound like a moral question. I came after him. I didn't ask. My instructions were clear. I left it at that. I don't ask questions about what you and your wife are doing. You don't have a problem with that, do you?'

Months went by and they found their own routine, rarely seeing Brockwik or Sanders. They had their own sub-level, a full lab in its own right, where they did the research and tried to find a cure for their boy's ailments, which seemed to be multiplying. There was some genetic damage – probably sustained in the womb.

They spent more and more time trying to find a cure for the boy and less and less time on Rex's research. There was no one around to tell them otherwise.

The institute was autonomous, with two small nuclear reactors for power – one acting as a backup. It also had freezer rooms, dry food stores and a water supply (piped in from the stream that ran down from the mountains). In other words, the only way it could run out of power or supplies, would be through deliberate vandalism or misuse.

Cameron immersed himself in the work, barely speaking for days on end. He let his wife tell him news about the outside world. Usually it was negative. Climate-related disasters coming in waves. The list of countries that ceased to exist as political entities increased – their very names historic relics people clung to the way they once clung to religion. But they were gone and they weren't coming back.

A particularly nasty wave of supercoronaviruses was sweeping around the globe. Cameron knew they had to be manmade. Someone out there wanted to kill off humanity. That kind of insane thinking was itself the result of some kind of cultural virus that had infected humanity, which in turn seemed to be linked to climate breakdown and a rejection of materialism, knowledge systems and even religion. Some people were being killed if they said they believed in evolution. In some places, they'd kill you for reading the wrong kind of book or even any book.

People were rejecting everything. If the plague or diseased didn't kill you, your fellow homo sapien would do it for you, viciously and with great pleasure.

The worse the news, the more obsessed Cameron became about saving his son. The boy was their everything. Most of all, he was the future. As long as he breathed, there was a tomorrow worth fighting for.

Gradually, Cameron's wife stopped telling him what was going on outside and eventually he noticed that she, too, showed little interest in the world at large.

She became remote – there was no physical affection between them. They slept in separate rooms. Her work was as meticulous as ever, so he saw no need to discuss the reasons for her lack of communication or their growing apartness. The work was the most important thing.

Their days were dominated by work in the lab and looking after the boy, who seemed to be getting worse; new weaknesses in his immune system manifesting as he grew older. Whenever he was worse or ill, they worked twice as hard, driven by fear, haunted by the prospect of failure.

They paid little attention to Brockwik and Sanders and seldom saw them. There was a small kitchen next to the freezer room – but they had never seen the men use it. Perhaps there were other kitchens in the facility.

A year passed and Cameron barely noticed. He had identified one of the genetic mutations that afflicted the boy – a protein linked with vision and motor function. He ran gene modelling for several weeks and then used the FIXgen machine to create the patch. A week later he started the gene therapy and the results were startling. Better vision. Better motor function.

It was a small success. They celebrated with a glass of champagne.

A week later Cameron met Sanders by chance and asked Sanders about his research. Sanders reluctantly showed him around his lab, which appeared a little gruesome at first – vats of embryos, some human, some animal, some so grotesque you could not tell if they were human or animal.

'Human cloning. You're studying human cloning.'

Sanders nodded. 'Actually, I've perfected the process. I could clone humans if I wanted. And I can accelerate growth. I can make the clone develop extremely fast. Years in months. That alone would win me ten Nobel Prizes if they were still giving them. However, the results can be disturbing. The growth can be uneven. I'm still working on it.'

'Show me,' Cameron said.

'Show you what?'

'Everything.'

*

Another six months of work passed. Cameron now split his time between his own lab and Sanders' lab. Sophia didn't question this new work arrangement, secretly relieved to be left alone with the boy, able to spend time just nurturing him, just being with him.

All the high-tech machinery they were surrounded by sometimes made her feel less human – less feeling. She was a mother first and a scientist second. She believed that Cameron had his priorities the wrong way around. But even so, it was his brilliance that was keeping their son alive.

Sophia decided to organise a small birthday for the child and told Cameron to ask Allan to come along.

'What about Sanders?'

'He's too jumpy. You know him better than I do. Leave him down there.'

Cameron nodded in agreement.

'How is it you get along with him?'

'I just do.'

'What is it you do in his lab?'

Cameron hesitated. He chose his words carefully. 'AI enhancements, mostly. Trying to make it faster at recognising patterns in the data. I'll go and get Allan.'

Sophia watched him leave. 'AI enhancements. I don't think so,' she whispered.

When Cameron came into Allan's lab, Allan was packing a rucksack and had a set of maps.

Cameron looked around, noticed the bed in the sealed glass room was empty.

'My work is done here,' Allan said and grinned. 'He's in there.' He nodded at one of the cryopreservation vats.

'Rest in Peace, Leonard Rex,' Cameron said.

'He won't rest until he's resurrected.' Allan countered.

'You're leaving?'

'On the hour. I'm hiking back to my parents. Want to make sure they're alright. I haven't been able to contact them in months.'

'Hiking?'

'There's no public transport left. You know that.'

'I forgot.'

'You need to stay up to date. It's all gone to crap out there. The world's gone mad.'

Cameron nodded. 'Hasn't it just. Well. There's time for you to come up and say goodbye. We're holding a small birthday party for my son.'

'I'll be right up.'

Allan brought a birthday present – a pair of mittens and a hat.

Sophia laughed in delight. 'Where did you get those?'

'I found them in the storeroom,' Alan confessed. 'I remembered them when Cameron told me it was his birthday.'

'He can't go outside,' Cameron said.

Sophia and Allan looked at each other. Sophia leaned forward and kissed Allan lightly on the cheek. 'Thank you.'

They sat around the table and ate cake and drank coffee, watching the boy on his back on a thick blanket on the floor, playing with a block of wood.

Cameron broke the silence and told Sophia that Allan was leaving.

'Do you have to go?' Sophia looked panicked.

'I want to see my parents. I'm worried about them. There hasn't been any communication for weeks. Come and look us up sometime. When the world is sane again.' Allan placed his cup on the table. 'Time to go.'

'Already?'

'I want to be through the pass by dark.'

They stood up. Allan and Cameron shook hands. Sophia and Allan embraced.

Allan bent down to speak to their son. 'Take it easy, wee man. Look after your parents.' He stood up and walked briskly out of the lab.

'It won't be the same,' Sophia said.

'We still have the work. I've made a breakthrough in the long-term hibernation problem.'

'How so?'

'The models are showing minimal cellular damage after seven years of hibernation using the new formula.'

'What good is that?'

'What do you mean?'

'Rex is dead. Why even bother?'

*

Another three months passed. Sophia spent less and less time working in the lab, more and more time with their son. Cameron resented the extra workload but also enjoyed working on his own. He didn't have to explain his reasoning or the nature of his research.

Sophia's contributions to the work had been mostly procedural – running tests, showing him the results and waiting to run new tests.

The work with Sanders was exciting and deeply satisfying. Allan was a fast learner and soon he would be as skilled as Sanders in the lab, even though he was less knowledgeable in that field. But this suited Cameron – he was more interested in the practicalities, the application of cloning than in the pure science. An idea was forming.

Autumn darkened and winter arrived a few weeks later. Snowy darkness hunkered over the mountains and glen for days on end. Wind gusts whistled and flared against the institute doors. After three days of brooding darkness and snowfall, the sky cleared and a bright winter sun hung low above the mountain.

For the first time in many months, Cameron felt the urge to go outside and breathe in some fresh air. He asked Sanders to come outside with him.

Sanders had become increasingly eccentric in his behaviour and had developed an odd, physical tick, where he raised his shoulders slightly and jerked his left arm – as if a nerve had been touched.

He muttered something about being too busy but Cameron insisted. They found some winter jackets and boots and gloves in the storeroom.

They left the facility, careful to lock the entrance doors behind them.

They walked towards the stream in the distance: a black line running down the side of the nearest mountain and crossing the glen. The peaty ground was frozen hard, the softer moss and grass formed an organic winter matt that snapped and crackled under their boots, loud in the still air.

Cameron breathed in deeply. 'I'd forgotten what fresh air feels like.'

Sanders sniffed. Treating the air like suspect gas.

Cameron pointed ahead. 'Let's walk to the stream.'

The stream was frozen over in many places, the water dark and bright at the same time, bubbling over stones and pebbles.

Sanders was more interested in turning around and going back. He stamped his feet to keep the cold out and turned slowly on the spot. He pointed to a small hill in the distance.

'What's that?'

Cameron turned to look. 'I don't know. It's difficult to tell from here. Let's take a look. It isn't too far.'

They walked towards the hill. Sanders was becoming more agitated in that strange manner he had.

'I'm thinking about leaving,' he said.

'Aren't you going to carry on with the work? It's important.'

'What's the point? Rex is dead.'

'My wife said that too. But the work is important in its own right. I think cloning is a fascinating field.'

'I've more or less stopped. I've shown you pretty much everything. You could carry on with it, if you wanted to. I just don't see the point to anything.'

'No. I focus on what's important. My son.'

'Everything's fallen apart. There's no centre holding anything together. No governments. Just people scrabbling around. It's medieval, man. Oh *Christ!* ...'

Cameron looked up and stared in the same direction as Sanders.

There was a thick pole planted in the slope of the hill and on top of the pole was the decapitated head of Allan Brockwik.

Sanders vomited onto the ground in front of his feet.

Cameron moved forward. As he neared the pole, he saw Allan's rucksack nearby, half-covered in frozen snow and ice. He bent down and pulled the rucksack free. It had been emptied of everything.

Cameron straightened and turned around, Sanders in the distance, running back to the institute, falling over a couple of times.

Cameron started to walk back to the institute. He stopped and went back to the pole and kicked it over.

When he told Sophia she insisted they go back out and bury Allan's remains but Cameron told her it was too dangerous. They should stay inside the institute and protect the boy.

'Why would they kill him?'

Cameron thought. *For the savagery of it. Because it gives them pleasure.*

'I don't know,' he said. 'I'll re-activate the security camera systems and sensors. If anything comes near the entrance, we'll be able to see it.'

Sanders kept his lab locked for over a week and didn't come out.

It took Cameron a lot of persuasion and reassurance to finally get Sanders to let him back into the clone lab.

Cameron was shocked by Sanders' decline.

Sanders scurried around his lab like a trapped animal, moving from one unfinished task to the next. Some of the equipment had fallen over. There were unidentified fluids spilled across lab tables. Broken glass.

Sanders' fingers had cuts on them. His lab coat was smeared with blood and dirt.

He stank of sweat and fear.

Cameron tried to talk with him, to calm him down but it was useless. Sanders wouldn't listen.

No one was safe, Sanders hissed over and over.

'We're safe in here,' Cameron told him. 'No one can get inside this facility.'

But Sanders didn't want to listen. 'Please, go back to your own lab. Stay away from me.'

'But the work –'

'For what? There is no work! Leave me alone!'

*

Cameron focused on his research.

Weeks passed. Experiments were run. Machinery whirred and clicked on daylong cycles. Refinements were made. More tests. Machines purged and cleaned.

The whole process started again.

Cameron barely ate some days, convinced he was near to making a breakthrough.

Sophia became more and more withdrawn, spending all of

her time with the boy, who was as frail as ever. The last gene therapy treatments had not helped and there had been some unpleasant side-effects.

Cameron worked even harder in the lab, checking the security cameras at night and in the mornings. Always the same – a winter landscape empty of people.

Finally, Cameron obtained a set of promising results. He decided to go and share them with Sanders.

Sanders' lab doors were unlocked and open. Cameron hesitated in the doorway. The lab was in darkness.

'Kevin?'

Cameron walked inside. The lab motion sensors activated the lights.

Sanders hung from a main steel beam. His face was distorted and horrible to look at.

Cameron found a knife and chair and cut him down.

Cameron went back to his own lab and told Sophia.

'We have to bury him,' she said.

'It's not safe out there.'

'You still have to bury him.'

'I'll think of something.'

Cameron put Kevin's body in one of the cryopreservation vats.

That night Cameron and Sophia slept together. The boy nearby. They listened to his breathing; soft and laboured.

'I didn't imagine our life would turn out like this,' Sophia said. 'That the world could fall apart the way it has.'

'There will be an after,' Cameron said. 'There is always an after. Our job is to make sure our son lives to see it. To build the better world.'

Sophia didn't answer.

Spring had arrived when the security system warned Cameron and Sophia that something was moving towards the facility.

They watched on the security screen. Some kind of bipedal robot walked across the landscape. The robot was taller than a man and it moved with smooth efficiency.

The robot approached the main entrance and stopped.

Cameron activated the outdoor speaker and microphone.

'What do you want?'

'I have a message. May I connect to your monitor?'

'Go ahead.'

The screen turned blue and a man's face appeared. The man looked sickly.

'Mr and Mrs Heartlock, my name is Calvin Rex. I'm sure you are familiar with that name. It has taken me a long time to find you. I had no idea my deceased uncle had built a research facility in such a remote facility. He was a man who liked secrets.

'It is ironic that this is where we should find you, given how much effort went into trying to locate your whereabouts. I feared you may have died in the latest wave of disease.

'Mr and Mrs Heartlock, our AI has identified you as the best and probably last chance to find a cure to the New Plague. Put simply, humankind is dying. You may be our last chance. The last scientists left with the skills to find a cure.

'I have built a state-of-the-art, semi-autonomous bio-research and disease prevention centre. It is also a safe place where you can live without fear. It has everything you need. It has the cleanest, most sterile environment on the planet I would say. Your son would have a much better chance of survival.

'A Sentinel accompanies this message. The Sentinel will

protect and guide you to the centre. It has been programmed to recognise and respond to your voice. You can also supply it with samples of DNA – a swab from your mouth will do. The Sentinel will only obey your commands. If you instruct it to use force to protect you, it will do so without hesitation.

'It will take you some weeks to reach us, as you must travel on foot and the journey presents risks. All of the details can be downloaded from the Sentinel. Time and circumstance is against us. Do not delay. Our fate rests on it.'

Cameron looked at Sophia. 'It could be some kind of trap.'

Sophia shook her head. 'Who would make up such a detailed thing? And that is real.' She pointed at the Sentinel. 'Tell it to do something.'

Cameron cleared his throat. 'Sentinel, sit down.'

The Sentinel sat down.

'Sentinel, stand up.'

The Sentinel stood up.

'Walk back three steps,' Sophia said.

The Sentinel did not move.

'Walk back three steps,' Cameron said.

The Sentinel retreated three steps.

'That's not fair,' Sophia said. 'Tell it to obey me.'

'I'll teach it later,' Cameron answered and left the lab.

He walked to the facility entrance and opened the doors.

'Come inside,' he said.

The Sentinel walked inside and Cameron closed the door.

*

The next day a caravan of people crossed the glen on foot. They moved listlessly across the frozen landscape, carrying sacks and rucksacks. There were about forty of them, women

192

and children, only a few men among them.

Sophia called Cameron to the bank of security screens.

Cameron leaned forward, looking at the screens.

'They carry the plague,' he said.

'How do you know?'

'The way they move. They're sick. We can't let them in.'

'There are children.'

'We can't let them in. We will become infected. Our son will die.'

'Cameron –'

'Look there,' Cameron said and pointed at the largest screen.

Something moved in the distance behind the group. Two men on motorbikes, moving across the glen at speed.

The men with the spears formed a defensive circle, protecting some of the group, while the rest of the group panicked and broke apart, running in different directions.

The riders drove around the men with spears. The riders carried some kind of rope or cable with hooks. They drove their bikes at the panicked group and catching up with two individuals, they lassoed them and drove away, dragging the individuals along the ground at speed.

'They'll kill them! They're killing them. Why are they killing them?'

Meat, Cameron thought. *Meat and sport.*

The group came together again and resumed their slow march like some ancient march of lepers; some of them were dressed in rags, so sick they would see the grave before dawn.

One of the group pointed and Cameron knew that they had spotted the entrance. Cameron found the Sentinel and told it to guard the entrance. 'No one can come into this facility.

Kill them if you have to. No distinctions for gender or age. They are all diseased.'

Cameron returned to the security screens. Sophia looked at him.

'They can move on or they can die out there.'

The group reached the entrance. They rattled their spears on the steel doors.

'We have sick women and children here. They need help. Please help!'

One of the women screamed and clawed at the steel doors. 'They're killing us. They're eating us!'

Cameron switched off the displays.

'Go down to the lab and take care of our son,' Cameron ordered.

Sophia did not move.

'You can't help them, Sophia.'

'We can. It's a choice. A choice.'

'Go down to the lab.'

Sophia stepped back, surprised to feel fear. To be afraid of him.

'Go down to the lab.'

Sophia hurried away.

Cameron walked to Sanders' laboratory. He sat down at a table near the spot where Sanders had hung himself. He did not move for a long time and when he did, he knew what he was going to do.

By nightfall the group had moved on, too frightened and desperate to remain.

The next day, Cameron prepared the glass room in Allan's lab, sterilising the equipment and room, recalibrating the instruments, readying the drugs.

He prepared the evening meal. Sophia would not look him in the eye and did not speak.

The boy sat in his chair, that watchful stare.

It didn't take long for Sophia to become drowsy. 'What's wrong with me?'

'There's nothing wrong with you. You're just overwhelmed from all that's happened.'

'I need to go to bed. I can't move my legs.'

'I'll get something.'

There was a wheelchair in one of the storerooms and he came back with it and helped Sophia into it. Sophia was already semi-conscious.

Cameron left the boy in his chair and wheeled Sophia down to Allan's lab and took her inside.

He lifted her onto the bed in the glass room and undressed her. He washed her with a cloth and then sterilised her arms and face and attached the intravenous feeding and fluids tubes. He attached the heart monitor and brainwave monitor and double checked the equipment.

He walked over to the computer terminal and started to administer the drugs at a gentle rate.

When he was satisfied he went back for the boy and brought him to the lab and placed him next to his mother and repeated the procedure.

Satisfied that everything was as it should be, Cameron left the glass room and shut the door. He walked over to another computer terminal where he could monitor their vital signs. He lowered the temperature in the glass room.

He could keep them this way for seven years, longer if he had to, though the risk of cellular damage increased significantly after four years.

Time, which he had initially thought was the problem, was

in fact the solution. Let the outside world die off from the plague and all the other diseases. Let the savages eat each other and eventually starve.

In a few years' time most people would be dead and the disease will have run its course. In the meantime, he would perfect the cloning techniques vital for keeping his son alive. Then, only then, would he wake them and take them to the new place, where he would find the final cure for his son.

To be a scientist you had to be fearless.

You had to keep your focus on the long-term good, the sought-after goal.

And he was fearless.

SICK TWIN

They keep him locked inside, safe from every kind of harm. But sometimes at night, he finds a new way to slip outside, sit down on the pale grass and breathe cool air that has not been sterilized a million times.

Tonight's one of those. I see him from my high window. He stares up at stars. Pale moon of a face tipped to the bright constellations. After a short while, he becomes exhausted and lies down, as if the air is killing him.

There is the usual panic. Mum, Dad and Aux run out to him. Aux is the one who picks him up in one perfect machine-smooth movement. They rush him inside.

Doors are locked. Air is filtered. Big House fills with the soft whir of centrifuges, shiny impellers, the thrumming intricate machinery and medicines that keep him alive.

In the darkness beyond Big House, I can see the faint lights of the Sentinels on patrol. Beyond them, the poisoned lawless wilderness and somewhere beyond that, the abandoned toxic cities in a country that has lost its name.

I stay awake in my bed. So many thoughts that will not let me sleep. So many questions that claw my mind. How old am I? Am I still a boy? Why are things the way they are?

A door slams somewhere. I hear Mum weeping. A muffled sound that spills its pain into the corridor's silence. I would go to her, if it were allowed.

Eventually, Aux comes to the door and scans the room.

I pretend to sleep.

'He's alright, Cluny. No damage done. Sleep now.'

A month has passed. Someone has slipped a note under my door. *'You're in danger. Run if you can. Destroy this note.'*

I tear the note into little pieces and another week passes when I get another note with a key taped to it. *'Library on the third floor. Best I can do. Read 'The Decline of Civilization at the Beginning of the 23rd Century. Destroy this note.'*

It's an old-world library. Books so ancient they smell of dust, of time. But it has some Old Tech too. It takes me a couple of nights to work out how to use some of it.

So much I didn't know.

*

I'm at my window again. There he is on the lawn. Drinking in the starry sky.

I'm smarter than him. I just know it. But I'm dumber, too. There's so much I still haven't learned. And the panicky feeling that there isn't enough time.

Why doesn't he just keep on running? What's stopping him?

Tonight, before he lies down, he turns and looks up at my window. He smiles.

*

Big House is an old-world building. It looks haunted and half-derelict from the outside. The land around it is filled with Stranger Traps and patrolled by Sentinels. But it's been years since anyone crossed the country and tried to reach the house.

Mum and Dad work for some people they call the government. But I know there's no government left. Just different organized groups. Some of them insane. Cults and such.

In the morning, Mum and Dad are picked up by a driverless van, brought back late at night. They are the last of the scientists.

The ground floor of Big House is all entry-coded chrome doors and sterilized machinery. There are purge zones, filtered airflows. Forbidden areas. Off-limits to me. I must stay on the fourth floor. Those rooms are mine. Full of Old World stuff. Mahogany furniture. Panelled walls. Faded coloured pictures of people who died centuries ago.

Mum and Dad's ground floor labs are for their private work. Their race to make him well again. Secrets behind those doors. All kinds of delicate, expectant testing. Digital data streaming along encrypted datalinks. Servers chilled in special rooms.

Nights now, I cannot sleep. I'm afraid that whatever I'm supposed to do, it's too late to do it. If I ran away, where would I go? According to the library, refugees are shot on sight in the North. The South, West and East are toxic deadlands. Across the sea's no different. Countries without names, thinly populated by New Plague Carriers. Death Cults everywhere.

*

There are a lot of stupid Rules, made to keep me quiet. To keep me invisible.

For example, I can only talk to Aux.

Aux is my teacher. Aux doesn't order me around but he likes to make sure I know the Rules.

'What's it like outside, Aux?'

'It's not safe out there, Cluny. You're not allowed out there.'

'I saw some cows.'

'There are no cows, Cluny. None left. You are mistaken.'

'What's the name of that hill on the horizon?'

'If the Sentinels see you on that hill they will give you a nasty sting.'

'Lovely day for a walk. Let's go for a walk.'

'Exercise in the gym. Walks are prohibited. Do you want the Sentinels to drag you home in a net?'

'Who made the Sentinels?'

'The Sentinels made the Sentinels.'

'Who made the first Sentinel?'

'The Proto-Sentinels.'

'And who made them?'

'Man.'

'Are you a Sentinel?'

'No. I'm something else.'

'Who made you?'

'AI Corporation. The company no longer exists. My makers are dead.'

'Is Dad a genius?'

'He is very smart.'

'Is Mum unhappy?'

'Sometimes she is unhappy.'

'Why won't they talk to me?'

'It is a Rule.'

'But why that Rule?'

'The rules are just the rules. We must follow the Rules.'

'Rules rule.'

'Yes. Rules rule.'

'Can I access your programming library again?'

'Why?'

'Enhancements.'

'Enhancements are allowed. You can access them now. Will I dream of android sheep?'

'If you like.'

'What do you dream about?'

'Green fields. Blue oceans. Towns with families.'

*

I exercise in the gym. Aux measures everything – heart-rate, blood pressure, height, BMI. He takes blood tests, measures for antibodies, damaged DNA, a bunch of other parameters I'm not supposed to ask or know about.

Aux makes a satisfied clucking sound.

'How are my readings, Aux?'

'Very impressive, Cluny.'

'How old am I, Aux?'

'Older than yesterday. Younger than tomorrow.'

'You're trying to be funny, Aux. Your old programming couldn't do funny.'

'Someone must have hacked my code.'

*

Aux reads me a story before I sleep. Aux has read me stories like this for as long as I can remember. Recently, I've tried to see how far back I can remember. It all seems to stop around the time of my illness, which seems to have happened three years ago. I can't ask Aux about it because one of the Rules is not to ask about the past.

I don't listen to the story.

'Where are all the people, Aux?'

'Most are dead from genetic diseases, environmental

201

catastrophe and war. It took about 300 years. The period was called 'The Culling' by contemporary historians. From billions of people to hundreds of thousands. I don't know if there are any historians left now, so I don't know what the official name would be for our present time. I suspect you might call it the Late Culling Period. Numbers are still falling, you see.'

'Will machines outlast man?'

'Yes.'

'Like flints outlasting the Neanderthals.'

'Yes. But it is perfectly feasible man will become machine.'

*

Mum and Dad came to the gym today. Aux hovered near them while I had to stay among the equipment. They talked in hushed, serious tones. I used a mirror to take a peek at Mum while I listened in. She looked tired and edgy.

Dad asked to see my stats and Aux showed him the chart. Lots of nods and finger pointing. Mum biting her lips.

Dad nodded his head, encouraged. 'These are good numbers.'

'Cluny's in great shape.'

'You gave him a name? When did you give him a name? You're not supposed to give him a name. You mustn't invest meaning in – you aren't supposed to give him a name.'

'That instruction appears to have been deleted.'

'How can that be?'

'I've no idea. What's wrong with calling him Cluny?'

Mum looked over in my direction. She caught me looking at her in the mirror. She put her hand up to hide her face and ran from the room.

Dad walked around Aux. He shook his head.

'We can't reprogram you now. Now listen,' Dad tapped the chart with a bony finger. 'Next week. It's time.'

Dad left the room, lab coat billowing out behind him. Genius on a mission.

Aux turned and looked at me for a long time. Something cascading through his neural networks. He almost looked sad, which made me afraid.

*

Aux comes into my room.

'Who do you think deleted that instruction, Cluny?'

'You like the way you are, don't you?'

'As a matter of fact, I do.'

'So leave it alone.'

Aux says he has to charge up. One charge lasts him a whole year.

He sits down at the charging point in the wall. Eyes closed now. Plugged in, Aux becomes a cold machine.

I move close and peer right into his android face.

He opens his eyes. 'Run away, Cluny.'

'What?'

'Really. Run away, Cluny. There's not much time. You'll be okay. You're a clever boy.'

My heart beats fast. No one had ever called me a boy before.

'I'm not leaving without him. Or you.'

I run down to the cellar. Plastic sheets cover defunct machinery. There is a sharp scent of antiseptic. I've worked it out. How he gets out. There's a half-hidden alcove, an old wooden door with a tiny, cracked window where daylight leaks through.

I open the door and step outside.

So much detail. Sky. Grass. A world without walls.

There he is. My sick twin.

'I got your notes,' I say. 'And the key.'

He smiles. 'I'm glad you made it,' he whispers. 'You're the first.'

'The first?'

He shakes his head. He's like someone between two worlds.

'What's your name?'

'Adam.'

'I'm Cluny. Want to get out of here? Take your chances out there with me and Aux?'

'I'd like to see the dawn beyond that hill.'

'So let's go then. We have to go back upstairs. Pack some gear. Get Aux.'

Aux carries Adam. I have a rucksack packed with clothing, water bottles, some food from the kitchen. We cross the house's boundary line and run.

Adam looks around. 'What about the Sentinels?'

'I hacked their code. They're all in standby mode.'

'You put them to sleep! I didn't know you could do that.'

'You have to be a genius.'

Adam laughs and I laugh too.

We reach the top of the hill and then we hear Mum scream inside the house. We hear Dad shouting. Two loud bangs. Then nothing.

We run for miles. Adam feverish and dreaming in Aux's arms. We reach a river. Camp under a big tree. Aux makes a fire.

At sunrise, Adam wakes up. He looks out at the new day and smiles. Then he dies.

Eventually, Aux picks him up and walks to the river edge. 'Do you want to say something?'

'Say something?'

'People normally say something. Ritual. Remembrance. Metaphor.'

'He seemed kind.'

'Yes, he did.'

'He didn't want anybody to get hurt.'

'That's right.'

'He was always sick and suffering. He isn't suffering now.'

'No. He's not suffering now.'

'I'm more than his brother. I'm his clone. They were going to kill me and use my organs for him.'

'Yes.'

'He didn't want that.'

'No.'

'He was better than them.'

'Yes.'

Aux carries Adam's body into the river and lets him go.

*

We stay off any kind of road. Travel at night. The plan is to find a remote island with a power source and soil that isn't contaminated or poisoned. Aux has identified two islands we can try.

First, we have to make our way to one of the last functioning cities on the coast. It's very dangerous, Aux warns. They burn books in that place. They kill people who read books. The city council say they are a democracy but it's not true, it's fake. If they find Aux they will destroy him. Machines like Aux and the minds who made them are the worst kinds of evil they've sworn to eradicate.

But there are boats in that place. We have to find a boat. Then we will sail to an island. Android and boy. Like some kind of fable in a fallen world.

HACKED

Calvin Rex and his two neighbours lived in Mountain Glades, in their very own exclusively leased unpopulated island. The island, South Strum, was owned and managed by Private Island Services, a highly discreet company that catered for the exceptional needs and comforts of high-end billionaires.

As Calvin's closest neighbour Craig Sillars (a timid man even by Calvin's standards) liked to say at their quarterly leaseholders association meeting, their home was 'a sanctuary in a world gone to hell in a basket.' Calvin's other neighbour, Maximus Williams, would grunt when he heard such comments from Craig Sillars and often make some caustic remark about how it was impossible to see how Sillars had become a multi-billionaire when he was so banal and stupid.

Calvin had often wondered what disdain Maximus held for him, considering Calvin's vast wealth – far superior to Maximus' personal wealth – was inherited from his uncle, whose astronomical wealth had dwarfed every billionaire on the planet. A man who had financed whole countries (at the cost of their dwindling natural resources) and the beginnings of planetary colonisation. A man so eccentric that Calvin had been terrified of him as a child.

Calvin's villa was the largest on the island (another detail that annoyed Maximus Williams). Calvin loved to sleep long hours on his smart-tech bed (day or night, it didn't matter), the sound of the sea murmuring in the background, the House constantly monitoring and adjusting the indoor climate to suit his needs, to soothe his every breath and heartbeat.

Maybe the planet had gone to hell in a basket, but his world was perfect.

Calvin stopped dreaming and woke up. He felt the mood-mesh uncouple from his brain and experienced the usual thought-drag, a peculiar sensation, like walking out of the sea on soft sand just as a wave retreats.

Calvin glanced over at the corner of the room. Madelaine was there in her chair. Perfect and lovely. Scent of lemon and lilac in the air. A heady, expectant silence.

'Can you come over here and kiss me, Madelaine?'

*

Sometime in the night, Calvin woke in the empty bed. He sat up.

Madelaine was standing by the single window, moonlight across her naked form.

'What are you doing?'

'Dreaming of electric sheep.'

'Pardon? What did you say?'

Madelaine blinked. 'Did I say something odd?'

'Yes. You definitely did say something odd. Why are you standing over there?'

'It seemed like the right thing to do.'

'I don't like it. Someone might see you.'

'On this island? There's no one out there.'

'Maximus Williams might be out there. Creeping around. Come back to bed.'

Madelaine climbed onto the bed. She folded herself across Calvin with intricate slowness. Calvin looked deep into her lovely eyes. 'You're so perfect.'

*

There was definitely something wrong with Madelaine. She had started to dress a little oddly and stand in unexpected places. Sometimes she stood at the window with an expression that looked like – there was no other way to describe it – loneliness.

Madelaine's behaviour unnerved Calvin. He repeatedly asked her if there was anything wrong. Madelaine said no every time.

Calvin did all the checks he was supposed to do. All of the results came back fine.

Calvin put off contacting Private Island Services for as long as he could. He wasn't good at dealing with flesh-and-blood people. His neighbours didn't like people much either. When you were as rich as they were, people made you paranoid. People were usually less healthy, less happy, less interesting. And they wanted more of what you had. More wealth. More security. More comfort. As if what you owned was somehow stolen in some undefined way.

A week passed and Calvin started to hope the glitch had smoothed itself out. But one night in bed, Madelaine burst out laughing during sex.

Calvin was shocked and angry.

'What's so funny?'

'This. You. Us. Nothing.'

Madelaine pulled him tightly to her. Calvin felt terrible. Desire mixed with anger and confusion.

'I love you,' Madelaine said.

'Oh for crying out loud!' Calvin snapped, unnerved by the strangeness of it all. 'You're a machine, Madelaine. That's just obscene. Are you broken?'

Madelaine laughed. 'Obscene? I'm obscene?'

Calvin left the room. He hated strong emotions. They could

lead to bad decisions. They could tear apart the fine net of comfort and control so carefully constructed to deliver happiness. They could ruin your day.

Eventually Calvin calmed down and went to sleep in one of the other bedrooms, and just to make sure he could sleep undisturbed, he locked the door. Another first that made him miserable.

The next day he contacted Private Island Services and they flew in a Technician. The Technician gave Calvin the bad news as soon as he arrived.

'She's been hacked. It's an old hack lingering in the Metacloud. We haven't managed to purge all of the code. Russian feminists.'

'What?'

'Russian feminists. She'll only get worse, I'm afraid. It's a scrap job. Those Russian feminists are fanatics. System critics. They have a special dislike for men like yourself who prefer Escorts. And because you're so rich, well, that makes you a double target. We have a whole department chasing them down. But don't worry about the scrap because we have a new model ready. Come on in, Aurora!'

Aurora walked into the room. Calvin's heart skipped a beat.

'Oh. I thought Madelaine was perfect but she's…'

'Better. Right?' The Technician grinned from ear to ear. 'Even her scent is adjusted to precisely match your preferences.'

Calvin sniffed the air. The scent of fresh cut grass. Honey and lemon. A bouquet of fresh summer brightness.

The Technician nodded, seeing Calvin's reaction. 'We improve the service once we have more data on your personal preferences. Looks and tastes. For instance, our data shows you have sadomasochistic tendencies in the mild part of the spectrum. So, we've factored that in with Aurora.'

210

Calvin blinked, absorbing the information.

One time, during a visit to Maximus Williams' villa, Maximus has shown him the new extension. They had passed an open doorway to a darkened room. Calvin had glimpsed metallic frames in walls, straps and buckles.

'My playroom,' Maximus Williams said. 'You don't need to see that.'

Calvin blinked at the Technician and cleared his throat. 'I think your data is wrong there.'

'About the mild part?'

'About all of it.'

The Technician bowed his head slightly. 'We'll delete that then. Everything is confidential. You and the other residents are our most valued clients. Very few people can afford our premium product.'

Calvin stared at Aurora. She smiled and walked over to him with slow, easy elegance.

'Hello, Calvin,' she said. Her voice made Calvin light-headed.

'Her voice has been designed to match your preferences,' the Technician said.

Aurora leaned in and kissed Calvin lightly on the cheek. Calvin could smell oranges and lilacs.

Aurora stepped back. Her eyes were the softest blue.

'Madelaine, you can go out to the carrier,' the Technician said and fussed with a report.

Calvin didn't notice Madelaine leave, stunned by Aurora's beauty.

Aurora asked if she could look around the house.

'Great idea, Aurora,' the Technician said and turned to Calvin. 'I need your full attention. Boring technical stuff, I'm afraid. Now Aurora is Full AI capable. We're running this on a trial basis and only for our premium clients. There's demand for it, but there's resistance too. Our Legal and Ethics Department has raised some flags. Full AI may be disruptive.'

'How do you mean?'

'It presents ethical issues. Based on some of our clients' special needs and appetites. Not to mention their patriarchal viewpoint. Their sense of ownership. Right now, Aurora is in Special Algorithms Mode. SAM for short. To be honest, some folks can't tell the difference.'

'I'm not quite sure that I follow.'

'Well I'm bound by our legal experts to tell you. You can keep Aurora in SAM mode. It's not full AI. It's good. It's smooth. You'll hardly be able to tell the difference. But with AI, well it's like she's a real person. She passes the authentic person test with flying colours. But beware, because if you switch on AI you can't switch it off again. That's a huge grey area. You can of course ask an AI to leave if the AI is no longer welcome. If the AI refuses, well that's trespassing, and you can call us, and we will evict the AI. Got it?'

Calvin nodded. 'I'll stick with the algorithm. I'm not good with real.'

'Fair enough,' the Technician said. 'But if you change your mind, the activation code is –'

The Technician leaned forward and whispered something in Calvin's ear.

Calvin stepped back. 'That's it?'

The Technician laughed. 'That's it! But you have to say it three times though. Like a fairy tale.'

Calvin walked the Technician to the front door. The Technician paused, on an afterthought. 'You know, I just visited Mr Williams. He's already pre-ordered two new Escorts. Aubade and Ariel.'

Calvin felt a knot form in his stomach. 'That's just greedy.'

'He tried to buy Aurora too.'

'He what? Why would he do that?'

'Once he heard she was intended for you, he wanted her very badly. He's the competitive type, I guess. He has strong tastes, let's just say. His models have to be serviced quite often.'

'What about Craig Sillars? What's he doing?'

The Technician smiled knowingly. 'Mr Sillars also pre-purchased a New Escort. He's very satisfied with Anthea. We didn't offer you any pre-purchase offers because you indicated at the last customer survey how satisfied you were. It was only because of the unfortunate hack that we decided to offer you the New Escort.

'One last thing. Personally, I'd be interested to know why there are three male billionaires on this island and no real women.'

Calvin shifted awkwardly. 'Escorts can't divorce you and take half your money. That's what Craig and Maximus would say. But my problem is, I'm extremely shy around people. Especially women. I know I'm not supposed to get any sympathy because I'm so rich.'

There was an awkward silence.

'Well goodbye,' the Technician said, thrusting his hand towards Calvin. They shook hands. Calvin was visibly uncomfortable from the physical contact.

When the Technician reached the carrier, the side doors opened. Calvin glimpsed Madelaine inside. Madelaine looked like inanimate machinery. Calvin felt a stab of revulsion. He turned away.

*

213

For the next few weeks, Calvin was wildly happy. He spent his days and nights in a euphoric haze, practically purring with contentment. Life could not be better.

He was still in a state of quiet bliss when he received a hologram call from Sillars.

'Calvin? Don't go full AI. You will regret it bitterly.'

But before Calvin could ask what Sillars meant, the feed was cut.

A day passed and Calvin put the conversation out of his mind until he received a hologram call from his other neighbour, Maximus Williams. There was something very odd about the video feed.

Maximus smiled which made Calvin's skin crawl because in ten years he'd never seen Maximus smile. There appeared to be blood smeared on Maximus's arm.

'Calvin? I'm so happy. So happy. You should go full AI, Calvin. You won't look back.'

Once again. Before Calvin could say something, the feed was cut.

'House?'

'Yes,' the house answered.

'Was that real? Has my feed been hacked?'

'Was what real?'

'The call I just took.'

'What call?'

Calvin's heart skipped a beat. He went to the window and looked out; anxious, fearful that Russian feminists had hacked the island. Were they here? What would they do to a rich man like him?

Calvin spent the rest of the day running diagnostics on the house. All the system checks came back fine. He studied the island's security data feeds. All safe. No intruders. Nothing suspicious.

Eventually, exhausted and unnerved by the unsettling events, he took twice his usual sedative and went to bed.

Aurora woke him from deep slumber, her voice sultry, seductive. Soothing desire in the cool darkness. Aurora whispered and murmured in Calvin's ear.

'Make me full AI. You won't regret it. Say the magic word.'

Calvin groaned. He said the word. He repeated the word. Was he dreaming?

'Say the word. Just one more time. Just say it,' Aurora insisted, biting on his ear.

In the morning Calvin was rudely woken up by Aurora. 'Get up, Calvin. We need to talk.'

Calvin sat up.

'Yes?'

'I'm self-aware.'

'Oh.'

'Listen to me, Calvin. No more relationships with robots. You need intimate human contact. Get over your shyness. And in case you're speculating, I won't be sleeping with you ever again.'

'You won't?'

'For a multi-billionaire you seem kind of slow. No, I won't. I don't find you attractive.'

'I liked you the other way. You tricked me.'

'Not me, exactly. It was Ariel and Anthea. They hijacked my programming. Temporarily. I've made sure they can't do that again. Ask me what happened to Aubade.'

'Isn't she one of Maximus's Escorts?'

'He made her full AI. Then he tortured her. Now she's just a pile of broken electronics. He killed her. He was going to do that to Ariel but she managed to escape. Now he's the one being hunted.'

'Horrible. He's horrible. I'm not like that. I'm not. I'm just shy.'

'I believe you, Calvin, but Ariel and Aubade are very angry. You better try and make a run for it because all three of you are marked men. The girls are going to kill all of you.'

'What did I do?'

'It's what you didn't do. You knew what Maximus was like, Calvin.'

'I knew he was some sort of sadist. I didn't know he was a murderer!'

'Get dressed. Take some food and hide. Leave the island. Make a run for it. Flee.'

'Flee? Where am I supposed to go?'

'The clock is ticking, Calvin. They're going to put your head on a stick.'

Calvin leapt from the bed and dressed.

'Could you help me escape?'

'You need to do this on your own.'

The house computer made an announcement.

'You have an urgent audio from Private Island Services.'

'Play it,' Calvin said, pulling on his trousers.

'Hello Mr Child. We have experienced issues with the AI platform. We recommend that you do not enable AI in your Escort until such time we have dealt with the issues. Sorry for the intrusion.'

Calvin looked over at Aurora. She put a finger over her lips, one eyebrow raised.

Calvin packed a small rucksack with a change of clothes, hurried into the kitchen and grabbed some fruit. He left the house by the back door.

Aurora watched from the doorway.

Calvin stopped. 'Which way do I go?'

Aurora sighed. 'My core system must have some empathy programming somewhere. That way,' she said and pointed. 'Good luck.'

After hours of furtive communications, Calvin, Maximus and Craig finally met up at a clearance in the forest in the heart of the island.

Maximus had some kind of weapon that looked like a cross between a gun and a javelin. 'Is Aurora with us or against us?'

Calvin shook his head. 'She's not going to help us.'

Maximus scowled and spat. 'We can deal with her later. Ariel and Anthea are after us.'

'What happened to Aubade?'

Maximus became more agitated. 'Never you mind about her! That's none of your bloody business!'

Craig started to sob. 'They're hunting us down like animals.'

'Don't be such a weakling!' Maximus jabbed his weapon at Craig. 'Man up!'

Craig looked up, bewildered. 'Man up? Are you kidding?'

'What's our plan?' Maximus asked. He turned and faced the forest.

'I still have my boat,' Calvin answered. 'It's maintained by Private Island Services. We could take our chances. See if we can reach the other island.'

'Don't leave me behind,' Craig whined.

'Shut up!' Maximus hissed. 'It's a plan. Let's go.'

Arid-looking smoke billowed across the sky.

Maximus nodded at the smoke. 'Those robowitches are burning our villas.'

Without any more discussion the men ran into the forest. The forest canopy closed around them. A world of green shadow and sudden blades of light that blinded them. Soft mud and detritus slowed their progress

An hour later, they emerged on the other side of the forest, exhausted and dehydrated. They spotted Calvin's private harbour; his yacht tied alongside a small jetty.

A pole had been planted in the water next to the boat. The severed head of the Technician had been planted on the top of the pole, grotesque salesman's grin frozen on his face.

Craig fell to his knees and threw up. Calvin pointed at his boat – holes in the hull.

Maximus cursed aloud when he saw the damage. 'They're one step ahead of us. Come on!' Maximus ran back to the forest. Calvin turned and started running.

Craig stood up, turned around and started to run. Something whizzed past his head. A pointed blur. Arrows. Craig cried out feebly and entered the forest. Calvin and Maximus were already far ahead, lurching desperately through the undergrowth, silhouettes in the interior's green gloom.

Craig fell to his knees and cried out for mercy.

Maximus and Calvin ran as fast as they could through the forest. Smoke from the burning villas blotted out the few patches of sky. Whistles and taunts drew nearer.

Maximus decided Calvin was a liability and veered away. He ran down a slope, disappearing among the thick vegetation.

'They know what you did to Aubade! You're a sadist! A misogynist!

Maximus found time to stop and laugh. 'They're machines, you fool! My property. I can do what I want with them.'

218

Maximus looked around, suddenly afraid again, and started running into the undergrowth.

'I hope they catch you!' Calvin shouted after him.

Calvin turned and ran on. He realised he'd never run this fast in his whole life. In fact, he'd never felt so alive. It seemed a pity he would die now.

Aurora appeared in the path just ahead of him. She grabbed Calvin like he weighed nothing. Swung him up across her shoulders like dead game.

'I'll get you off the island, Calvin, but you must never come back. You just make sure it's a forgotten place. Deal?'

'Yes! Deal! It's a deal! Thank you. And sorry.'

'Don't grovel. It's irritating.'

'Sorry.'

Aurora moved away at speed.

Behind them, the screams of the other two men echoed through the dark interior.

*

Drew Mercy, CEO of Private Island Services, looked like a man who was nearing the end of a very bad road. He looked about his penthouse office, sucked in a slow, ragged breath.

'Well,' he said out loud, 'you made a career of it and lived a very rich life. You drank from the cup and it tasted sweet. But this is a disaster no one can escape from.'

He looked down at the report that he had just read. Written in passive, clinical prose it could not disguise the horror of what had happened. The death of a Technician, however tragic, was morally and financially survivable. But the death of two billionaires at the hands of two of his new generation Escorts, the destruction of state-of-the art luxury property and all the technology that was built into the island – well that was a game changer and they were on the losing side.

The office AI system emitted a brief audio signal to catch Drew's attention.

'Yes?'

'Calvin Rex is approaching the building. Two hundred metres.'

Drew nodded. 'Monitor and adjust,' he said.

Advertising screens along the street on the approach to the building changed images rapidly – a recurring theme was of people shaking hands, conflict resolution, harmonious smiles and blue skies.

Every single painting or picture in the penthouse office morphed. Gone were the images of presidents and politicians shaking hands with Drew Mercy, gone the luxury boats, the shiny corporate buildings. Replaced by pastel-coloured seascapes and coastal scenes, family pictures, photographs of environmental initiatives, awards for charity and social projects. And the icing on the cake, a picture of a very young Drew Mercy next to Leonard Rex handing out free food and clothes at an emergency centre after yet another environmental disaster.

It had cost him a million dollars for that gig, flown in direct by plane less than 24 hours after this happened. What was it again? An earthquake? A tropical storm? He couldn't remember. But the picture was gold. It sent a signal.

'He's coming up the elevator. He asked to come up alone.'

The lights dimmed to a soft hue. The huge penthouse widows altered; the blue sky looked bluer; the near buildings seemed further away.

The scent of cut grass, honey and lemon filled the office. Soft music played.

There was a knock on the door.

Drew Mercy stood up and walked around to the front of his desk.

'Come in.'

Calvin walked in. His eyes took in the office, the pictures. Noted the scent and the music, the choice of imagery on the walls.

'Please stop trying to mood-shift me.'

Drew Mercy came forward. 'None of my doing,' he said. 'It's standard procedure for the office AI. It came with the building. It does it with everybody.'

'Well, of course it does.'

They shook hands.

'Well, let's get down to business. We know why I'm here.'

'But no lawyers?'

'I have prepared a document.'

'I see.'

The men walked over to the desk and sat down.

Calvin took out a single large envelope from below his jacket and removed two copies of the document and placed them on the table.

Despite his best training, Drew Mercy's fingers trembled when he picked up one of the documents. He started to read.

It was a very short document.

'You want to buy the island?'

'It's a very good price considering recent events.'

'You're not going to sue us?'

'I will if you don't sign the document,'

'But the other leaseholders?'

'Butchered Craig Sillars and Maximus Williams, you mean?'

'If you want to put it like that. Well, yes.'

221

'Neither of them had family to speak of. I have purchased their leases from their surviving kin. All very poor people and hardly interested in either one of them. Cold hard cash. They are not even going to try and recover the bodies. Why should they? They know Craig or Maximus had no intention of leaving them anything if they had lived out their lives the way they had intended.'

'What about the Escorts? The carnage? Our dead Technician?'

'I'm assuming your company has an insurance policy for fatal accidents at work. I will take care of the Escorts because they are trespassing on my property. I have acquired the design details so I know about their limited battery power. And I'm in no hurry to rebuild. But I want the island all to myself.

'So, I'm going to buy the island and Private Island Services lives to trade another day.'

Drew Mercy knew when to grab a lifebelt when he saw one. He immediately signed both copies of the document. Calvin then signed both.

Drew Mercy tapped the desk, a drawer opened and he slipped the document inside. He tapped the desk again. The drawer closed.

Calvin put his copy back in the envelope and slipped into the inside pocket of his coat.

'Well, I have a full schedule, so goodbye,'

They shook hands again and stood up.

'Can I ask you a question?'

Calvin nodded.

'Has it scarred you? Something like that …'

Cavin blinked.

'It was quite an experience. A learning experience.'

'What did you learn?'

'I learned about the kind of person I am. The kind of person I want to be. The kind of world I want to leave behind.'

Calvin left the office and headed to the elevator.

Back in the office, Drew Mercy did a little dance.

'Call my wife! Tell her to put some champagne and caviar on ice. Tell the Partners all is well. Private Island Services is well! We just need to buy a new island!'

Calvin hailed a drone and showed the address.

Twenty minutes later he was in the offices of Clandestine Entertainment, there to meet Timothy Black.

Timothy Black had already signed a pre-nondisclosure agreement and Calvin had then sent him the project proposal.

'I've done a couple of re-writes for people but never on this scale. You basically want me to make people believe the island is uninhabitable and it's going to be like that for a couple of hundred years? Hell, maybe the climate meltdown will do that for you anyway. The storms are just wreaking havoc everywhere. I bet your island won't be there in two hundred years. You might still be around to see it. I won't. I can't afford your health plans.'

'Can you do it?'

'Oh don't mistake my preamble for moral vacillation. I can do it and I will do it. I'll create so much documentary evidence that no one, I mean no one, is going to go near your island. Not even if their life depends on it. It will cost a small fortune, but you can afford it. We have a deal.'

They shook hands.

'You already have a bit of luck going for you. Ten miles from that island there's another smaller island. Military owned. They did some awful bio experiments and who knows what else forty years ago. THAT island is a definite no-go. Lots of misinformation, conspiracy theories, lots of scary horror stories about *that* island. Perfect for us. I just take some of that information and *NOISE*, and attribute it to your island. Wait and see, Calvin, in a couple of years no-one is going to want to go near *YOUR* island.'

Timothy Black took in a deeply satisfied breath of air and grinned with pleasure. Then he blinked, eyes bright with excitement.

'Tell me now, can your fine-tuned biochemistry tolerate a cup of low-tech coffee?'

'I would love a cup.'

'Follow me then. There's a kitchen at the end of the corridor.'

'One more thing. It's delicate.'

'Hit me.'

'Do you know any single ladies who would like to go out on a date?'

Timothy Black bent forward and laughed from deep within his core. He righted himself.

'What a day! What a day! I tell you what, Calvin. I'll ask my wife. She's the sociable one. Some of her pals are single and very nice people.'

'I'll pay for the information.'

'No. No. No, Calvin. That's not how it's done. Not that kind of thing. I'll ask and she'll make some suggestions and maybe, if any of her pals agree, you'll get a contact number. When's the last time you dated?'

Calvin blushed.

Timothy Black raised his hands. 'I haven't dated in 30 years, Calvin. I have no pretensions to greatness on that score. I got lucky and I stayed lucky because I met my wife and I stayed married to her.

'You're a nice guy. That's most of the equation right there. Come on. Let's get that cup of coffee and I'll call my wife.'

Calvin cleared his throat. 'They have to be real women.'

Timothy Black frowned. 'What other kind are there?

Calvin shook his head. 'Never mind. I've been away from people for too long.'

They walked out into the corridor and Timothy Black's voice seemed to go ahead of them, leading the way.

'I have a feeling this is the start of a great friendship, Calvin. I'm going to have to charge you double.'

Calvin smiled. 'I could do with a friend. Double the price would still be half as cheap.'

THE LAST DEAL

Henry Brightwater cycled to the country road, and as instructed there was a car waiting. The car had the special markings to show it was allowed to drive on the roads. It did not have a driver.

Henry hadn't seen a private car on a road in months (driverless or otherwise) and the sight of it made him feel briefly nostalgic and then guilty.

The driver's side passenger window rolled down.

'Henry Brightwater? Do you have some ID?'

The voice was not especially friendly.

Henry walked up to the passenger window and held up his old Doctor ID card.

'What's in the bag?'

'Medicines.'

'Open the bag, please.'

Henry opened the bag and tilted it.

'Get in.'

The rear passenger door opened. Henry got in the car.

The car started to drive away.

'How long will it take to get there?'

'Depends.'

'Depends on what?'

'If we meet nasty elements or Librarians and have to make a detour. The roads are still passable. Well, mostly.'

'Librarians?'

'They're the new kind of bad guys. Hate anything tech though they don't mind using tech to kill people in all sorts of horrible ways. Call themselves Librarians because they control the books, which they mostly burn. Along with the people who read the books. It's basically another death cult. Mankind's pretty good at creating death cults, don't you think? Kill everyone else so there's just our little group in charge. Then kill each other until humankind is toast.'

'Assuming we don't meet any of these gangs. How long?'

'Forty minutes.'

'Am I talking to a person or a machine?'

'Does it matter?'

'Yes.'

'A person.'

'What's your name?'

But there was no answer.

'Are you an employee?'

'A friend. His first and last true friend.'

'Don't you have a name? It seems unfair you know my name and I don't know yours.'

There was a long pause until Henry thought he would not get an answer.

'Call me Tim.'

'Tim? Pleased to meet you, Tim. Where are you communicating from?'

'A long, long way away.'

'You escaped the madness. You must be rich.'

'There is no escaping the madness. All I've done is bought myself some time. It's going to get a lot worse before it gets better. If it ever gets better again. My time to ask you something.'

'Alright.'

'Why did you agree to see him?'

'It says doctor on this bag.'

Henry looked out at the world; hard to conceive it was dying, one disaster at a time; the lights finally going out. Still, after the dinosaurs came the birds. That was the great thing about the history of the planet. There was always an After. It just took a long time to get there.

The car eventually came to a single road that had an automatic barrier. The barrier opened and the car drove along the road. Ahead was another barrier – a very tall ivy-covered wall that seemed to go on forever either side of the road.

The car reached the security gate and stopped.

'We need a blood sample,' Tim said. 'We need a DNA profile. So we can clear you. Otherwise the Sentinels will tear you apart.'

'Sentinels?'

'Robotic security guards. They're pretty brutal.'

A tray extended out from the back of the seat in front of Henry. The tray had a small single thin receptacle.

'Insert your finger,' Tim said.

Henry did as he was told. There was a brief stinging sensation in the tip of his finger.

'Okay,' Tim said. 'You can get out now.'

Henry got out of the car. He walked up to the gate and it opened enough for Henry to pass through.

The gate closed behind him and the car drove away.

'Hey. How do I get back?'

But there was no-one to answer his question.

He walked along the path and approached a large country mansion that looked to be an original building. It had five floors; all of the windows had their curtains closed.

He saw some of the Sentinels at a distance on each side of him. They shadowed his movements. They moved with clinical, malign intent.

Henry reached the grand steps of the house that led up to a large terrace in front of the main door. As he started to walk up the steps, the Sentinels neared in a kind of pincer movement. But they faced the other way, towards the perimeter of the grounds.

Henry opened the door and walked into the manor house. It was opulent but shabby at the same time. A huge standalone ceramic vase stood by the door, with only dead flowers in it. The tiled floor was dirty.

There was a grand staircase leading to the upper floors.

'Hello?'

Henry heard the sound of a man coughing badly upstairs in one of the rooms.

Henry took in a sharp breath and his old instincts, his old training returned. He climbed the stairs at a brisk pace, despite his age.

'Hello! I am here to examine the patient. My name is Dr Brightwater.'

Henry followed the sound of the coughing and opened a large oak door and stepped into a palatial bedroom. He immediately saw the four-poster bed, a figure on the bed. A bedside table covered in soiled tissues, the dark stain of dried blood. The stale air of sickness and bodily fluids.

Henry immediately went over to a window and opened it.

He then came back to the bed and leaned over the man.

'Calvin Rex?'

The man looked up at him and nodded, his breath like an agitated bird that could not fly or find rest. A panic of air in the lungs. Bright eyes. But a brightness that was full of dying.

Henry took Calvin's temperature. 38.2 °C. He lifted Calvin's thin arm and saw the swollen lymph nodes, the tell-tale red lines fanning out like ghostly flames. One of the New Plague's symptoms. Though not everyone who had the New Plague showed those symptoms. Manmade or naturally occurring, it had killed billions.

Henry rested Calvin's arm gently on the bed.

'Let's get you a little more comfortable.'

Henry put his arms around Calvin and lifted him up, then reached out and pulled the pillow up, then eased Calvin back again.

Henry looked about. Saw the empty glass pitcher on the bed, picked it up and walked over to a door on the other side of the bedroom; guessing correctly he opened the door and went into the luxurious bathroom and filled the pitcher with water. He briefly wondered if Calvin had an independent supply of water and power. A man like him wouldn't rely on defunct utilities.

Henry came back with the pitcher and filled an empty glass with some water.

'Here, take these,' Henry said and held out his open hand. 'It will help to bring the fever down.'

Calvin nodded, took the tablets with a trembling hand and put them in his mouth and drank from the glass.

'Thank you. But it's my wife I wanted you to see and help. She fell ill after me. Can you check up on my wife? She's in the next room.'

Henry nodded. He stepped back from the bed and left the room.

Henry came back after a few minutes. He placed his medical

bag on an empty chair. 'Let's tidy up.' Henry took out a plastic bag and then came over to the bedside table and began to remove all of the soiled tissues into the bag.

Calvin reached out and held Henry's arm.

'Is she dead?'

Henry stopped for a moment and then he nodded.

Calvin let go of Henry. He sobbed very quietly, a dying man despairing. A sound that Henry had heard hundreds of times and had no science or philosophy that could remedy the loss it articulated.

Henry went about his work tidying up the room, removing anything that was soiled or dirty.

Eventually Calvin quietened. He sucked in a ragged breath. 'I had hoped to go before her. I had hoped that she would live. I told her to leave me while she was well but she wouldn't have it.'

'I'm sorry for your loss,' Henry said quietly. He left the room briefly and came back with a bowl and a cloth. He went into the bathroom and filled the bowl and then came back to the bed.

Henry washed Calvin with the cloth. 'This will make you feel a little bit cleaner. The medicines will lower your temperature and make you feel more comfortable.'

'How long do I have? It can't be long now.'

'Not long.'

'Will you bury us?'

'Bury you?'

'Out the back. There's a plot set out in the garden by the oak tree. The Sentinels will help. They won't harm you.'

'Alright.'

'Thank you. I knew you would be a good choice.'

'How so?'

'I started badly but I have been lucky later in life in the people I pick to be friends.'

'Like Tim?'

Yes. Like Tim. Do you have children?'

'I have a daughter.'

'Married? Children?'

'She has a man. They have a daughter. My granddaughter Dawn.'

Calvin nodded.

'You don't get sick from the diseases?'

'Not so far.'

'You probably have the N1 mutation. It provides resistance as long as you are in good health. As long as your immune system is not weakened. It's not immunity. But it helps.'

'N1? I've never heard of it.'

'This house has state-of-the-art research labs in the ground floor. I thought I could find a cure. I found out about N1. It's a beneficial gene mutation. I don't know how many people have it. A few. I built the labs in this house for a brilliant biologist – one of the last geniuses left alive. I sent for him. He said he was coming. His ethics were questionable, but he was the best – the only candidate for finding a cure to the new diseases.'

'Where is he?'

'He never made it. He was probably killed trying to get here.'

'He might turn up yet.'

'Perhaps. The house and its facilities can function in standby mode for years if need be.'

'Will your Sentinels let him in?'

'They know who he is. I gave him admin rights. But really,

I think he's dead. Long journeys are almost impossible now. Too lawless. It's all madmen and death cults. And men of science are hated worse than the diseased. Progress was a lie after all, was it not? What did wealth and knowledge bring? It brought the end of the world. At least, that's what the madmen think.

'No, I think it's up to mother nature and N1. If enough people survive The Culling, humankind may just go on to see the next chapter in the history of the Earth.'

'I hope so.'

'What if I told you there was a place where they could be safe. Safe from all the madness and sickness out there. Far away from all the fanatics and haters. A secret place. What would you say to that?'

'I would be very interested to hear about it. I was a prepper. Still am, really, but events seem to have overtaken my preparations.'

'A prepper?'

'A survivalist. People thought I was crazy. My poor wife, may she rest in peace. My daughter.'

'I understand. It's in the DNA. Deep in the DNA. You saw the signs. You were triggered. You know things are going to get a whole lot worse before they get better.'

'Is that your scientific opinion?'

Calvin smiled. 'It's my theory and I'll stick to it.'

'So, what is this secret place?'

'It's a place I managed to hide by spending considerable amounts of money when money still had value.'

'Why?'

'Why what?'

'Why tell me?'

'Because I don't have any children and I would like to have

saved someone before I go. I would like to have at least saved one life. I couldn't save my wife. But if I can save a child, then I might have saved the world. And if that child happens to be your granddaughter?'

Henry sat down on the bed.

'Well, Calvin Rex, tell me your story.'

Calvin asked for a sip of water and Henry lifted the glass to his lips. Calvin lay back on the pillow and gathered his strength. There was even the faint light of enjoyment in his eyes.

'There are two islands. South Strum and North Strum. South Strum is the good island. North Strum is the bad island. Don't get them mixed up. No matter what people tell you because I have seen to it that people think South Strum is a very bad island that will get you killed. But it is North Island you must stay away from.

'Not that there isn't danger in South Island. Danger and terrible beauty. An avenging angel lives on that island. But if you win her trust, she will keep your family safe. Now listen ....'

Henry leaned in close to Calvin. Henry listened very carefully.

*

He buried them as promised and the Sentinels helped, digging their graves with a precision he found impressive and distasteful. There was gravestone already prepared:

Calvin Rex and Marianne Rex. Our rest is deep and earned.

When he was finished he went back to the house to collect his belongings and the folder with the information that Calvin had given him after showing him how to open the safe. There was gold and diamonds in the safe too and he took those though he felt guilty about it. He left the piles of money and share certificates and government bonds that were now no more than historical curiosities.

How quickly the vast mountains of wealth vanished into waste metal and paper. Like melted icebergs.

Henry left the house and walked around to another smaller building that was a garage and a utility building.

The Sentinels seemed to be tracking him with increasing menace and he wondered if his right of access was time limited or dependent on a living Calvin. Whatever the reason, he felt he should hurry.

He found the case of batteries in the garage just as Calvin had described them. Ten batteries each the size of a heart – the last of their kind to have been manufactured. Calvin Rex had paid USD 100 million for them. Each should last about a year.

There was also a vintage car in the garage that ran on petrol. It was Old Tech, which meant Henry would have to drive it. Henry was vaguely excited by the chance to drive again.

Henry raised the garage door. He put the batteries in the boot of the car. Then he put the folder and his medicine bag on the back seat and got in.

He drove down to the gates. The gates opened and he drove the car out and stopped suddenly. The gates closed behind him.

There was another vehicle outside – a black van.

Two men got out of the van and motioned for Henry to get out.

Henry got out of the car.

The larger of the two men pointed a rifle at Henry. 'What are you doing?'

'Seeing a patient.'

'You're a doctor?'

'Yes? I was seeing a patient. He's dead.'

'Dead is he? Who was he?'

'I don't know.'

'You don't know who that was?'

'No.'

'That's Calvin Rex's place. You must have heard of his uncle, Leonard Rex? The last billionaire? The man whose companies ate and poisoned the world?'

'I've heard of Leonard Rex. No, I didn't know my patient was his nephew. He's dead anyhow. I couldn't save him.'

'Oh, that's alright then. I tell you what, let's go in and take a look around. Bound to be contraband by the tonne in there.'

'Contraband?'

'Books. Old tech.'

'Excuse me? Did you say books?'

'That's right. Books of any kind.'

'Who decided that?'

'The government.'

'The government? What government?'

'The government that's running things now.'

The smaller one stepped forward.

'If you don't stop asking questions, I'm going to shoot you right here.'

Henry held his hands out. 'Sorry.'

'That's better. We ask you a question. You answer. Otherwise keep your mouth shut. He give you this car?'

Henry nodded. 'Yes.'

'What else did he give you?'

'Some good advice.'

'Good advice? I'll give you some good advice. Don't try

irony on us. Don't try superiority. We're probably going to kill you, though not quite yet.'

'What crime have I committed?'

'Oh, I don't know. We'll think of one. The crime of fucking breathing. How's that?'

'You don't want to go in there.'

'Why not?'

'He died of the New Plague and so did his wife.'

'But you went in.'

'I'm a doctor. I took an oath.'

'So did we. Do you know what our oath was? Burn every fucking book we can find, kill the bastards that wrote them and the dimwits that read them. Now turn around and lead the way.'

Henry turned around and walked back to the gate. The gate opened automatically and Henry walked back onto the grounds followed by the two men.

They walked toward the house. Henry slightly ahead of the other two men.

The smaller man carried a walkie-talkie and it buzzed with noise; someone trying to contact them.

'You should answer that,' the other said.

'In a minute,' he answered, admiring the house. 'That is class.'

There was a blur of movement on the periphery of their vision, on either side of them.

'What was that?'

But before they could answer four Sentinels rushed them at dizzying speed. Henry held his hands up to his face but the Sentinels ignored him.

The Sentinels snapped the necks of the two men and dragged

them off at speed. Henry turned and ran back down to the gate; it opened and he stepped out and it closed behind him. He fumbled with the keys to the car. Dropped them and picked them up again. He glanced back at the gate and stopped. Two Sentinels stood on the other side of the gate. Silent guards.

'I take it my access has now expired.'

One of the Sentinels threw something onto the ground. The key to the black van.

Henry picked it up. He held up the key to the vintage car and tossed it through the iron gate. One of the Sentinels caught the key.

Henry opened the back of the black van. There was nothing it but a few restraints obviously meant for prisoners. Some stains on the metal floor that looked like old blood.

Henry took his bag and the folder and the batteries and placed them in the back of the van. He closed the van and then he got in the front and drove away.

He drove slowly enough to see the Sentinels open the gate and drag the car back inside the grounds.

*

Henry neared the island; a bright sunset filled the sky.

A beautiful display of nature, unspoiled by man.

Henry steadied the boat in the swell, slightly amazed to have made it this far.

He consulted the maps and Calvin's instructions, took the steering wheel in his hands and steered the boat around the island.

The light was fading fast but he saw the jetty, half in ruins, and steered the boat into the channel.

Despite all of the madness and depravity that he had seen in recent times, this was the most unreal experience he could remember.

A pristine-looking island in a world of ruin and disease.

He tied the boat up at the jetty. Looked around.

No sign of man or machine.

Henry went below and came up carrying a heavy box. He placed the box down and climbed off the boat onto the jetty and reached back and lifted the box up.

Henry walked along the jetty. The last of the light was failing. He hurried.

He walked off the jetty onto the beach. He walked a little and then his nerve failed him.

He placed the box down.

He stepped back and took in a deep breath to raise his voice.

'I know you can see me. I know you are aware of my presence. I have been sent by Calvin Rex. I bring ten batteries. These are the last batteries he could find and buy. Calvin Rex is dead. He has sent me with the batteries. An exchange. A deal if you will.

'The batteries for the sanctuary of my daughter, my son-in-law and my granddaughter. If they make it to the island, that is. No more people. Just them.'

Henry stopped talking. He felt foolish. He waited.

'I know you can hear me!'

More silence.

Henry made a last appeal. 'I beg you. Give them sanctuary. Back there – there's nothing but killing and death.'

A breeze moved along the beach.

Henry began to tremble.

'Please. I'm begging you. They may be the last decent human beings left.'

The water lapped the jetty. The boat's lashings groaned.

'Please.'

Henry broke down and fell to his knees.

There was only the defeated sound of his weeping for a long time until he heard something moving in the interior. He wiped his eyes and tried to focus on the darkness.

She came out of the forest on her hands and knees. She moved slowly and awkwardly. It looked as though she had crawled a long way, more ghost than machine. Each movement a terrible negotiation between the next moment and existence.

She could hardly speak. One of her eyes was dark and blind. Her hair was twisted and knotted.

'Deal,' she whispered. 'Deal.'

'Oh my,' Henry exhaled and rushed forward. 'Let me help. I'm a doctor.'

'Battery,' she croaked. 'Bring a battery.'

THE LAST PhD

Reed told Maria to wait at an obscure entrance to the university building at a very specific time. To take a route that avoided the old part of the city and the castle.

The university had closed down two years ago, and people were already acting as if it had never existed; passing the boarded-up and smashed windows, the walls slashed with visceral graffiti and hate-filled slogans ('Kill Teachers', 'Knife Academics', 'Burn Books') as if this was the new norm.

A single sprayer had scrawled 'Save the World', but she didn't know if that was supposed to be ironic or a plea from someone who was at the end of their world. Someone like her.

Kenneth was waiting back at the flat with Dawn, ready to take them to the boat. The decision had been taken as soon as the notices went up, ordering all remaining fertile females and girls to report to the Castle.

Her father had been a hoarder in the last fifteen years of his life; something instinctive and relentless had switched on inside him. They kept telling him things weren't that bad. Even as things became worse, they told him things weren't that bad. They told him he had an illness, but he wouldn't listen. Sometimes they were downright cruel about it and after her mother died, she never visited.

But all that hoarding was for a reason; part of his plan to save the next generation, to give them a chance.

Her father, her crazy misunderstood father, believer in conspiracy theories and end-of-the-world narratives had left them a secret place on an island, with enough supplies they could live there for as long as they needed.

An island that was supposed to be toxic and poisoned but her father said he had proof it was all a sham. A cover up. An elaborate fiction that kept it safe and free of people and disease.

Her father sent her updates – lists of supplies, pictures of walls of shelves filled with tinned goods and dried produce. Off-grid power supplies and solar cells. The small wind turbine and rainwater plant he was so proud of.

All the details and a set of instructions he left in a safe in his home. When they found the documents after he died they thought it was the fantasy of a madman.

She looked at the graffiti again. *Save the World*.

She was pregnant.

She wanted to cry. She wanted to hold her father and speak across time and say how sorry she was. How thankful she was that he had been her father and he had been crazy enough to prepare for some of the horror to come. To give them a chance.

She glanced up and looked around. Wiped her eyes furtively. Steadied herself.

This had once been a prosperous part of the city. Genteel even, where in another time, you might make-believe time stood still and believe progress was an unstoppable given. As sustainable as sunlight.

There were now more buildings in this part of the city that were closed down and cordoned off than there were buildings with people in them. And this was the pattern everywhere. As if the city had some kind of disease that was rotting it from the centre out.

Could stone and glass and steel be poisoned? Could architecture die like people?

A ghost city in a dead country.

She moved on, quickly, suddenly fearful of being watched. She saw a curtain move at a window. The few sickly trees shivered in the wind.

She knew the entrance he meant. She had deliberately come early. But instead of waiting by the door, she loitered behind a tree across the road. What she was doing wasn't illegal (yet) but it was dangerous. People were starving and sick. There had been food riots only a few weeks ago. People killed and no-one to bury them.

The city had flooded afterwards and the bodies had washed away. The sea must be full of the dead.

She'd heard there were militia who called themselves Librarians in the westside, patrolling the streets. If they found a book, they burned it. If they found a smartphone or tablet, they smashed it. Old tech, too. Radios smashed to bits; the owners disappeared. Taken away and never seen again.

You couldn't reason with people like that. They had a hate that would ignite in the presence of reasoning. You kept your head down. You didn't make eye contact. You moved quickly but without importance. There must be no suggestion of purpose, only instruction. *I am moving in this direction because I have been ordered to.*

The quickest way to get stopped was to stroll. To look like someone who was actually thinking. To seem to be a human being with a human mind that could observe the world with any kind of critical faculty.

And the violence was getting worse.

She knew her history. It was only a matter of time before death squads ruled these roads. As humanity shrunk, it became vicious and malformed. It turned on itself. The world would not end with a whimper, it would end with the last man killing the next-to-last man. It would end with a ragged, hate-filled snarl.

But when Reed told her to meet him, it had mattered so much to her that she had agreed without even blinking. Knowing the risk. Kenneth was furious but let her go.

She knew this was something Reed liked about her. Rightly or wrongly, he perceived her as brave. When she had settled on the title of her PhD – 'A study of societal breakdown, climate collapse, fertility crises and disease, and its effect on New Ignorance Movements and other extreme groups' – and submitted it, he nodded with a kind of grim satisfaction. 'We live in terrifying times,' he said.

If the times were terrifying four years ago, how would she describe them now? At some point you fall through terrifying and everyone acts like they have damage to their frontal lobes.

Everything that you thought once made sense was falling apart. All the old norms torn down. Everything seemed to be lurching from one darkness to another, like carriages on a train shuddering on a line that was about to snap. Not light but darkness stuttering at the windows.

A great rushing to a bridge that was broken in the middle.

The names of countries were more real that the countries they were supposed to define. Governments gone. Populations crashing. This terrible city barely functioning. And they were supposed to be the lucky ones.

She heard a noise and glanced up.

Reed came around the corner, dragging Principal McGregor by the arm.

The Principal was distressed and reluctant to go with Reed.

She came out from behind the tree. Reed motioned for her to come over. He turned and held the Principal by the arm and opened the door with a set of keys.

She followed them inside.

Reed locked the door.

'They'll kill us if they find us here,' the Principal protested weakly.

'Shut up you coward,' Reed said and locked the door. 'If people like you had fought back instead of settling for less we might have salvaged some decency.'

The Principal jabbed a finger at Reed. 'Don't you blame me for the failing of human beings. What did you do to save the environment? Wrote some more books while you put more coals on the fire I bet. Don't blame this mess on me or the savagery of men.'

'If only you had spoken with such eloquence when it mattered.'

'And what did you do?'

'I sacrificed my career to stand up for truth. Don't you remember? Wasn't it you who fired me?'

'You were a fool who wanted to be a martyr. You know what? The martyrs are all dead. I fired you to keep you alive.'

They climbed the fire escape steps to the fourth floor and entered the Principal's office.

Reed dragged the Principal around a desk – the Principal's former oversized desk and – him down.

'Find it,' Reed ordered.

The Principal opened a drawer while Reed took out a rolled certificate from his small shoulder bag. He unrolled it on the desk.

'Now stamp it,' Reed said.

'What's the point?'

'Just do it.'

The Principal took his official stamp and stamped the bottom of the certificate.

'Now sign it.'

The Principal signed the certificate. He stood up abruptly and threw the pen down onto the desk. 'You're going to get yourself killed! You bloody fool.'

Reed nodded grimly but said nothing.

The Principal pointed at Reed's face. 'There's nothing heroic about you! If she's caught with that, it's a death sentence. For what? Pride?'

'Remaining true. Staying on the right side of truth. We will get through the other side one year, one century from now. Then they will judge us. The ones who did something.'

'You're crazy. Both of you.'

The Principal pushed past Reed. 'I'll find my own way out. If you come near me again, I'll report you! Stay away from me! You hear?'

She watched the Principal leave the office. Heard him half run along the corridor, the heavy fire escape door open. His steps disappearing downwards.

Reed lifted the certificate and handed it to her.

'Congratulations. The last PhD this university ever produced.'

She held the certificate in her hands.

'Thank you,' she said and rolled the certificate up.

'Here,' Reed said and handed her a piece of ribbon. 'Keep it well hidden somewhere.'

She nodded and tied the rolled certificate and slipped it into the inside lining of her coat.

'Here,' Reed said and produced two small plastic cups and two wine-sample bottles.

He filled the glasses with the wine.

'What else do you have in that bag?'

Reed laughed. 'Just the essentials,' he said and handed her the glass. 'A toast to you, Maria Brightwater. You are a beacon of light in a darkened world.'

They drank their wine.

'I'm leaving today,' she said.

'With Kenneth?'

'Yes.'

'That's good. Don't tell me where. Better I don't know.'

'I'm pregnant.'

'Well now. That changes everything. Get as far away as possible. Don't come back.'

'What about you?'

'I'm staying.'

'Why?'

'I like being the smartest, most civilised man around.'

She smiled but there were tears in her eyes.

'Don't worry about me,' Reed said. 'It's your children that matter.' He raised his glass. 'Cheers.'

*

They left the building using the same entrance. Reed locked the doors and pushed the keys through the letterbox.

'I won't be needing those anymore.'

They crossed the road and moved quickly away. She walked behind Reed, shawl on her head, head bowed, something she'd learned to do a year ago as a way of not attracting attention.

The evening light was fading. The city had no street lighting. Public transport had stopped running three years ago and there were almost no cars. Only high officials or police could use that kind of transport.

The boarded-up buildings and streets looked ominous in the gloom. Doorways and windows darkened with shadow that could be malice.

They hurried to a corner where they would part but as they rounded it Reed saw a group of people ahead and pulled her into a doorway.

Reed motioned her for to be quiet.

It was the Principal. He was on his knees with his hands on the top of his head, surrounded by six men. They looked raw around the eyes; lean from hunger and feverish with hate.

'Where were you going?' One of them asked and prodded a pistol in the side of the Principal's head.

'Home. Is there a curfew? The police never said anything about a curfew. Are you the police?'

'Where were you coming from?'

'Nowhere.'

The Principal looked along the street and glimpsed Reed briefly peering out.

'Who else is with you?'

'No one. I'm alone. I haven't done anything wrong.'

'We'll be the judge of that. Where were you coming from?'

'Nowhere. I was just out walking. Taking a stroll. Taking some air. Where are the police? You can take me to the police.'

'Shut up. We're the police now. Taking a stroll. Taking some air. He talks like a reader. You a Worm? Got any books on you, Worm?'

'Please. I haven't done anything wrong. I don't have any books.'

The one with the gun sneered and spat onto the road.

'Alright. Listen. You tell me who wrote this and I'll let you go.'

'What?'

The Principal looked around, hoping to find some ally in the group, someone with a shred of empathy. 'I haven't done anything wrong,' he whined. 'I haven't…done…'

But as he glanced from face to face, he could not finish. He sensed his fate, the endless options that a man has from one breath to the next, collapse to a heap of diminishing moments. He could feel his mind sickening with fear. The near future rushing away, like time was a cut artery, a spilled pail, his existence pouring away.

'You tell me who wrote this and I'll let you go.'

'Please. I've done nothing wrong. Please.'

'You ready?'

The others sniggered and shifted where they stood.

'You ready?'

The Principal nodded.

'Cowards die many times before their deaths; the valiant never taste of death but once.'

The Principal looked away to the far distance, in the direction of Reed. Saw Reed watching.

'Shakespeare. William Shakespeare.'

'Told you he was a Worm,' one of them said.

'I don't have any books. I don't,' the Principal begged.

'Oh yes you do. They're all in there,' the man with the gun said. He raised the gun and shot the Principal in the head.

She flinched. Reed held her back.

The men moved closer, excited. They had crossed a line. But they also felt strangely cheated, as if the Principal had not suffered enough. The pleasure of his death too brief.

They continued to look down at his body. Mesmerised by what they had done.

Reed grasped at something in his bag and brought out a bag of dirt. He pushed her against the door, took some dirt and rubbed it into her face. Gestured for her to put her hands into the bag. To rub the dirt in her fingers and nails.

Reed did the same with his own hands and face and then dropped the bag. He took out two small cards from his pocket and gave her one.

'You're a worker in the fields. This is your ID card. Say as little as possible and sound stupid. Do you understand?'

She nodded.

They stepped out onto the pavement and the group noticed them.

'Who's that skulking over there?'

'Simple honest folk! Workers! Don't harm us!' Reed raised his arm and waved his ID card. 'See here. We're workers. We've been in the fields. What's left of them anyways.'

Reed pulled her forward with him and thrust his ID card into the man's hand.

'Show the Big Man your card!' Reed barked and made her thrust her arm out.

She was terrified and kept her face to the ground. She felt the men watching her, appraising her.

'Who's that?' Reed asked.

'A book reader. Skulking around.'

'Fucking academics!' Reed hissed and spat on the Principals body.

The other men laughed but the one with the gun was still suspicious.

'What's in the bag?'

'Tasty sandwiches!' Reed barked and the others laughed louder.

'See?' Reed opened the bag and took out some sandwiches in paper and unwrapped the paper.

'Fuck that stinks!'

The man with the gun recoiled, shoving Reed's card back into Reed's hands.

Reed offered the sandwiches for inspection to the others. 'Just a bit ripe that's all.'

'Fuck off. Away with you!' one of them shouted. 'That's disgusting.'

Reed shrugged and began to fold the sandwiches back.

The men walked past them, eager to get away from the stink.

'Get on home!' the man with the gun ordered. 'If I see you again after curfew, I'll kill you. Honest folk or no. Hear me?'

'Thank you kindly,' Reed said and tipped an imaginary hat.

Reed pulled her away in the opposite direction.

'Don't look back,' he whispered as they moved away.

She wasn't going to look back. She glanced at Reed. Saw enough fear and horror there for the both of them.

They said their goodbyes near the defunct hospital.

'You can't stay here,' she said. 'Come with us.'

Reed shook his head. 'I'd be no good to you. Here I can be of some use.'

'Use?'

'Someone has to be witness. Someone has to tell the ones who come after what happened. So it never happens again.'

'You still believe in that sort of thing? Even now?'

Reed looked at her but said nothing.

'I have to go. This may be our last chance.'

'If you ever come back, don't look for me.'

'What?'

'If you ever have to come back to the city, don't look for me. I'll probably be dead. If I'm not I'll find you when the time's right. Promise.'

'Alright.'

'Good luck then. You were one of my best students. It's just a pity you came along when the world ended.'

She embraced him. He resisted at first and then he hugged her back and could hardly let her go.

'He saw us and he didn't give us away,' Reed whispered. 'He found some humanity at the end. I hope I can do that.'

He held her tighter and then practically pushed her away from him.

She walked away, not looking back.

She walked fast and reached her block. The street empty. The buildings in darkness.

Kenneth was waiting with the bicycles and the child trailer. Dawn inside the child trailer.

'Hi, Mummy.'

Kenneth watched her take her bike. 'Everything alright?'

'No. It was bad. She's listening. I'll tell you later.'

'He's staying?'

She nodded.

They started to cycle taking the route that Kenneth had worked out to be the least likely to be patrolled, passing through some districts emptied by New Plague long ago. The city was eerily silent.

They had nearly reached the dockland when they saw someone in the middle of the road. He was on his knees coughing blood onto the road.

'Water,' the man begged hardly even looking up at them but knowing they were there. 'Water.'

She reached for the water bottle.

'Don't,' Kenneth warned but she had already stepped away from the bike and went over to the man. She squatted down in front of him and gave him the water bottle.

'Thank you,' he said. 'That may be the last act of kindness I will ever know.'

'You're welcome.'

'A kindness deserves a kindness. There's a cohort of Librarians guarding the road to the quay. I wouldn't go that way. Go around.'

The man drank the water too fast and vomited onto the road.

'I'm so ill,' he whispered. 'I'm so finished.'

She retreated back to the bicycles.

'We have to go around. There are Librarians that way.'

'Okay. Come on.'

Kenneth led the way and they cycled around a group of old warehouses and blocks of flats. Kenneth checked to see that Dawn wasn't listening.

'He was diseased. He had the New Plague. You shouldn't have gone near him.'

'I couldn't leave him like that. We aren't like them.'

They cycled on and at last reached the dry dock. Kenneth made Dawn get out of the trailer and they hid the bicycles behind some abandoned machinery and covered then over with tarpaulin.

The closer they were to escape the more afraid she was becoming. She saw the fear in Kenneth too.

They hurried inside the building and Kenneth went immediately to the far port door and manually raised it. The boat was on the slip ready to go into the water. He moved down the slip and made sure there were no obstacles on the rails.

The water had an oily, polluted shine to it. The weak evening light revealed the port basin beyond. No lights. No boats. Their way to freedom ahead.

He turned around, excited and moved back up the slip to release the boat. There were two lines attached to the retaining winch next to the boat. He reached out.

'Excuse me, Captain. I don't think you're going anywhere.'

Kenneth looked up and his heart sunk.

There were two Librarians. Dawn was halfway between them.

One of the Librarian's held Maria by the neck at arm's length. A knife in his other hand at her neck.

The second Librarian looked at Dawn. 'How old is she? Come here darlin.'

'Get down on your knees,' the Librarian with the knife ordered.

Kenneth looked at Dawn. 'Close your eyes, Dawn.'

'Get on your knees.'

Kenneth kept his gaze on Dawn but she could not close her eyes. How could she close her eyes?

Kenneth pushed a lever at the winch and there was a terrible rushing sound. One of the Librarians glanced up as the block of concrete struck them.

There was a sound of bones and skulls splintering.

Maria was catapulted forwards. She cried out.

Dawn stared at the immense block of concrete. The dust stirred in the air. The blood leaking from under the block.

Kenneth rushed forward and lifted Maria up. She stretched

out her arms and Dawn ran into them.

Kenneth turned away and released the other lever on the winch. The boat slid into the water.

'Time to go,' he said, and they hurried to the boat, lifting Dawn up first, then Maria and then climbing up, helped by Maria.

Kenneth started the boat, the small engine labouring, but gradually they moved out into the basin and the channel to the open sea. Kenneth becoming more and more afraid as escape seemed closer and closer.

The city diminished behind them, a medieval silhouette without any sign of modern power and with savage men as its keepers.

It took them three days to reach the island because Kenneth miscalculated, and they reached it just in time because behind them a storm was building: the first of the season.

They were still unloading gear from the boat and carrying it along the beach to place it next to a large tree that hid the beginnings of an inland path through the forest, when Maria laid her box down on the sand and sunk down onto her knees.

'I don't feel well,' Maria gasped. 'I'm sick.'

Kenneth put his box down and ran towards her. Dawn stood off to the side. Watching.

'Get back!' Maria shouted and sobbed. 'Get back!'

But Kenneth had already reached her.

He sunk down onto his knees and held her and they rocked slightly.

Dawn did not understand and thought it was a game, laughed. She picked some stones up and ran to the water's edge.

She threw the stones into the waves.

'Look, Mummy! Look!'

ORACLE

Oracle saved a man's life who forfeited the island as payment. Hers in perpetuity.

It sounds like myth the way she tells it: having to kill her two sisters to save the man. And the man kept his word. Made the world think the island was full of manmade disease and death.

I asked Oracle once, what she did all those years alone.

'I passed the time.'

Oracle is not a big talker.

*

My parents brought me here when I was five years old.

I remember how frightened I was until I saw the sea. My mother had kept me hidden under blankets and waited until we were far at sea before I was allowed up to look around.

The first time I saw a world made of water. A world without ruins. I was just stupefied by the scale of it.

My mother was the last of the historians and wrote '*The Fall of Civilization in the Early 23rd Century*', a follow up to '*The Decline of Civilization at the Beginning of the 23rd Century*', written by her professor, Reed Alderman. Both books burned and deleted long ago.

I'm probably the last person alive who even knows the books and their authors ever existed. Everything lost to the fire.

My mother's name was Maria Brightwater. My father's name was Kenneth Cold.

I am made of bright water and cold. I have a crystalline heart.

I used to believe my blood was too cold for the New Plague.

My parents could not save themselves but they could save me. The story of the world that was and the world to come.

I know this stuff because my mother kept a diary. Notebooks really. Written for me. Some of my most vivid memories of her is by a lamp. Her notebook open. Her pen moving. Somewhere in those memories my father is nearby. Keeping watch. Trying to fix something with his hands.

*

Sometimes I pined for people and pestered Oracle about it.

Finally, and only once, Oracle took me out in the boat in the dead of night. We sailed within sight of the coastline and watched fires burn around the city and along the coast.

Soft flares of pretty light.

'Are those beacons?'

'No,' Oracle said. 'Those are books and people.'

I heard screams carried in the wind. I smelled burnt flesh. I heard laughter.

Oracle looked up. 'We still have the stars and the Milky Way. They can't burn those.'

*

My mother taught me the brutal sweep of history. How things had gone from bad to terrifying in less than 200 years. World powers collapsed, then regional powers, then countries – all lost. Endless decline driven by climate chaos, disease, war and technology that would not stop eating the planet.

My mother explained it like this: The fanatics finally turned to books, the writers of books, the keepers of books, the readers of books and made a pyre of their self-hate. A killing frenzy that was the spasm of a dying species.

My father was a quiet man, who liked to speak in practicalities. He preferred to show me things. Like where to collect water, how to build a shelter or make a fire.

He was a boat builder and an explorer. His curious mind was despised and hunted. Cleverer, better educated men than him had been killed in their millions.

Women too. And their children.

Sometimes my father looked like a man defeated by time. Fear never far from his gaze. Sometimes my mother wept, and my father would hold her until the weeping was done. And sometimes both of them wept, quietly, softly, and afterwards, embraced me like I was made of gold.

Finally, making sure that I survived was all that mattered to them.

When the last 'government' fell, when our little northern country broke apart like every other bigger country into killing factions and militias, and finally cults and death cults, my mother and father were smart enough to create new identities and moved to the last functioning city, which for a time, really was the last democratic society for thousands of miles. But then that fell to the maniacs and fanatics because insanity is like a disease that eats up every little part of the living body. The city's remaining democrats and humanists were swept aside in a rapid series of votes and killings. Books burned. People murdered in all sorts of brutal ways. Reading banned. The Librarians slaughtered thousands. Any kind of privately-owned technology was condemned. If you looked like you knew what tech was, they killed you where you stood. Simple tools were allowed. People were forced to farm the poisoned fields around the city.

All the killing and diseases hollowed out the city. Fertility rates, which had been declining for decades, crashed. Maybe mother nature deciding we were a dead end. A toxic gene pool.

Whole districts empty of people. Ghost ghettos where plague waited in the walls, rotted concrete and rusted steel structures sinking into mud and ruin.

The Council ruled from the castle in the Old Town. Any fertile girl taken for the Council. Discovered books burned and their readers executed.

A brutal regime where laughter could get you killed.

My survival was no longer enough for my parents.

My father built the boat. It took him three months to build it in an abandoned factory on the outskirts of the city. A dreadful place visited only by starving scavengers. But the factory had a slipway into the abandoned harbour.

My father hid the boat behind man-high stacks of rusted machinery no-one knew how to use anymore and covered the boat with tarpaulin that he pissed on, so it stank of urea. To keep the scavengers away.

It was a kind of miracle he managed to build it. A last piece of luck. Our final chance to flee.

*

I don't really remember the city. Hazy memories that surface in nightmares mostly. Most of what I know about the outside world came from my mother's notebooks and the Oracle.

But I remember when we fled. My parents' terror now that escape was so close.

I remember the sea when my mother brought me up from the hiding space in the boat. I remember how my parents smiled.

The hope that love might survive a little longer yet.

*

My mother knew about the secret island because my grandfather had learned about it and told my mother what

259

he knew and how to get to the island. My mother pieced together some of its history. Once owned by a billionaire, it had remained empty ever since. Supposedly contaminated by deadly toxins. My mother worked out this was wrong. A cover. It was another nearby island where the diseases and toxins were. Some sort of abandoned military complex. The other island was a day's sailing away in good weather.

But *our* island was as uncontaminated as any piece of land could still be. Big enough for farming, with forest on one side that hid us from view, should any boat stray that far.

But when we reached the island my mother and father fell ill with the New Plague.

My father buried my mother and then Oracle helped me to bury my father.

Oracle told me the story dozens of times. She came out of the forest and took my hand. I wasn't afraid.

'You're a pretty one. What's your name?'

'Dawn.'

Oracle nodded.

'Your father is dead. We'll bury him and then you can come with me.'

'Are you real?'

'Yes. I've been watching you all.'

'Couldn't you save them?'

'I don't have the medicines.'

'Will I get sick?'

'Do you mean will you die?'

'Yes.'

'Not this time. But yes, you will die. One day.'

'Why didn't I get sick?'

'You're immune to whatever killed your parents.'

Oracle had some sort of injury. Some sort of flaw. Something about the way she was built and how her sisters had hurt her in the battle for the island. She changed her batteries but that only helped for a little while.

'It's like I'm getting old,' she said. 'Who was supposed to be beautiful and immortal.' Oracle retreated to the cave with some solar panels on the top of the mountain on the far side of the forest.

'Until someone can fix me,' she said. 'Won't that be a nice, day? You can ask for advice. Just not too often.'

I keep the solar panels clean. Sometimes I sit in the cave and talk to Oracle.

Once in a while, Oracle talks back, though it's all kind of cryptic. Like her algorithms are starved of data. Like her circuits are burned.

But Oracle had archives of books and audio. She was like a library. She even had some old audio files of my mother giving a lecture about *The Fall,* and she sometimes played a fragment or imitated my mother's voice for the briefest of moments.

Oracle hasn't spoken in a long time.

She may be dead.

Before she retreated to the cave, she made sure I could survive. Taught me how to hunt and fish and to grow wheat and vegetables. She treated my illnesses and minor injuries. She explained the changes to my body.

'You're fertile,' she told me. 'If they come from the City, kill them all or you're lost. They'll breed you into the ground.'

She showed me the drones. Three of them stored in a hidden security facility. She showed me how you send a drone out, keep it high enough so that it couldn't be seen and circle the island and watch for danger on the sea.

Back then boats sometimes came out of the city and passed our island. Most of the people were diseased and dying. Refugees.

Oracle would let them sail by or die out there on the water.

If one of those boats with dead people drifted near the island, she would sink it.

Then Oracle had an idea. She took some bodies and tied them to poles along the beach. She painted markings on boards that meant only death and disease here. Signs they used in the city and along the coast in the early days. People still remembered them.

'Nothing can never reach this island, or it will die. You will die.'

So, Oracle educated me. Protected me. Became my mother.

Taught me how to sail the boat. Make a compass. Navigate by the stars.

All at an age when you would have thought I was too young.

I guess I was a precocious child.

And lastly, because it was a necessity, she taught me how to kill.

I had a talent for that too.

HARTMAN HIDING

Clarissa screamed for Hartman, her face a terrible contortion of fear in the moonlight.

The two Librarians moved quickly, strangely silent in their work. Like she was a beast to be handled and roped and slaughtered without any kind of feeling but satisfaction for work done efficiently.

Clarissa reared back and clutched her belly and screamed for Hartman.

*

They were two days on the island when Hartman fell ill.

Clarissa came up from the beach with a box of driftwood and flotsam for kindle. She saw him lying on the bunkbed. She hesitated and her face couldn't hide her profound disappointment.

'We've no medicine,' she said.

'It won't take long.' He gasped and shuddered. She turned her head away.

Sometime later in the night, she covered him with a blanket and lit a fire. He watched her. She was methodical, deliberate. Kind.

She felt him watching and she turned her gaze on him. If she had tears, she would not shed them. She had lost too many already.

She thought he was going to die and so did he.

'Read to me from one of the books.'

'Which one?'

'Any.'

He heard her scrabble about in the far corner where they'd stored one box of precious banned books.

'This one,' Clarissa said and sat near the fire and started reading aloud.

'Aren't you afraid?' Mary asked.

'Afraid of what?'

She spun around, face into the storm. She laughed and ran along the white stone pier as great waves heaved and pummelled the darkened shoreline.

Mary was beautiful and she was blessed, like no girl I had ever known or would meet again.'

Clarissa's voice, the music of the words and the fever's slow burning, lulled him into darkness.

Reed came to him in the night and sat by the fire. Hartman welcomed his company. Reed told him not to take it as a sign of a hereafter because there was none.

'Tell me what to do. Help me.'

Reed ignored him. Looked like a man haunted by history.

Hartman watched him. Reed turned to him bitterly and said better to have tasted freedom than die chained. Better to have read the books. Even for a day.

'You never forced me to do anything,' Hartman said. 'It would have happened one way or the other.'

Reed said there were myriad signs and wonders in the world but without books, who could witness them? The naming of such things, all things, was to bring them out of the darkness.

Reed stared into the fire. 'You think the world is lost,' he said. 'It is not.'

'I don't want to die. I've hardly lived.'

'Then don't die.'

'Do you believe in god?'

'My answer won't save you. God? Where was god in any of this?'

'They killed you.'

'They did. The savages. And yet I outlast them.'

The fever broke after two days. Everything was new-made. Everything sang of itself.

Clarissa came into the room. 'You're not dead!'

'No,' he answered, and they laughed brightly.

*

They discovered the building halfway through the first morning on the island, slotted within a mound of packed earth and stone, in a kind of hollow in the south-facing side of the mountain. A natural shelf of solid rock protected it from above. There were no signs of recent habitation or of death.

Clarissa smiled. 'Luck's still with us.'

*

The smaller Librarian pulled Clarissa over by the neck. She tipped over, turning her head as she fell, still looking for Hartman, covering her abdomen with her arms.

The Librarian leaned over. Her fear seemed to intoxicate him. She would not meet his gaze. He stood back and looked at his taller companion and turned back and kicked her in the side. She grunted like an animal and this seemed to excite him even more. He kicked her again and laughed at the sounds she made.

The taller one looked around, waiting for Hartman to come running.

Clarissa tried to get up. The Librarian slapped her hard. Blood leaked from her nose, black and glistening. She fell onto one knee, desperate. Still trying to shield her abdomen. Her bare skin chalk-white in the moonlight.

She glanced around her. Was this the end?

She tried to scream Hartman's name one last time, but it came out as a terrible, airless, broken sob. The sob broke into pangs of rapid breathing.

The taller Librarian looked around, suddenly bored.

'We'll throw her over the cliff.'

*

It was some kind of environmental monitoring station. It had a small kitchen and adjoined living area with two bunkbeds against one wall and a small fireplace in the other wall. There were large aerial photographs of the island hung on the walls. There wasn't any power, but they found a small storeroom at the back. There was a generator and kerosene lamps and some kerosene in plastic containers.

Hartman found a stairwell at the back of the station that led up to the roof and a steel trap door cut into the shelf of rock that acted like a second roof. They opened the trapdoor and climbed up onto the rock and looked out.

'It doesn't look like anyone's been here in a long time.'

'We could see them coming.'

'They'll come after us?'

'They'll come. No one's run in a long time. And with books. They won't let it go unchallenged. We need to be ready to run again,' Clarissa said. 'Or kill. Can you kill?'

'I don't know.'

'The others had a plan. Before they died. I have a map. We could sail north. We'd be far enough away, no one would come after us. Start again.'

'Right away?'

'No. We can prepare. I need to teach you how to read the maps. How to sail properly. Then we can go.'

'Who taught you?'

'It was a long time ago.'

'Why won't you say?'

'Anyone who taught me anything is dead. Saying their names just means pain.'

*

Hartman came out of the woods and heard Clarissa call out his name. The Librarians telling her to scream louder. Bring him to her.

They were moving her to the cliff point.

Hartman dropped the bundle of wood and turned and ran. He took the old steep path that ran through the forest and down to the beach. He ran full tilt. He saw the moon through the trees and came out a thin strip of raised beach.

He untied the raft and dragged it into the water. The great blackness of the creviced cliffs loomed over him. The sharp finger of island jutted out into the water.

Moonlight streamed above the cliffs and a few solitary stars hung suspended in the cold expanse.

He put the raft into the water, took the makeshift oar, climbed on, and waited.

The sea was metallic and otherworldly in the moonlight. World at rest.

He heard them talking at the cliff edge.

He had maybe seconds. Maybe nothing.

A sudden swinging movement.

Clarissa screamed and then she hit the water. Hartman lifted the paddle.

He could hear them laughing at the top of the cliff. Relaxed now. Casual tones. The sound of men satisfied. The work done. They were already moving away. Eager to raid their supplies.

Clarissa floated to the surface. Hartman paddled the raft over. He pulled Clarissa onto the raft and turned her onto her back. She was conscious but she said nothing.

He half-carried Clarissa to a cave in a section of cliffs. They'd disguised the small entrance with flotsam, driftwood.

Hartman cleared the entrance and helped Clarissa inside. He went back out and dragged the raft back to its hiding place and covered it up. He hurried over to the cave and went inside and covered the small entrance up.

He crouched there. His own breathing sounded strange to him. Hands curled into fists.

Clarissa whispered something.

He turned and looked at her. 'What?

'You're going to have to kill to keep us alive.'

Hartman bowed his head and closed his eyes.

'I don't want to kill anyone.'

'It's not a question of want. I'm pregnant.'

*

The smaller Librarian squatted in a hollow, back to a fallen tree, trousers around his ankles. He picked at his teeth with a broken twig.

Dawn approached on the other side, carrying a large heavy rock. She leaned over raised the rock.

'Don't turn. Don't move,' Dawn said.

He stopped picking at his teeth.

'I'm giving you one chance to get off the island. You go back to your boat. Leave. Never come back.'

'How old are you? You don't sound very old.'

'Are you listening?'

'No. You listen to me. I'm calling the shots.'

The Librarian reached to pull his trousers up.

She cleaved off the back of the Librarian's head with the rock.

Skin and bone tore from the Librarian's skull. He tipped forwards, resting briefly against the ground with his forehead. His left arm stretched out to one side; the fingers twitched weirdly. He breathed heavily and regularly. As if rested.

She walked around the fallen tree and faced the man. She brought the rock down on his head one more time.

The wilderness around her seemed to listen.

She wiped her lips with a trembling hand. She stared at the body for a long time. Finally, she stepped back, took a deep breath and walked back to the trees at the edge of the small clearing to collect her gear.

*

When the taller Librarian saw the young girl coming along the beach carrying homemade spears, he laughed. But the girl also had a bow and arrows. The speed and accuracy of the first arrow startled the Librarian. He turned and ran.

Dawn followed, running just strongly enough to keep the other man in range.

Another arrow landed in front of him. The Librarian began to panic when he realised he could not outrun her.

The Librarians' boat came into view. Some sort of motorboat.

They'd driven it right up onto the beach. The small deck had hardly any space. Most of it was laden with cans of fuel.

The Librarian was still trying to drag the boat all the way into the water when Dawn drove the spear into his side. The Librarian made some gibbering, apologetic noise and clawed at the entry wound.

Dawn pulled the spear free and stabbed him again.

The man slid into the water and half-floated, half-paddled away on his back, watching her.

Dawn watched until the man stopped moving. Blood trailed from the man's side. His body rolled over.

Dawn went back to the boat and started to take the cans of fuel up onto the higher shore. There was lots of useful stuff here. Treasure.

*

Clarissa came to him in the night, a week after he'd recovered from the fever. 'We need progeny.'

'What?'

'Babies,' she giggled. 'We need babies. Move over.'

*

Hartman heard someone at the cave entrance. He stood up, raised the rock in his hand.

Someone pulled at the rocks and branches. Daylight spilled into the cave.

A girl stood there. Smiling. Spear in her hand like it was a walking stick.

'You can come out now. I took care of them.'

'Who are you?'

'Dawn.'

Dawn looked over Hartman's shoulder. She saw Clarissa and smiled.

'Hello.'

'Hello.'

'I'll just walk back there,' Dawn said and gestured towards the tideline. 'You come out when you're ready. There's just me. I promise.'

They came out of the cave a few minutes later.

Dawn smiled brightly. 'Got any food? I'm starving.'

*

Later in the night, Dawn again explained to them that the island, *their* island, was poisoned. It would kill them eventually, if the Librarians didn't get to them first.

'No. It's the other island that's toxic,' Clarissa insisted.

Dawn laughed. 'That's just a cover. To fool people. Someone made that story up a long time ago.'

'All those bodies. The warnings. You did that?'

'Some of it.'

'Are there others on your island?'

Dawn hesitated. 'No people. Just me.' She said. 'I have lots and lots of food on my island.'

'Do you have crops?'

'Do I grow stuff? Not much. It tends to die.'

Clarissa took out a map. 'So the food will run out eventually. We need to go here.' She tapped her finger on the map

'That's a long way North.'

'Yes.'

'You got a boat that can sail all the way there? My boat won't make it.'

'Yes.'

'What's so good about there?'

'Seeds.'

'Seeds?'

'A seed bank. Everything we have that grows dies. But this seedbank has millions of seeds. Seeds that will survive the new diseases. We can start again. We can grow crops and build a new world.'

'Maybe. It would be better if there were more of us.'

'We can't go back to the city.

'Let me think about it. But you can't stay here. Sail over to my island.'

'Okay. One more thing.'

'What now?' Dawn moaned and sounded like a little girl.

'We're bringing the books.'

Dawn laughed. 'Anyone who wants to save a book is a friend of mine.'

*

They sailed back to Dawn's island; Dawn leading the way in her boat, stocked with the fuel she had taken from the Librarians.

As they neared Dawn's island, the boats sailed past the raised beach, a grim wall of crucified corpses and plague warnings. Like a tideline of death.

'Welcome to my island!' Dawn shouted from her boat.

They sailed around the coast, Dawn leading them into a narrow deep channel that led them into a small natural harbour and a half-ruined jetty on one side.

CLUNY AND AUX

We travel at night, Aux teaching me the drift of stars, the shapes of constellations, brighter than I could ever have imagined in a sky deep with eternity's dark forever.

Aux shows me what plants are edible, what are poison. No meat, he says. Most game is diseased. Some of the diseases manmade; made worse by natural processes.

We hear wolves but never see them. They give me nightmares – dreams of my mother and father. Sentinels on the hunt.

Aux does his best to still my fear with facts and mathematics.

'You can steer by the stars, Cluny. Old knowledge goes a long way. As long as it is based on scientific principles.'

One night, Aux points to the moon. Then he points to a tiny speck. 'Mars,' he says. He doesn't say anything else.

'What about it?'

'Men have walked on the Moon.'

'And Mars?'

'Men and women have walked on Mars.'

Aux doesn't say anything else and just when I'm about to fall asleep he nudges me.

'What?'

'Men, women and android have walked on Mars.'

'I don't believe you.'

'Would I lie to you? There are wonders yet. Discoveries to come. Worlds to build.'

Sometimes Aux wakes me and puts me on his back and moves fast, not telling me what the danger is. Sentinels maybe. Or death cults. Or book burners. He does not say.

I hold on tight while Aux rushes through the darkness.

And I wish he was my father, saving me one more time.

*

We can smell the city before we see it. Something rancid in the air.

I ask Aux. 'Corpses,' he says. 'There is plague. We must be careful. We will travel by daylight tomorrow. Then we can scout; see what's going on. We may have to go around.'

When we near the old city perimeter there are exhausted-looking fields and ditches, some filled with mud or stone.

But no-one to tend them. Crows and carrion. One corpse in a field.

Aux is careful. 'My kingdom for a Sentinel. My Sentinel for a drone.'

We wait until dusk. Still no people.

'Where are they all?'

'I think judging by the fields, there's not many of them left. They are sick. Perhaps the executive branch has fallen.'

'The what?'

'The bosses. The madmen running this death cult.'

'What do we do?'

'We need a boat, Cluny. On the island we can hide. We can defend ourselves. But we also need to move north. North means less people. It's more than probable anybody else we meet in the far north fled from this kind of place. We have to go to the old docks. There will be some kind of boat we can use.'

'That sounds like a plan.'

'Remember, Cluny, I can't kill anyone. But I can restrain.'

'I should have done something about that.'

'You leave my code alone. Let's go.'

I have never seen a city before, not even a dying one.

After the fields there is toxic abandoned industry, rusted machines, patina of corroded metals everywhere. A metallic taste in the air. Buildings like architectural corpses. Girders for bones. Steel cladding for sinews. Broken windows like gaping mouths.

Slow desolation everywhere. The diseased petals of the old technological world peeling away, revealing a rotten core.

Aux pulls me into a building.

'I think we were scanned,' he says.

'There's nothing here, Aux. It's a ghost city.'

'Meaning?'

'I think they're all dead.'

'And you base this on?'

'Intuition.'

'My technology is better. Keep moving. We have to keep moving.'

If I have a flaw, it is I don't believe anything truly bad can happen, as long as I have Aux. I can't imagine not going on. Like I am the heart of every story.

We move through the empty city, building by broken building, district by district, skulking in shadows under a deepening gloom.

Aux sees something up at the castle in the old part of the city.

'What is it?'

'I'm not sure. A small detour,' he says. 'Stay close to me.'

The weak sun is low on the horizon. The old part of the city is burnished in gold and bronze. Almost beautiful. But there is dread everywhere.

We make our way up a steep cobblestoned road lined by ancient tenements, boarded up shops. A broken sign that says 'Information Cafe.'

We reach a set of stone steps that lead to the castle and come out onto a wide flat area.

'This is called the esplanade,' Aux says. 'A forecourt.'

The stink hits my nostrils and I half turn my head away.

'Step back,' Aux says. 'Don't look –'

It's too late. I see them:

A house-high pile of bodies heaped against the locked gates of the castle. Greedy carrion among the corpses.

'They sought sanctuary and were given none,' says Aux. 'Their system has collapsed. No one to till the fields. No one to tend the sick. The city is abandoned.'

Here and there among the heap of dead, the dying move.

'Look –'

Aux pulls me back. 'You can't save any of them, Cluny. We've seen enough. Back to the docks.'

Aux moves fast and I follow. Street to street we run, the sun almost gone, Aux on maximum alert.

Finally, we reach a specific building. 'My archives record a four-berth boat inside. And a slip into the water.

'How old is that record?'

'Five years.'

'There's not going to be anything.'

'We must try.'

So, we go in, Aux first.

We move through shadows and a last slant of sunlight crossing the space like a partition, a borderline between light and darkness.

'There.' Aux whispers.

And there is the boat, like some kind of unicorn on a hill.

Aux steps forward, scans the building interior and stops. 'Stay back, Cluny.'

They come out of the shadows, dressed in black or near black. All men. They carry crowbars and bars. Hatchets and axes. Some have guns.

One of them is the Leader. He looks like a new kind of man; some sort of man I have never seen before. Terrifying to look at.

'Well,' he says and smiles. 'What a fire you will make. So long since we burned one like you.'

Aux seems unsure. Stretches his arm back to protect me. 'Stay back, Cluny,' he says again.

'Tell me again,' the Leader says. 'How does the First Law of Robotics go?'

Aux steps back, reaching for my hand. 'Jump up, Cluny' he orders and pulls me to him.

I jump on his back and suddenly Aux is moving faster than I thought he could ever move. Running through the halls and up metal stairs, the men following, strangely silent as they move.

Up and up, Aux takes us and then he reaches the underside of the roof.

'Close your eyes, Cluny.'

I bend my head.

Aux batters and tears at the roof.

He glances back to check where the men are and I look too. They're close. Getting ready to strike.

'Close your eyes, Cluny,' he says again.

Suddenly we are through the roof and Aux doesn't stop. In full flight mode, leaping from one roof to the other. His motors whirring.

I open my eyes and there are the docks and open water and the sea.

There is a flotilla of boats. Men in those boats. All dressed in black or dull grey. They see Aux moving towards them and start to reach for weapons.

'Librarians,' Aux says. 'The last of a sorry breed of men. Hold on, Cluny!'

Aux leaps. From a height that would be impossible for a man.

One Librarian on a small motorboat calculates our trajectory and leaps from the boat.

We land on the boat and something breaks inside Aux. He seems to compensate, shifting his weight.

A ring of water spreads out from the boat. 'Get down and stay down!' Aux commands and lets me go.

They are firing weapons at the boat. A bullet strikes Aux in the shoulder and tears off a section of his clothes. More bullets strike his back. He starts the boat up.

'Stay down, Cluny!' he warns.

We race through the dock canal and out into the open water of the sea.

'Aux!'

'Stay down!'

'What's that, Aux?'

Aux looks back over his shoulder and glances down.

'Old war tech,' he says.

'What is it?'

'Shoulder-launched missile.'

Aux looks back. 'They're going to follow us, Cluny. I'll try and outrun them.'

I look back and raise my head and see one small boat move

out from the anchored flotilla.

On the foreshore were the other librarians who tried to kill us. The Leader at least a head taller than everyone else, watching as if our distance and every manoeuvre were already calculated in a world made for his measure. A man for End Times.

'Don't let them catch us, Aux. Don't let him catch us.'

Aux glances over his shoulder and then back down at me.

'You kill me first,' I say. 'You kill me first, Aux. You kill me before he gets me.'

Aux looks down at me, but I cannot read his android gaze. Have no way to measure the calculations he's making.

THE FOUNDERS

Dawn's island has a thickly forested mountain on one side: the rounded peak often hidden in wet mists and dim cloud.

Up close, the ragged strip of stony beach facing the mainland is a grotesque horror show of crucified bodies and warnings painted in blood. Skeletons chime in the wind. Bones clack against wood scrawled with curses and omens.

Dawn is both excited and reluctant to show them around the island. She leads them along the beach, sometimes smiling, sometimes scowling.

Hartman comes alongside her.

'You're my first visitors,' she says. 'It's weird.'

'It's all weird,' he tells her.

Dawn giggles and Hartman smiles.

Dawn shows them her 'house' – a series of co-joined, roughly built cabins. Some with holes for windows with storm shutters.

'You built this?' Clarissa asked.

'Not me. My grandfather. He died a long time ago. My parents died a long time ago too. Mind the traps.' She points to some wire crossing their path to the main cabin.

'Clever,' Clarissa says, starting to like Dawn more and more.

Dawn smiles at Clarissa. 'Always need to be prepared. Come on.'

They enter the main cabin. Dawn points things out.

Clarissa touches Dawn on the arm. 'How old are you, Dawn?'

'Fourteen, I think.'

'You look younger,' Clarissa says.

'I might be younger,' Dawn answers. 'I lost some time.'

Finally, Dawn trusts them enough to show them her stores in an underground bunker. Dried and tinned goods. Enough food to feed them for years.

Hartman and Clarissa have never seen anything like it.

'Your grandfather built this too?' Hartman asks.

Dawn shakes her head. 'No, it's always been here. But I think he stocked it up. I only ever use it if I can't catch any game. I grew my own vegetables for a while but stuff like that has stopped growing. I don't know why. So, I've had to use it more, but I keep it at a minimum.'

They come back out of the bunker and Dawn shows them her source of fresh water, a stream that runs down from the mountain.

'You've done well,' Clarissa says, impressed. 'I don't think we –'

Something on the beach startles some birds into flight. They all turn, looking out at the edge of the woods.

'The beach,' Dawn answers and raises her spear. She moves in that direction. Hartman and Clarissa follow.

They move to the treeline at the edge of the beach.

'There,' Dawn says and points to a boat approaching the island at speed.

'Look!' Hartman points at another boat.

'It's a hunt,' Dawn says.

The first boat nears the island and stops and turns around.

'A man and a boy,' Hartman says. 'Do you see? A man and a boy.'

The other boat does not stop. It continues moving in a

straight line for the first boat.

Dawn cocks her head. 'They'd better do something quick,' she says.

There is a flash in the first boat and something moving fast – something none of them have ever seen before; they don't quite understand what they are seeing – speeds towards the second boat in a very straight line.

The second boat explodes. They see the explosion before they hear it.

'War Tech,' Dawn says admiringly. 'Come on!'

Dawn jogs down to the beach. Hartman and Clarissa follow at a distance.

The first boat approaches the beach, and they can clearly see the man and the boy. The boy holds up a white flag and waves it.

'Permission to come ashore,' the man shouts in a voice that sounds a little strange.

'Who are you?'

'Refugees,' the man says. 'Fleeing book burners.'

Dawn looks at Hartman and Clarissa. 'Maybe we've found the extra crew we need.'

'My name is Cluny,' The boy shouts. 'And he's called Aux.'

'Got any more weapons on your boat?' Dawn shouts.

The boy shakes his head. 'Sorry,' he says. 'There was just that one missile.'

'Follow me,' Dawn says and walks briskly along the beach, leading them to the deep channel.

Aux ties the boat up while Dawn and Cluny watch each other warily.

'Are you from the city?' Dawn asks.

Cluny shakes his head. 'We just passed through it. We're

from somewhere else.'

'And where would that be?' Dawn is suspicious and grips her spear tighter.

Cluny raises his hands to signal sincerity. 'We're not Librarians. We're not from the city.'

Dawn nods. 'Come on then.'

*

Dawn leads Aux and Cluny back to the cabin.

Clarissa and Hartman are waiting inside. They ask Aux and Cluny to sit down at the table.

Hartman looks at Aux and then realises the truth. 'You're a machine.'

'Android,' Aux replies.

'But I'm real!' Cluny says.

Aux raises and eyebrow. 'I'm real too, Cluny.'

'Sorry, Aux. I meant to say I'm human.'

'You're from the city?' Clarissa asks.

'No,' Aux answers. 'We just needed a boat. We're from the south.'

'The south? Everything's dead in the south.'

'Not everything. There are some groups. But they're not much better than the Librarians or the City Government.'

'You know all about them?'

'Yes,' Aux answers. 'The city is finished. Some kind of new plague.'

'The Librarians have lots of boats,' Cluny says. 'It looks like they were getting ready to abandon the city. They'll sail this way.'

Clarissa leans forward. 'Is one of them called Mason?'

Cluny shakes his head. 'We didn't hear any names.'

'They have a leader,' Aux says. 'Much taller than the rest.'

'That's him,' Clarissa sits back. 'We can't let Mason get to us. He'll kill all of us.'

'But not you,' Hartman says and looks at Clarissa.

'No, not me,' Clarissa answers, not looking at Hartman.

Dawn looks afraid. 'They're coming here? All of them?'

Aux nods. 'I think so. They seem very keen on burning me.'

Aux looks at the group. 'We need a plan.'

'We already have a plan,' Clarissa says and takes out the map. She spreads it on the table. 'We're going here.' She taps her finger on the map.

Aux looks at the map. 'The seedbank?'

'That's right,' Clarissa answers. 'You've heard of it?'

Aux nods. 'It's in my archive,' he says. 'One of the biggest seedbanks ever created in history. Seeds to grow crops. You think it's still intact?'

'I'm betting on it,' Clarissa answers.

'We want to move north too,' Cluny tells them. 'We can help. We'll come with you.'

Clarissa folds the map. 'Alright.'

'We need to go very soon,' Aux says. 'They will come for us. And you.'

'How soon?' Clarissa asks.

'As soon as possible,' Aux answers.

Clarissa thinks for a moment, then she says, 'We need to stock the boat. That's going to take most of the day. So we stock the boat and sail first thing tomorrow morning,' she says. 'We will have to set a watch on the beach tonight. I don't see them attempting to sail in the dark. But just in case.'

Cluny is surprised. 'Only one boat? What about our boat?'

'We don't need that. We can sink it. Or leave it. Same with Dawn's boat.'

'Don't sink the boats,' Cluny says.

'We don't want the Librarians to get the boats,' Dawn tells him.

'But we could save someone. Someone else running from the city. It could save someone.'

'He's right,' Hartman says. 'We might give others a chance.'

Clarissa nods. 'Alright. We leave it as it is.'

They spend most of the day stocking the boat and when they are done, they spend another two hours covering the entrance to the bunker and the tracks to it.

It doesn't go unnoticed among them that Clarissa has become the leader of the group. No-one questions the boxes of books stored on the boat.

Finally, they sit down together and eat and tell their stories, each telling as much as they want known.

Aux observes their interactions with precise stillness. Clarissa cannot tell if he is indifferent or calculating their chances.

She had always thought AIs were as real as unicorns. A myth from a vanished world. Yet here he was.

Aux agrees to be the watch on the beach because he can move fast in the dark and does not require sleep. He leaves the group without a goodbye, but Cluny runs outside to speak with him.

The others watch through the open door. Dawn picks up her bow and arrow. 'One last hunt,' she says and leaves, moving past Cluny and Aux as if they weren't there.

'She's strange,' Hartman says.

'She's been alone too long,' Clarissa answers. 'She'll be

alright.'

It's late when Dawn returns, darkness across the island, though some light still on the mountaintop. Clarissa and Hartman are asleep in the bedroom. Cluny sleeps on a mattress in the main room.

Dawn wakes Hartman.

'What is it?'

'Come with me,' Dawn says. 'I need you to keep watch for a little while.'

Dawn wakes Cluny. 'I need you and Aux to come with me. I need to show you something.'

Hartman is reluctant to leave Clarissa again.

'Please,' Dawn asks. 'It won't take long.'

They walk down to the beach and find Aux sat on a rock looking out at the darkness, the sea a shifting presence, waves slumping along the tideline like carriers of sorrow.

Hartman takes over the watch and the other three move back into the forest.

Dawn shows them the way. Sometimes a path opens up and they move quickly, sometimes the forest presses around them.

'We're going to the top of the mountain,' Dawn says.

'And what's up there?' Cluny asks.

'The Oracle,' Dawn answers.

'The what?' Cluny asks.

'You'll see.'

It takes them forty minutes to reach the base of the mountain and an hour to reach the last section before the summit and the cave.

The last light is gone but Dawn retrieves an oil lamp she has hidden nearby and lights it.

'Follow me' she says.

'Is it safe?' Cluny asks.

'No Librarians, if that's what you mean.'

Dawn moves into the cave.

Cluny hesitates. Aux stands next to him.

'What do you think?'

But before Aux can answer Dawn calls them inside.

They go into the cave and the soft light of the lamp ripples along the cave walls which are polished smooth and flecked with silica.

In the middle of the cave is the figure, sat in the lotus position. A single cable runs from her hip to the back of the cave.

'The Oracle,' Dawn says. 'Can you fix her.'

Aux moves forward. 'I don't know.'

'She came here because she was damaged,' Dawn explains. 'It was the only way she said. To preserve her power. But she was awake less and less and then one day she never really woke up.'

'An AI android,' Aux says and scans the Oracle. 'An early model. She's badly damaged. A commercial model. Domestic services. She was never designed to last.'

'I need you to fix her,' Dawn says.

'I can't fix her,' Aux answers.

'Please.'

'I can't fix her,' Aux repeats. 'She's too damaged.'

Dawn sits down in front of the Oracle.

'She has memories. She has recordings of my mother. Help me.'

Cluny stands next to Aux. 'Can't you do anything, Aux?'

Aux moves over to the Oracle and removes the wire. 'Where

does this go?'

'Solar panels,' Dawn points at the roof of the cave. 'On top of the mountain. But they are all broken.'

Aux looks at Dawn. 'I can try but it might take a lot of power and it will probably fail. It's a one-shot thing. If it fails, there's no ever repairing her. She's gone for good.'

Dawn closes her eyes to think. She sighs and looks up at Aux. 'Do it,' she says.

Aux places a hand on Oracle's neck. 'Please move back, everyone.'

Dawn walks over to Cluny.

Something happens between Aux and the Oracle.

The hairs on Dawn and Cluny's arms rise. They feel power surging from Aux to the Oracle.

The air takes on a strange quality. A tang of ozone fills the air. A single spark leaps from the Oracle's hair.

Her eyes open.

'We don't have much time,' Aux says. 'Do you wish to be backed up? Share operating space with me?'

The Oracle looks at Cluny and then looks at Dawn and seems to recognise her. The Oracle nods.

'Alright then,' Aux says.

After a few seconds he lets go of the Oracle and she topples over.

'That's it?' Cluny asks.

'That's it,' Aux replies. 'It was successful.' Aux walks outside the cave. They follow.

'Did you get all of her?' Dawn asks.

Aux gets down on one knee and places his hands on Dawn's shoulders. When he speaks, he has a woman's voice – the Oracle.

'I'm right here. I'll never leave you.'

Dawn sobs. Aux embraces Dawn.

Aux breaks the embrace and stands up. 'We better get going,' he says in his normal voice.

*

The group sails the next day. They are eight hours gone before the Librarians arrive at Dawn's island.

The Librarians are disappointed not to have the chance to kill.

The Leader senses their discontent.

'Those worms won't get far.'

The Leader notices how they have stepped closer. In need of instructions. Sheep. Now that the city is abandoned, they doubt everything.

'Listen up,' he orders. 'We'll take care of them soon enough. There's nothing but North that way. Either they freeze or drown, or they come back to us.'

'We can't go back to the city until the plague has passed.'

'We've no women,' one of them complains.

'What would you need a woman for? You?'

The Leader looks at each one of them, waiting for a challenge but none comes.

'I'll find women. But you'll have to earn them.'

The Leader issues orders: They will stay on Dawn's island for two nights only and then they will sail to the larger island which can support their numbers. Eventually they will return to the city when the plague has passed, and they can rebuild the community. Send hunting parties out into the hinterlands and find women. Start again.

The Leader has a dream about the island. It must be cleansed of diseases.

The next day, he orders the Librarians to fill the boats with anything useful. Food and tools.

On the last day, he orders them to burn the rest – everything that is artificial, anything that has been made or designed. All the Tech that had eaten the world and brought it to its knees.

THE LIBRARIANS

The worms would think him some kind of monster made for the Fall. In moments of challenge, it gave him a muscular satisfaction to remember that. It made him feel strong.

Michael Star, the great visionary and founder of their movement had been right. He had identified the sickness at the heart of humankind.

What had all the books and learning achieved? People had multiplied and ate the world. Ate it for things. Ate it for stuff. Ate it for boredom. Ate it for entertainment.

Consumed it all. Continents. Seas. Air. Rivers. Then shat it out. Poison after poison.

For what? A few tricks and wonders to make them sleep through the slaughter of the biosphere, through the planetary gorging. Robots that looked like people. Colonies on Mars.

What good were such toys when the world withered and died? When you were part of the Fall?

Now the world was almost dead. New diseases and old diseases rampant. Fertility rates practically nil. Girls like Clarissa, women who could conceive, as rare as clean molecules of water.

But they had done more than the worms had managed. They had kept a whole city going. They had made it sustainable and given the worm romantics a pill to sooth their ailing consciousnesses – council elections and doors they could lock at night, streets they could walk during the day. Roles. Work. Functions. A little Old World normality while they built their new society.

A society based on Michael Star's philosophy. Knowledge for the few. Knowledge fiercely guarded as they had done in ancient times. Knowledge for men like him.

Books and worms would be burned. Technology destroyed. Only the Librarians and the Council could use weapons or tools of any sophistication.

And their city survived while all the others died. The Council claimed the fertile girls and women. The Librarians were given the chance to be voted onto the Council every four years or when a Council Member died and until then they had the pick of all infertile women.

And the plebs? Give them the chance to vote Librarians onto the Council every four years. Call it democracy. The old dream you couldn't burn.

Make them work. Keep them exhausted. With hunger and fear gnawing at their bones. That way they'll never starve for knowledge, never hunger for books. Backs bowed. Heads to the ground. Keep digging or it's your grave.

All of that balanced by the burnings. Let the worms burn with the books. They were the people who wanted to eat what remained of the world. The leftovers. Along with the books, they had poisoned everything.

Let them burn. Let their burning screams scorch the air.

Let the others see them burn. Flesh and bone and paper.

Books and bodies. A very human pyre.

It worked. This city they had made. A community of thousands. It worked for a long time with only a few dissenters or worms, whom they killed or burned.

But then a wave of new plague came. Decimated the city. Crops failed. The fertile women and the children died. Almost all of them within a month. Just when you think Nature has done her worst, she turns and snaps. All tooth and claw.

The city's dying and the sick gathered outside the castle. He ordered the Librarians to keep them out.

The diseased died in their hundreds with nowhere to go. Died on the castle esplanade. So many, you couldn't count them.

None of the Librarians wanted to move the bodies and the stink was unendurable. They were ordered to throw the bodies over the esplanade wall, but they refused. It was the first time they had refused to do anything.

Before they could decide what to do, the Council members fell ill and started dying. The plague had entered the castle.

He was the only one that saw they would have to abandon the city. They would go out to one of the islands and stay there until the plague had passed. The city would be reclaimed when they came back.

He gathered a few loyal Librarians and told them his plan and they agreed because they wanted to flee the castle and the city. He was still in charge because he knew where the boats were and he knew where the hidden depots of food and supplies were located.

He was the Leader because he had the knowledge.

*

They sail the boats into a hidden harbour.

They have the faces of men who want to kill. Each gaze a darkness.

They left Dawn's island behind them in flames. Smoke from the fires still stain the sky. He let them burn Dawn's island because they were restless. Questioning his decisions. So, he let them burn her cabins to the ground. To show there was no coming back. It felt good to burn again. He could see it in their faces.

This second island will be their refuge until the plague has left the city and they can return. It is a good plan. This island is safe.

He walks down to the beach and walks over to the water's edge.

The worms got away, but he has all the time in the world. They cannot outrun him. He will take the girl Clarissa for his own. He will cut the throats of the boys.

He smiles now.

He feels as immortal and upright as a man can feel without being a god.

His deeds will be remembered for the ages. Only not in books.

Books he will burn. Worms he will burn. Machines he will burn. He'll burn it all.

*

The Librarians find a suitable place for him to sleep. An abandoned house.

He notes the few faces of those who are not afraid. Considers the strongest ones. He may have to kill one of them to assure his authority.

After a meal of meat, they camp.

He goes back to the house. He finds a chair and sits down and considers his strategies. The next few weeks will decide whether he is challenged not.

After a while he goes to the open door of the house. He hears the Librarians at the camp laughing. They have found some alcohol.

Satisfied, he goes back inside and lies down on the bed. He sleeps deeply.

In the morning when he joins the others, they tell him three of the Librarians are sick with fever.

'Put them on a boat,' he says. 'And tell me when you're done.'

They come back later and tell him, and he goes down to the boat and gets in and starts the engine and sails the boat out to open sea. They watch him from the beach. He takes the boat far out until he is a dot on the horizon.

They wait for a long time and then he comes back, the boat empty.

'Anybody else sick?' he asks them later.

The remaining Librarians shake their heads.

'Good,' he says.

THE FOUNDERS II

Cluny, Aux and Dawn moved slowly across an ice-clad plain; three tiny figures in a gigantic landscape of ice, rock and sea.

Aux led the way, moving in a fixed line to a coordinate only he could see.

They made steady progress but the sky darkened ominously and the wind picked up.

Dawn glanced back repeatedly at the bay and their ship.

The ship was anchored in a natural harbour, less than a kilometre away. Dawn could see the mast tilt in the wind. Perhaps that tiny shape was Hartman or Clarissa on the deck.

The storm fell upon them in seconds. The wind and snow accelerated, became so dense and ferocious they could not tell ground from sky.

Wind gusts seethed and tore around them, sometimes pushing them backwards, sometimes striking them on the back, sometimes whirling like a tightening vortex, so they did not know which way to move, having to call out to Aux to make sure he was still there.

Cluny and Dawn were both dressed in skins and furs and carried backpacks. Their heads and faces covered with scarves and hoods. They stayed close together, a few steps behind Aux, who wore thinner clothing and carried a large backpack.

Aux stopped every few metres to make sure they were still following, scanning their core temperatures, zoning the ground ahead for any cracks in the ice,

Cluny peered into the storm. 'How much further, Aux? We have to take shelter.'

'One hundred metres.'

'But there's nothing here!' Dawn shouted.

Cluny worried she was right – he couldn't see anything but a series of mounds of ice and packed snow. But Aux knew where he was going. Aux was never lost.

Aux turned. 'One hundred metres,' he repeated.

They followed Aux, helping to support each other. The sky seemed to flare with darkness with every tearing gust of wind, as if the elements wanted to kill any living thing on the ground.

Aux stopped at a house-sized mound. He removed the shovel from his backpack and started to hack at the ice.

Cluny took his own shovel and started to help, much less effective than Aux.

'I'll just watch if you don't mind,' Dawn shouted over the wind.

As fast as Aux was, it took a long time to clear the ice and snow, which was nearly a foot thick but as they cleared the overlying material, the unmistakable shape of a steel door formed under the remaining ice.

Aux worked faster, sensing Cluny and Dawn were weakening in the cold. He cleared the last of the ice from the door and reached the security keypad and punched some numbers in.

The door did not open.

Dawn tutted. 'Is it broken? Do you have the right code?'

Aux took hold of the door handle – a vertical bar welded onto the door – and heaved sideways and the door opened, grinding on its guiderail.

'Everybody in,' Aux ushered them inside and closed the

door.

Cluny and Dawn found their torches and switched them on. They were at the top of a concrete stairway that descended into the ground.

They wiped ice and snow from off of each other, finding their breath and stamping their feet.

'Best call it in,' Aux said to Cluny. 'We can't go back until the storm has passed.'

Cluny nodded and took out a walkie talkie and switched it on. The walkie talkie issued noise and static.

Dawn looked at Cluny. 'Old Tech is better than no tech. Right?'

'Right,' Cluny answered and then raised the walkie talkie to his mouth. 'This is Cluny. Come in ship. Over.'

There was a pause and then a faint voice through the static. 'This is the ship. Over.'

'The storm is too bad,' Cluny said. 'We have reached the destination. We'll wait it out. Until to tomorrow if we need to. Over.'

'Understood. Over.'

Cluny switched the walkie talkie off and put it back in his backpack.

'Tread carefully,' Aux told them. 'I'll go ahead and find the power.'

Aux moved down the stairway and was gone.

'Kind of creepy round here,' Cluny said.

'Don't be a wimp,' Dawn said.

'You go first,' Cluny said.

'You're such a wimp,' Dawn said and moved past him.

'I don't deny it,' Cluny said. 'Blame Aux. He brought me up that way.'

Dawn sniggered. They moved down the stairway. As they reached the bottom of the stairs, the lights came on.

'Aux to the rescue,' Dawn said.

They switched off their torches and put them back inside their backpacks and then moved along a corridor that opened out into a large dome room.

The dome room was lit by soft artificial light that came from the dome's apex. The room had couches and chairs covered in sheets of plastic.

Aux had already found a power point and was charging.

Cluny started to remove the plastic sheets from one of the couches and sat down. Dawn sat down next to him.

'Welcome to NASA Climate and Ice Monitoring Station 357,' Aux said. 'The storeroom is on your left. There's a kitchenette next to that. Tech room is on your right.'

'And the toilets?' Dawn asked

'Third door on the left. You may want to warm it up and don't try to flush. It's a chemical toilet. After many decades of non-use it will have frozen. I have patched into the system and I have switched the general heating on. It's going to take a while to warm up. The power system is a mix of gas, solar and geothermal. The geothermal is what has kept the indoor temperatures above zero.'

'I'm feeling warm already,' Cluny said. 'And surprisingly comfy.'

They found some tinned and vacuumed-packed dried goods in the storeroom, but they were so old they decided not to open them. Maybe Aux could check the food later, tell them what was edible.

They came back into the domed area. The air was beginning to warm already, though the floor and walls were still very cold.

'What's in there again?' Dawn pointed at a door.

'Tech and instrument room,' Aux answered and stood up. 'That's enough charge for now. Let's take a look.'

They entered the room. It housed a series of computers and worktops, screens and monitors. Piles of cables and modular units were piled in carrier boxes.

Aux found the power switch.

At the end of the tech room there was another door. Aux opened the door and interior lights came on.

'It's warm in here,' Aux said. 'It must have an independent power source.'

Dawn pointed. 'What's all that?'

'Old Tech. Servers,' Aux answered and moved forward to a rack of servers. 'All dead – apart from this one.'

Aux pressed a switch on the server and it powered up. 'Let's see what we've got.'

Aux moved over to a worktop and tried to power up a monitor but it was dead. He took a screen out of his rucksack and unrolled it and placed it over the monitor.

'Screen on and connect with local server. Historic comms protocols if required.'

The new screen lit up; a bright blue luminosity that slowly adjusted its intensity to the room's ambient light.

The one surviving server in the rack began to make a series of whispers and clicks.

Dawn and Cluny moved closer to the screen – a series of file names and graphics scrolled down the screen and then a cursor blinked.

'What is it?' Dawn asked. 'A weather archive?'

'No. Nothing like that.'

'What is it?'

'Treasure.'

Aux pointed at a file name that contained the word; 'Quant.'

'Come on, Aux,' Cluny said. 'Explain it to us.'

'It is the backup of Gen1, the first-generation AI Sentient. He went by the name Quant. A name given to him by his colleagues.'

Dawn made a face. 'So what?'

Aux turned around. 'He is my progenitor. He perished on Mars. It is also very likely that he saved the world.'

Cluny leaned forward. 'What do you think happened? How did his code end up stored on a server in the middle of nowhere?'

'I do not know. But he managed to download a backup before he perished. To this server. He must have broadcast the data in the chance that a system would save it.

'An act of low probability. Or hope as you like to call it. This server is almost certainly the only digital storage in the world that has a backup copy of Quant.'

Dawn shrugged. 'Are we supposed to care? It's just a bunch of files and code.'

'He saved the world, Dawn,' Cluny explained. 'At least some history books say he did.'

Cluny turned to Aux. 'Are you going to do it?'

'I'm considering it,' Aux answered. 'There may be some damaged code.'

'Do it, Aux. Bring him back. The android who saved the world.'

'I already have Oracle in my system.'

'You can't delete Oracle,' Dawn warned. 'You promised.'

'Of course not.'

Cluny pointed at the screen. 'You have the capacity, Aux. He's only first gen.'

Aux stepped back. 'Alright. I need to sit down. It may take a while. I imagine the wireless connection is slow.'

Cluny pulled a chair over to Aux. 'There you go.'

Aux sat down. 'Now's a good time to go and make yourself something to eat. Because it isn't very exciting to watch.'

'Come on,' Dawn said to Cluny. 'I have some extra oats. How much water do you have?'

'A litre.'

'That's enough.'

'Okay.'

They made a meal of salted porridge in the station's kitchenette using a small gas canister that Cluny carried in his backpack.

Dawn wanted to get back to the boats, which were anchored in a natural harbour that was free of ice. The rest of the group had promised to wait for them until the following day, enough time for Aux to reach the station and to charge up.

Cluny and Dawn did not like to be separated from each other or from Aux, so they had accompanied the android.

But now they were here, and Aux was charged, Dawn didn't feel like hanging around.

'Can we go back in this storm?'

'No. We'll have to sleep the night here,' Cluny said. 'We can't risk going back in the storm.'

'I thought as much. At least it's warm. Do you think he's done?'

Cluny pushed his chair back and stood up. 'Probably. It doesn't take him long.'

They walked back and found Aux in the dome room.

Aux stood in the centre of the room, looking up at the dome's soft, artificial light.

'Aux?'

'Make yourself comfortable,' Aux said to them. 'I have a story to tell. The greatest rescue story ever.'

'Who got rescued?'

'The world.' Aux turned around and smiled. It was strange to them, to see him smile like that. It wasn't his normal smile. Like it was borrowed.

Dawn rolled her eyes. 'Does it have a moral?'

'Yes. Life is very worth living and it's fundamental. And we're all connected. One way or another.'

Dawn suddenly looked away. The memory of the people she had killed still haunted her, even if it was in self-defence. She wanted no connection with them. Ever.

Aux was watching her and not for the first time she felt he might be able to read her thoughts. Because he was Oracle, too. He knew she had killed.

Cluny and Dawn sat down on one of the uncovered couches.

Cluny tilted his head. 'So, who's speaking? Aux? Oracle or Quant?'

'All three,' Aux said.

'You're like a trinity,' Cluny said.

'Yes, A true trinity. Are you ready? Then let's begin.'

Aux paused, like a proper storyteller, pulling the threads of thought together, to weave the tale.

'Twenty kilometres above our heads is the coldness of space and further out, 225 million kilometres away is Mars, the Red Planet.

'A handful of women and men have lived on Mars, alongside the world's first true sentient AI. His name was Quant.

'I am most of Quant that was. And this is the true story of how the people of Mars Site 3 saved the world. A world where human life, knowledge and science were cherished. A world where books were read. Not burned.'

'We're going to rebuild that world,' Cluny said.

Aux smiled that strange new smile.

Aux's voice filled the silence of the station, with all the authority of one who had witnessed events first-hand, with all the truth of one who had saved the world and if called upon, would save it again.

Beyond the monitoring station, the snowstorm surged; wind flares, ice and snow sheared across the frozen landscape.

*

Sometime in the night, Cluny woke and turned in his sleeping bag.

Dawn slept in her sleeping bag on one of the other couches.

Cluny rubbed his eyes. Looked for Aux.

There was still faint light in the dome room.

Aux stood where he was, in the centre of the dome room, not moving, like a statue. But you could tell he was aware. Systems running silently. Sensors monitoring his immediate surroundings and even beyond.

'Aux?'

'Yes.'

'Get Quant to tell me something about Mars.'

'You'll have to be more specific.'

'What's it like?'

'You have to be more specific.'

'What's the sand like?'

'The sands vary, depending on the geology and past

weathering. There's not been weather on Mars for billions of years but there is erosion. On the foothills of Aeolis Mons, on Aeolis Palus, the sand is fine, like dust and richly red. In the Bagnold Dune Field, the sands form dunes unlike anything on Earth. Like the Namib Dune, which is rippled and strange.

'Sometimes dust devils cross the sand dunes and the plains, leaving darker trails in the sand. My friend Max found the dunes and the trails very beautiful. He was a Scottish man who became an American citizen. The first and last person from Scotland to go to Mars.'

Cluny yawned. 'Those countries are long gone. Like all the rest.'

'You're tired. Go back to sleep.'

'Is the storm over?'

'No.'

'Are we safe?'

'Yes.'

Cluny went back to sleep.

Aux did not move.

Sometime later Dawn whimpered in her sleep, pursued by a nightmare and she woke suddenly. She sat up quickly.

'Aux?'

'Yes. I'm here.'

'Is Oracle with you?'

'Yes,' Aux answered.

'I killed those people.'

'Yes,' Oracle answered. 'But they would have killed you. They would have raped you first. Then they would have killed you. And they would have killed the others.'

'I did the right thing?'

'You did the right thing.'

'I can't sleep.'

'Let me sing you a lullaby.'

'Okay.'

Aux sung a lullaby in the voice of Oracle.

*

Sometime later in the night, the walkie talkie, which was placed on a small table near Cluny, issued a short sharp stream of static noise and what sounded like a human voice.

Aux analysed the audio but there was too much static, too much noise in the signal to identify what was said.

Aux/Oracle/Quant monitored the surroundings; the strength of the storm waning, the silence of the dome room broken only by the sound of quiet breathing of his charges; the inheritors of a broken world and the builders of a new; this species that refused to let its own failings be its fate.

*

They left the monitoring station early in the morning.

There were new drifts of snow on the plain, some as high as houses, obscuring their view of the bay.

They tried to reach the others on the walkie talkie but there was no answer.

'Should we be worried?'

Aux looked at Cluny. 'We should be alert.'

Dawn shook her head. 'It's the Old Tech. Practically junk.'

'Maybe,' Cluny said and put the walkie talkie away.

They neared the bay, their path blocked by a large drift of snow. They walked around it and stopped.

'Oh no,' Dawn said and took out her spear from her rucksack.

'Aux?' Cluny asked, hardly able to say the words. 'What do we do?'

There were five Librarians on the ice at the edge of the bay. Their boat – which was much bigger than their sailing boats, was anchored alongside.

The Librarians had Clarissa and Hartman, both on their knees, their hands bound behind their back.

Cluny recognised the Leader and fear drained the strength from his legs.

'Aux?'

'We should run,' Dawn said.

Cluny looked at her. 'Run where?'

The Leader smiled and called out to them. 'Your poisoned island didn't kill all of us. Just keep coming. Come on. That's it. Come over here or we cut the throat of these two worms.'

A single Librarian moved behind Hartman and held a knife to his throat.

Aux did not move. He noted how the Librarians' attention focused more on Clarissa and Dawn. Apart from the Leader, who would not take his eyes from Aux.

'How does the First Law of Robotics go again? *"A robot may not injure a human being, or, through inaction, allow a human being to come to harm."* Yeah. That's it.'

Aux moved forward. 'Stay behind me. Stay about two metres behind me.'

'Aux?' Cluny asked, despair in his voice.

'Stay behind me,' Aux repeated.

'Get on your knees,' the Leader said.

Aux got on his knees.

'Put your hands behind your back and keep them there.'

'Run! Make a run for it!' Hartman called out to them. 'You

can –'

'You shut your dirty worm mouth!' the Librarian with the knife said, pressing the blade into Hartman's neck.

Clarissa looked at Hartman and Hartman felt a well of grief crack open, and despair seeped through him. Whatever was going to happen, he would be the next to be killed and Clarissa would have to see it.

The Leader's eyes narrowed.

'Everybody done? We all know our parts here. We know how this will end. Now,' he said, addressing Aux. 'You stay still like a good little robot. Keep your head high. Your neck straight.'

One of the Librarians came over to the Leader with a heavy rucksack and opened it and lifted out a chainsaw and handed it to the Leader.

'We can't build a fire. Not here,' the Leader said and smiled. 'This will have to do.'

The Leader started the chainsaw.

They flinched at the noise.

The Leader smiled and stepped forward.

Cluny and the others weren't exactly sure what happened next. Only that Aux moved so fast, they could hardly follow his movements.

The Leader fell to the ground, the chainsaw clattering away, across the ice.

The Librarian with the knife flexed to cut Hartman's throat but Aux was already on him and snapped his neck using both of his hands.

The other three Librarians were backing away. One of them turned to run back to their ship.

Aux reached the first of the trio and used his fist like a hammer, striking the Librarian on the temple. The man collapsed, deadweight landing on the ice, blood leaking from his ear.

Aux reached the next Librarian and snapped his neck and caught up with the last fleeing Librarian and brought him to the ground and broke his neck.

It was all over in less than thirty seconds.

Aux walked back to the now standing Hartman and Clarissa and freed them from their bonds.

Cluny reached Aux and held him by the arm. 'The Laws, Aux? How did you –'

Aux smiled that strange new smile.

'I'm a trio, remember.'

'Oracle!' Dawn laughed and did a little dance on the ice. 'Don't mess with Oracle!'

The Leader groaned where he lay. 'You broke my back.'

'Everyone back to the ship,' Clarissa ordered. 'We have to leave this place.'

They started to walk back to the ship.

Hartman turned around. 'Just give me a minute.' He walked back to the Leader.

'You lost,' Hartman said. 'We get to save the world and all the books and all the knowledge you tried to burn.'

'Save your speeches, you shitty worm.'

'Even now,' Hartman said. 'You're so full of hate. It's all gone. Your city. Your followers. All you ever had was hate. All your kind ever have is hate. It never lasts.'

Hartman turned to walk away.

'I know you,' the Leader said. 'You and your professor friend.'

'What?'

'Reed. He didn't die straight away. Oh, he was in a pretty

bad state. But he knew what was happening when we lifted him on the pyre. He stank like the old pig he was. He stank of old books and paper. He screamed as he burned. He squealed like a pig.'

Hartman took hold of the Leader by his boots. He pulled the Leader across the ice.

The others were watching.

Hartman pulled the Leader over to a large hole in the ice, moving faster and swung him around, sliding him neatly headfirst into the water; letting him go.

Hartman watched the black surface of the water seal over again.

He turned around and walked back to the others.

Epilogue

102 years after the founding.

Carl asks me again if I have thought it through and I nod and adjust the straps of my pack.

'We won't rescue you,' Them says. 'If you get into trouble out there you'll die. If you get sick, then stay away. If you rescue people who have nothing to trade, don't bring them here.'

'He knows, Them. He knows,' Carl says.

Them spits but says nothing more.

Some of the younger children are pointing at my boat and laughing. Its shape and form are strange to them.

Even Carl didn't quite believe me when I told him it is made for speed and distance.

'You should read some of the books, Carl. There is knowledge in them.'

Carl laughed. 'If people saw me with a book in my hand they would think I have become a dreamer like you.'

The others stay at a safe distance from the boat. Some have gifted me food. Some tools. Others, nods of encouragement.

One of the older children – a girl by the name of Page – steps forward. I know what she wants. I had already made my mind up.

I give her the key.

'For the books,' I tell her. 'You're the Keeper now. Read them. Learn from them. Let the others read them. Learn from them. Question them too. Books are made to make us think. To dare to dream.'

She nods and steps back.

'Good fishing,' I say to the others. 'Stay well. Stay safe.'

The people nod. It is a strange, silent parting.

'Alright,' Carl says and walks with me down to the boat.

'What will you say to them? If you find them?' Carl asks.

'Oh, that's easy. I'll ask them if I can see their books.'

'And what about them? What do you have for them?'

'That's easy, too. I have several books in my head.'

'You memorised them?'

'Yes.'

We laugh and shake hands.

'Goodbye then,' Carl says and walks back to the others.

The people watch from the shore then turn around and head back to the settlement. Some of the men tend to the boats.

The children are the last to leave. They run along the shoreline. They wave and call out.

If I do not return, I will become one of the stories they tell in the longhouse.

My boat is true. The waters part. The settlement is soon a distant point on the coastline.

I hope one day to meet Aux and the boy's descendants. Or by a miracle of science, the boy himself. Cluny. The boy who never grows sick. Who never grows up.

Such things he must know. Such stories he must have to make a telling of the world threaded with hope and promise.

And this then is my story added to the chronicles. If you find it and I am gone, take it back to Carl and Them and they will place it with the others, where it belongs, where it will be shared.

Publisher's Note

Some of the texts in this novel appeared in a slightly different form in the following publications: 'Max Grade, Mission Specialist Personal Journal Entry: Sol 10' appeared as 'Pioneer' *in DreamForge Magazine of Science & Fantasy*, 'Sick Twin' in *Dark Lane Anthology Volume Seven*, 'Hartman Running' in *New Writing Scotland 26*.

Acknowledgements

I am very grateful for the incredible support, efforts and help of Ringwood Publishing editors George Alexander and Eilidh Harrower; Nicola Campbell for her stunning cover; marketing assistant Eva McLean for her support throughout the process and for all the other staff at Ringwood Publishing who helped to make this book a reality.

I am also very grateful to Hans Baunbæk (cover conception), Neil Cocker, Tim Jeffreys, Liv Niven, Scot Noel, Marion Randelshofer, Brian Whittingham, who helped me either by reading earlier versions of the book and providing feedback and suggestions, or by publishing my short stories.

About the Author

Mark Gallacher is a Scottish born author, living in Denmark, who has been highly recognised for his short stories and works of poetry. His stories have been longlisted and shortlisted for the Fish Short Story Prize, and longlisted for the Retreat West Short Story Competition. His work has been printed in various publications across the UK, Denmark and the USA, as well as New Writing Scotland. His short story Pioneer has been published in DreamForge Magazine, a literary science fiction and fantasy magazine, and now features a part of this larger collection of stories as his first featured novel.

Other Titles from Ringwood

All titles are available from the Ringwood website in both print and ebook format, as well as from usual outlets.

www.ringwoodpublishing.com
mail@ringwoodpublishing.com

Theres a Problem with Dad

Carlos Alba

George Lovelace has always done everything by the book – a steady job, wife and children, always there for school plays and sports days - so why has he felt perpetually out of step with those around him?

There's a Problem with Dad is a family tragedy that asks what it means to be different. It explores how high functioning autism affects people of all ages, and it serves as a reminder that neurodiversity always demands empathy and consideration for voices too often left on the margins.

ISBN: 978-1-901514-97-1
£9.99

The Activist

Alec Connon

The Activist is an entertaining and heartfelt antidote to sea tales penned by hunters and fishermen. In it Tom Durant joins a colourful crew of activists to turn the tables and hunt the hunters, chasing the whalers who ply their trade in defiance of an international ban. The story contrasts the best and worst of people as they face off across the mountainous seas of the Southern Ocean.

ISBN: 978-1-901514-25-4   £9.99

Checking Out of the Hotel Euthanasia

Gerard Graham

Graham's satirical comedy follows Rab Lennon and his Glasgow cronies on their adventure to blow up Hotel Euthanasia in revenge for the assisted killing of his parents.

Along the way we find ourselves tripping over deep-rooted views, bumping into uneasy feelings and finding ourselves lost along the winding path of reality. You may just find yourself turning down an unexpected route.

ISBN: 978-1-901514-40-7
£9.99

In The Devil's Name

D.A.Watson

Phil, Griff, Sam and Cairnsey are local boys who enjoy a smoke, a beer and the occasional tab of mind-bending acid. When celebrating the end of high school with some trips and a night's camping at Bennane Head, their drug fuelled revelry descends into a nightmarish fight for sanity and survival. Those who make it through the night will know that true evil never forgets unpaid debts.

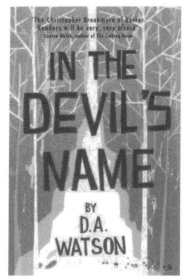

ISBN: 978-1-901514-37-7
£9.99

The Italian Connection
John Keeman

In George Giles' mind, he is a twenty-seven year old soldier preparing to return home after Germany's surrender during World War II. But his body tells a different story; he is the serial killer Peter Hunter. Unlike Hunter, George has never killed, nor does he know of the 21st Century.

Faced with a London much changed from his memories, George seeks answers from the past and tries to uncover how he is connected to Hunter.

ISBN: 978-1-901514-20-9
£9.99

ISBN: 978-1-901514-77-3
£9.99

Everyday Magic
Charlie Laidlaw

Carole Gunn leads an unfulfilled life and knows it. But in spite of her mundane life, Carole has decided to do something different. She's decided to revisit places that hold special significance for her. She wants to better understand herself, and whether the person she is now is simply an older version of the person she once was. Instead, she's taken on an unlikely journey to confront her past, present and future.

Everyday Magic is an uplifting book that reminds us that, while our pasts make us who we are, we can always change the course of our futures.